I0719565

THE
NAME GAME
MURDER

A Smiley and McBlythe Mystery

THE NAME GAME MURDER

A Smiley and McBlythe Mystery

BRUCE HAMMACK

To the REAL Paul...

Thanks for loaning me your name, but most important, for wanting to be immortalized in one of my books. You are officially part of the Smiley and McBlythe case files!

1

———

Heather looked on as Steve pushed silverware toward his plate and rested his hands on a white tablecloth. "Is Donnie Douglas alive or dead?" He didn't direct the question to Heather, but to her boyfriend, Jack Blackstock.

"It depends on who you ask," said Jack, as he returned his glass to its proper spot on the table at CHEZ VOUS, an upscale restaurant in The Woodlands, Texas.

"You lawyers," said Steve with a huff. "Getting a straight answer out of you is like trying to water your garden with a kinked hose." He pointed to Heather. "Her favorite answer to anything I ask is, 'It depends.'"

"That's because it does," said Heather, winking at Jack, giving him a cue to take up the conversation.

"I know the family and thought it wouldn't get complicated to have someone declared dead. Boy, was I wrong."

"Are we talking about a homicide or not?" asked Steve.

Jack directed his answer to Steve. "The family says yes. The insurance company is stalling because they think Donnie is still alive. To complicate things, he may have changed his name, perhaps multiple times."

Conversation ceased when a server delivered a basket of

bread. Once she left, Heather asked, "Do you want me to butter a slice of baguette for you?"

Steve nodded and readjusted the sunglasses hiding his sightless eyes. "Keep the bread coming. Unless I'm mistaken, the portions they serve in this high-dollar place aren't enough to keep a kindergartener alive."

"Don't be such a grump. Jack was nice enough to invite us to lunch, and this restaurant reminds me so much of Marseilles."

Jack returned to the previous conversation and offered a more complete explanation for the conflict between family and insurance company. "Donnie was a boy-wonder celebrity in the world of gaming. One of those self-taught programmers who only needed a high-powered computer and a quiet basement to make millions. His games still rake in seven figures a year, even though he's produced nothing new for years."

Steve nodded and expressed an "Uh-huh" to let Jack know he tracked the conversation.

"Years ago, he disappeared. We're talking about falling off the face of the earth type of disappearing."

"Let me guess," said Steve. "The family wants to have him declared dead so they can make a claim to the fortune?"

Jack nodded, which, of course, Steve couldn't see, so it did no good. "A family member came to me last year after the seven years of no one hearing from the missing man. Things are in limbo because an insurance investigator found weak evidence that Donnie might still be alive and living in Belize. The family is chomping at the bit to get the money."

"You're representing the family?"

"For now, but I wonder if I should tell them to find someone specializing in probate."

"Good idea," said Heather. "An insurance company fighting against a family doesn't sound like it should involve a criminal defense attorney."

"Interesting," whispered Steve, as the server arrived to take orders.

Heather ordered for both herself and Steve in French, asking for Steve's entrée to be cut into bite-size pieces. Jack closed his menu and asked the server for his recommendation. The man gave the French name for the recommended entrée and Jack said he would take it. Heather knew he spoke passable Spanish, but hadn't a clue with French. Not wanting to embarrass him, she said, "Excellent choice." She hoped he wasn't disappointed with roast duck.

Orders placed, Jack gave his head a nod and held out a hand for Heather to hold. "Thanks for the legal advice. I'll give Mary Ricks a call this afternoon and tell her to find another lawyer." He tilted his head. "Any suggestion on other attorneys I could recommend to her?"

"Mergers and acquisitions are my game. It would be a different story if Donnie showed up and wanted to sell his intellectual property and maintain his anonymity."

"What if the family gets it and wants to sell it?"

Heather raised an eyebrow. "That would be worth a look."

"You might change your mind after talking to Mary. She's something of a cross between a barracuda and a cougar."

Heather noticed Steve had stopped eating. "Tell us more about the family."

"The closest relatives are two cousins, Mary and her brother, Trey. Trey has some learning challenges. Mary... let's just say she's a bit demanding."

"Don't you mean she's a witch?" asked Steve.

A smile crossed Jack's face. "That's a better descriptor."

Steve leaned back. "What is it about money that changes people from decent human beings into something a mother couldn't love?"

"Not everyone," said Heather.

"No, but money had something to do with most of the murders I investigated," said Steve with an edge to his voice.

Heather took a long look at her part-time business partner. "You don't seem your normal happy self today. What's wrong?"

Steve took a bite of bread.

"Come on," she said with a challenge in her voice. "Quit stalling and tell us."

He swallowed and chased the bite down with a drink of water. "I had to fire another writing coach today."

Jack responded first. "Another one didn't work out?"

Steve shook his head. "I thought it would be easy to find someone who would be tough on me like Kate. This guy gave me some song-and-dance about not wanting to destroy my unique voice." He put air quotes around the last two words. "I'm wondering if writing stories based on my experiences is worth it."

Steve remained quiet for several seconds, which gave Heather time to come up with an opinion. "You've been idle too long. All you need is another murder to solve."

He nodded. "I'm sure you noticed how Jack's problem with the missing millionaire pricked my interest. That's not what I'm used to dealing with, but what if this Donnie guy is still alive?"

"He may be," said Jack. "If so, the Ricks family won't be happy."

With Christmas coming on, this could be the perfect opportunity to get Steve's mind busy doing something that kept him from falling into a well of depression. "Look into it. Who knows, someone may have murdered him."

"That crossed my mind, but we don't have a client."

"Now you're making excuses. Besides, you're getting rusty sitting around the condo all day. Tracking down a missing person will be good practice for when the next murder comes along."

Steve grumbled out something that didn't register as words.

Heather squeezed Jack's hand under the table. "You'll need to find another attorney for the Ricks family. It's a long shot, but I don't want my company involved if there's any chance Steve decides we need to investigate Donnie's disappearance."

"No problem," said Jack. He raised his eyebrows. "This is off the subject, but does this lunch count toward our weekly date?"

"No way," said Heather. "It's golf on Saturday morning and my treat for dinner Saturday night."

Steve tucked his napkin under his chin. "Jack, could you get me the contact information of the insurance investigator? I'll call him and try to pick up the trail in Belize."

"It's not a him. Her name is Marsha Pennywell. I can give you the company name, but I don't have any other contact information."

"That's all I need."

The server arrived with a cart carrying three covered plates. He removed the metal cover with a flourish and sat Heather's plate before her. "*Coq au vin pour la dame.*"

Jack's plate came next with a bold announcement of, "*Canard a l'orange pour vous, monsieur.*"

The server's announcement of Steve's lunch sounded tepid, almost apologetic. "*Saucisses et frites Francais.*"

"What's that in English?" asked Steve.

Heather answered for the man who'd already turned to walk away. "Sausage and french fries."

Steve nodded his approval.

Instead of going back to the office with Heather, Steve called Uber to shuttle him home to his two-bedroom condo. He opened the door and heard Max voicing his displeasure for allowing his bowl to run out of Beachside Party Mix cat treats.

"Sorry, Max. Heather had a luncheon date with Jack and she took extra time making sure she looked her best. She didn't tell me about it until this morning and I—"

Max let out something between a hiss and a howl. Steve interpreted it to mean the Maine coon cat wasn't interested in excuses. "All right, keep your fur on. I'm going."

Steve placed his white cane by the front door and moved

with no hesitation to the kitchen, where he reached under the sink and retrieved the plastic tub of treats and shook out a decent-sized helping into a bowl. He put it on the floor by the kitty door that separated his dining area from Heather's reverse image condo. He couldn't help but smile every time he thought of their strange relationship. Two people who lived separate lives until it came to solving murders and sharing a cat with fur like a mink stole.

With Max crunching bites of fish-flavored food, Steve checked the cat's water bowl, found it still full, then moved to the living room. He grabbed his laptop on the way and settled into his recliner. He instructed his computer to call the insurance company where Marsha Pennywell worked. It proved to be a major company with an office in Houston. It took a few minutes to work his way through the automated answering system, but when a human voice answered, it belonged to a woman who answered with her name, followed by, "Who's calling?"

"Ms. Pennywell, I'm Steve Smiley. This call is regarding a case you're working on concerning Donnie Douglas."

Before Steve could get out another word, she interrupted him. "Do you have information concerning Mr. Douglas?"

"That's what I want to talk to you about. I had lunch with Jack Blackstock, the attorney representing the Ricks family. Is it possible we could meet somewhere and discuss the case?"

"I don't want to waste my time, Mr. Smiley. Are you an attorney? Do you work for Mr. Blackstock?"

"Neither. I'm a retired Houston homicide detective who works part-time as a private investigator. My business partner is Ms. Heather McBlythe. It's Smiley and McBlythe Investigations. Check us out and call me back."

"Why don't you tell me what you want over the phone?"

"I give, and receive, more information in person."

"What does Mr. Blackstock look like?"

"You're testing me, Ms. Pennywell. Heather says he's a hunk."

"What do you say, Mr. Smiley?"

"I say you're the one wasting time. Do an internet search on me and you'll have all the answers you need in twenty minutes. Include Heather and you won't call back for at least an hour."

The phone went dead and Steve chuckled. Max rubbed against his pant legs and emitted deep purrs. "I like her, Max; she's cautious." He patted the arm of the chair and Max leaped to receive scratches behind his ears.

Forty-five minutes later, his phone announced he had an incoming call from Marsha Pennywell. He told it to answer and said, "You used your cell phone. That means you want me to have your private number."

"Where do you want to meet?" asked Marsha.

"It needs to be someplace public because you still don't trust me. Name the restaurant and I'll buy you supper tonight."

"Don't you want me to come to you?"

"You worked all day. No need driving past the airport and back again."

Marsha gave the name of a restaurant he was very familiar with. He swallowed hard and said, "I'll call and have a table reserved for seven o'clock." He didn't tell her that was the restaurant he'd taken Maggie to on the last anniversary they celebrated before that fateful night when he lost his sight and she was murdered.

After finalizing plans, he wondered if Marsha had dug deep enough to learn about Maggie. Even if she had, she wouldn't know what the restaurant meant to him. He also wondered how many sleepless nights he'd have after returning to their special place.

2

———

Steve pulled out a wad of folded twenty-dollar bills and counted off enough to pay the Uber driver, then one more and thanked him for the smooth ride. Evening traffic stretched the trip to over an hour, which gave Steve plenty of time to wrestle with memories of his life in Houston with Maggie. Once again, he concluded he'd made the right decision by moving from their home within the 610 Loop to a condo south of The Woodlands.

"You want me take you to door?" asked the driver through an accent Steve identified as originating somewhere in the Caribbean.

"If you don't mind. It's been a long time since I came here." He didn't add that the last time he had 20-20 vision and Maggie wore a blue summer dress that matched her eyes.

The driver not only took him to the door, but brought him inside. A soft voice said, "Welcome back, Steve. It's so good to see you again."

"Inga? I can't believe you're still working here."

"It's worse than that. Henri found the nerve to pop the question. That makes me half-owner, and an indentured servant."

"Congratulations."

He thanked the driver again as Inga placed a hand on Steve's arm. "I'm so sorry about Maggie. I meant to come to the funeral, but—"

Steve interrupted before she could stumble over any more words. "I wasn't able to go either." He cleared his throat. "I'm a little early and I'm expecting a guest. Has Ms. Pennywell arrived yet?"

"Not yet, but I have a table open for you. Or, you can wait in the bar, if you prefer."

"Lead me to a table. If you don't mind, I'll take hold of your arm. It might save broken dishes and apologies."

Inga placed his hand on her arm and walked at a slow pace. "I'll tell Henri you're here. It thrilled him to hear you'd be our guest tonight and that you're not dining alone."

She had laced in a presumption, so he made a preemptive statement. "Sorry to disappoint you or Henri, but the meeting tonight is business. In fact, I've never met Ms. Pennywell and I don't know what she looks like."

"All the same, it's wonderful you're here and we hope you come back."

The sounds of dishes clattering, iced drinks sloshing in glasses, and a dozen conversations going at once bombarded him. But the noise didn't compare with the aromas of seared steaks, sautéed mushrooms and fresh-baked bread that dredged up memories. He sat dumbstruck as thoughts of his many pilgrimages with Maggie to this, her favorite restaurant, attacked without mercy. Business date or not, he reached for his cane with every intention of leaving the haunting memories behind when a voice to his left broke through. "Here you are, Ms. Pennywell. Enjoy your meal."

"Thank you, Inga."

Steve attempted to stand, but didn't get far. "Please, Mr. Smiley, remain seated. Your chivalry is a welcome novelty in today's world, but unnecessary for a business meeting."

"How about a handshake? I know I'm supposed to wait until

the lady proffers hers, but under the circumstances, you might wait a long time for me to respond."

"I'll shake your hand if you call me Marsha and I can call you Steve."

"It's a deal."

Steve extended his hand and knocked over his glass of water. He groped to pick it up but knocked over his empty stemware for wine. With hands held up in surrender, he said, "I'll stop before I endanger the entire restaurant. I'm so sorry. I hope I didn't drench you, especially after you went to the trouble of showering after work."

Her voice came back with a hint of accusation. "How did you know I showered recently?"

"Lavender shower gel," said Steve. "The fragrance is soft, yet distinct. You sounded harried on the phone when I called. That led me to conclude you were having a rough day. Even though you wanted to soak in a hot tub, all you had time for was a shower."

"You're certainly living up to your reputation."

The next voice Steve heard belonged to Inga. She came with two servers and soon had the table cleared and reset with a fresh tablecloth, dishes, and cutlery. After the team left, Marsha asked, "Do you drive in from The Woodlands to eat here often?"

"It's been years." Seconds passed in silence.

Marsha's tone changed to something more upbeat. "My turn to do some deducting. You and your wife Maggie used to come here. It was your favorite place for special occasions."

Steve responded with a nod of his head.

"You should have suggested another restaurant."

"Some therapists might disagree with you. They'd say I need to face my past and come to grips with it."

Marsha issued a scoffing laugh. "Most therapists I've met are as screwed up as the rest of us, if not more."

"Good point."

Their server came to take orders. Marsha surprised Steve

when she ordered the blackened prime rib. He held up two fingers. "I'll have the same."

"Did you always order the prime rib?" asked Marsha.

"It took years, but Maggie gave up trying to get me to order something else."

"Does it bother you to talk about Maggie?"

Steve raised his shoulders and let them drop. "What about you? Do you mind talking about your ex, Bob?"

Instead of answering his question, Marsha kept the conversation on him. "You realize that talking about Maggie is a defense mechanism."

"How so?"

"It sets strict boundaries on any potential relations with women. It's your way of telling them you're not on the market."

Steve had to admit she nailed him, but her logic worked two ways. "I talk about Maggie and you don't answer questions about Bob for the same reason. We're both not ready yet, if ever."

"I'll drink to that."

They each lifted their water glass and saluted the mutual agreement.

"How's your daughter doing in college?" asked Steve.

Marsha's eyebrows raised. "You have done your homework."

Steve inclined his head and nodded. "As I'm sure you have also."

"To answer your question, she's doing well, but costing a fortune and insisting on law school. How is your old partner, Leo?"

"Better, since he and his wife stopped trying to repopulate the world. It took him six kids, but they found out those little bundles of joy cost a lot to raise."

"Tell me about it." She paused. "Your current partner, Heather, intrigues me. What makes her tick?"

"You'd like her," said Steve. "She's complicated, but to answer your question, two things get her heart pumping. The first is making money. It's a game her father taught her to play, and she's darn good at it. The second is solving murders with me. She's my eyes and a lot more. She has contacts all over the world in almost every branch of government and business resources galore."

"But why does she live in a two-bedroom condo next door to you?"

Steve couldn't help but chuckle. "She got used to living a frugal lifestyle when she was a cop for ten years. Also, we share her cat, Max. I'm a convenient cat-sitter."

The conversation flowed without effort. Steve knew they were testing each other, and the best way to do that was to keep asking and answering questions. Child's play for two seasoned investigators.

"What about Heather and the attorney she's dating?" asked Marsha.

"That's got me stumped," said Steve. "They seem content with regular dates for now. I'm not sure they're dissimilar enough to make a permanent go of it."

"You must subscribe to the theory that opposites attract. I'll keep that in mind if I ever date again."

Steve took his turn by asking a probing question. "Why did you leave the CIA?"

Instead of becoming defensive, Marsha came right back with an answer. "Three reasons: Bob, my daughter, and politics." She paused. "Not in that order."

Steve summarized, "Lost love, a strong-willed child, and people without a conscience."

Marsha laughed. "That's the best distillation of my reasons for taking an early retirement that I've ever heard."

Their server arrived with identical meals, which put further discussion on hold. They'd made a good start. Later, over coffee, they'd discuss the real reason for their meeting, the mysterious disappearance of Donnie Douglas.

Setting his coffee down, Steve brought the conversation around to finding the missing millionaire. "Did you know Jack Blackstock is backing out of representing Mary and Trey Ricks? The only reason he got involved was because he defended Mary Ricks's mother several years ago."

"That explains why a defense attorney got involved. I should have looked deeper into that." Marsha paused. "No doubt the family will hire a specialist who will press hard to have my company pay out the policy."

"Unless you can prove Donnie is still alive."

Marsha's fingers drummed on the table. "Why are you interested in this case?"

It hadn't taken her long to ask the one question he didn't have a suitable answer for. He sat up straight and hoped Marsha would believe the truth. "I suspect that Donnie isn't dead, or at least not yet. If possible, I'd like to keep the latter from happening."

The background noise seemed to disappear as Marsha remained quiet. Her lack of response lasted so long, he wondered if she might consider leaving. "In other words, you're curious."

Steve nodded. "Curious and bored."

The drumming on the table stopped. "What's in it for you?"

"Nothing but a chance to put my mind in gear and not think about Christmas. It's a tough holiday for me."

More long seconds strung together before Marsha cleared her throat. "If I hadn't done such a deep dive into your background today, you'd be sitting by yourself."

"And I won't blame you if you walk out now." Steve didn't wait for her to respond before he asked, "Why did you quit looking for Donnie?"

He sensed Marsha leaning forward with elbows on the table. "I stayed as long as my expense account allowed. Unlike my previous job, which had almost unlimited funds, private companies watch expenses. After a month of hopping from one

Caribbean island to the next on the company's dime, Donnie's trail grew cold, and the clock ran out on me."

"Did you prove he was alive?"

"He was alive, but I don't know for sure if he still is. You need to keep in mind how rich he is. That kind of money can buy you many new identities and passports. If he's still alive, he doesn't want to be found."

"What makes you say that?"

"I had a friend at that place I used to work do a psychological profile on him. Donnie is harmless as a butterfly. He's forget-table, like cheap flip-flops on a crowded beach. Shy as a Tibetan monk who's taken a vow of silence."

"Those are the hardest ones to track," said Steve, as though talking to himself. "They can disappear in a locked room with three other people." He reached for his coffee. "Where's the last place you tracked him to?"

"Belize, but I was only in the country two days. One person saw through the beard and long hair of the photo I had of him."

"Could you have found him if you'd stayed in Belize a while longer?"

"I believe I could, but that would take time and money that I don't have."

Steve finished his coffee. "Is there any chance Donnie came to harm while living in Belize?"

Marsha whispered. "I never reported it to my supervisor, but someone tried to make it look like he died. It was a clumsy attempt that involved a tiny amount of blood, a knife, and a spot on a beach made to look like a crime scene."

"Were there drag marks?"

"They went from under a palm tree, up to a road."

"There must have been a police report."

"I have a copy of it that Jack knows nothing about. Donnie used one of many aliases while in Belize, so the report isn't under his name."

Steve lowered the volume of his voice to match Marsha's. "If the new lawyer for the Ricks family digs, he, or she, might uncover the same thing you did. The court would have no choice but to declare him dead and your company would have to pay the claim."

"Fifteen million reasons to find him alive."

Steve considered the options and came to a quick conclusion that he needed to go to Belize to confirm if Donnie was still alive or dead. "Do you think you could pick up his trail if you went back to Belize?"

She hesitated. "No guarantees, but I believe I could."

"Can you get away from work long enough to get the results you're after?"

"I was close when they pulled me back to Houston. The boss that decided we'd wasted enough time and money on travel retired. The new one and I get along well enough that I can at least take time off."

"When can you be ready to leave?"

"Hold on a minute. Are you suggesting we, as in me and you, go to Belize?"

"Why not?

"Are you serious?"

Steve pulled his phone from the pocket of his sports coat and told it to call Heather. She answered on the third ring.

Heather had mischief in her voice. "How was supper with the former spook?"

Marsha chuckled, but said nothing more to acknowledge the slang name for a CIA agent.

"We're still at the restaurant and she's listening. We're talking about going to Belize to track down Donnie Douglas. Marsha's convinced he's still alive."

"When are you wanting to leave?"

"Let me check when Marsha can get off work."

Marsha spoke up. "Tomorrow's Friday. I can clear my schedule and be ready to go Saturday if we can find a last-minute flight."

Steve echoed what Marsha said to make sure Heather heard her. "The day after tomorrow. Marsha thinks she can pick up Donnie's trail."

"I'm flying to Naples, Florida, first thing in the morning, to look at a hotel that's coming on the market. I'll be back tomorrow evening. I don't have any trips planned for next week. The plane's all yours."

"Thanks."

"Do you need me to go with you?"

"Not unless you want to work on a tan."

Heather paused, but only for a second. "I had to cancel three dates with Jack last month. A mini-vacation to Belize should be enough to heal his bruised feelings. We'll play while you two work."

"Are you sure you're not coming along to chaperone me?"

"Now that you mention it, you do have a habit of finding trouble."

Steve tried to sound offended. "That's not fair. Trouble finds me."

3

Steve punched a button on his television remote and spoke to Max. "The weather around Houston isn't fit for either of us today. There are traffic accidents everywhere."

Max responded by issuing a deep baritone purr.

"Marsha should have been here fifteen minutes ago." He opened the front door, heard the steady patter of rain, and felt the sting of a chilly wind. He shivered and stepped back inside. "No wonder she's late, Max. I bet the freeways are a mess."

Steve traded his light jacket for something more substantial and waterproof. Footfalls sounded outside his door. "There she is."

"Where's Max?" asked Marsha as soon as he swung open the door for her.

Steve had his suitcase packed and standing by the door. "We're late."

"No, we're not. Heather called while I drove through the monsoon. She and Jack decided at the last minute they wanted to play golf in Belize. She'll be over when she finishes packing. They're staying at Cay Chapel. Max? Come here, kitty."

By the sound of Marsha's voice, she'd already made it to the living room. Steve turned to face her. "What's Cay Chapel?"

"It's an island off the coast of Belize with a Four Seasons resort and a Greg Norman signature golf course."

Marsha called again for Max to come to her. "While we're trying to find Donnie, Heather and Jack will chase a little white ball around one of the most beautiful places in the world."

Steve half-mumbled when he said, "Serves me right for mentioning she could work on her tan."

"There you are! Oh my goodness, you're the most handsome kitty I've ever seen."

Max didn't take to most people right away, but judging from his loud purring, he'd made an exception for Marsha. Still, Steve didn't want to read too much into the cat's judgement.

"He feels like twenty pounds of mink."

"A little under twenty pounds, but Max and I have a deal regarding our weight. We both think it's nobody's business but our own."

Using a child's voice, Marsha said, "Maxie, I'll make a deal with you, too. Don't ask me how much I weigh and I won't lie about it."

"Did Heather say when she'll be ready?"

The front door opening answered Steve's question.

"Let's go," said Heather. "Jack left for the airport with both sets of clubs ten minutes ago."

Steve heard his suitcase roll toward the front door as Heather spoke. "Marsha, can you take Steve in your car and follow me to Conroe Regional airport? I'm not counting on us all coming back together, even though Jack and I are taking off an extra day or two. From what Steve told me, you two don't know how long it might take to get a lead on Donnie."

The next thing Steve knew, his hand rested on Marsha's arm and Heather had locked his door behind him. He only had time to ask one question. "Did you arrange for someone to come feed Max?"

"Of course! Jack's niece will have him spoiled rotten by the time we get home."

Rain peppered down, making thumping sounds on the umbrella Marsha held over Steve's head. Being in close proximity gave him a hint of her height. She was every bit as tall as his five-nine. Other descriptors such as hair color, build, eyes, shape of face, glasses, and anything out of the ordinary would have to wait until he could get Heather alone to give him the lowdown.

"What kind of car is this?" asked Steve, as he slumped down into the seat.

"Let me get out of the rain and I'll tell you."

Marsha's door opened and closed with a solid thunk. "It's a Tesla. Have you ridden in one?"

"Once. They freak me out. I'm not used to a car that makes so little noise." He then asked, "Are you doing your part to save the planet?"

The car pulled forward with virtually no noise but the sound of windshield wipers slapping and the occasional artificial voice. "I'm not opposed to it, but I bought it because it made sense for my driving needs. Also, this car fits my personality profile. Nothing flashy, but it can take off like a scalded dog if the situation requires."

Steve cleared his throat. "Why didn't that last statement make me feel safer?"

"Are you mocking me?"

"Not at all. It's a smooth ride and you and your car speak in clear sentences."

"I'm not sure being compared to an electric car is something a woman aspires to, but I'll take complements wherever I can get them."

"Something tells me that's never been a problem for you."

"Let's just say the compliments aren't rolling off men's tongues like they used to."

Steve nodded. "It's a good thing I'm not on the market. I'm not sure there are any shoppers left."

Marsha chuckled, but it sounded tired. Perhaps she'd stayed up late washing, packing, and going over her case notes. Time to change the subject. "How does your daughter feel about you running off to Belize with a man you just met?"

"Just another of her mom's secret trips. We communicate by text most of the time. I'm afraid I imprinted her with too much of my DNA. You'll have to look hard to find a more secretive young lady. I'm hoping she grows out of some of it, and I didn't raise an ice-queen." She paused. "Sorry. I never open up to quasi-strangers like this."

Steve waited without speaking. It didn't take long for Marsha to add a post script. "I didn't go this deep with my therapist for six months."

He waved away the last comment. "It drove Maggie nuts when I'd shut her out to work on a tough case."

"How did she cope?

"Her therapy came through art. She'd lose herself in creating things that matched her mood."

"I read how sought-after her works are in today's market."

Steve cleared a lump from his throat. "I have over a hundred of her paintings in a special storage facility."

"Do you ever sell any?"

"I've given a couple away since she died. Can't bring myself to part with them, even though I'm blind." He turned to face her. "We need to come to an agreement. No talk of spouses or kids for the rest of the trip. After all, this is business, and we need to write off the expenses."

"Shake on it," said Marsha.

"Only if there's not a water glass in front of me."

Marsha chuckled. "Plenty of water outside, but none in here. Do you want to talk about the case?"

"Let's wait until we get in the air. I want Heather and Jack up to speed." He chuckled. "That's what's good about both of them, attorney-client confidentiality will protect anything we say."

"For me too?"

"You'll need to fork over a dollar to each of them. That's the friends-and-family discount rate."

HEATHER NOTICED JACK COMING TOWARD HER WITH HIS GOLF umbrella covering him. The pilot and copilot followed close behind. She glanced behind her as Marsha moved to the other side of her car with an open umbrella to keep Steve from getting drenched.

Once in the hanger, she and Jack separated, and he popped the umbrella shut and open twice to get the rain off. Marsha did the same, which gave Heather a chance to examine her in more detail. Marsha must have been a natural brunette whose hair had gone gray during her thirties. It might have been gray when she was younger, but now is was more like spun silver, cut to touch her collar and push toward her throat. It showed off a pleasant face with a strong chin and high cheekbones. Her figure remained hidden under an all-weather jacket and loose-fitting water-repellent pants, the kind that you could unzip the legs above the knees and turn them into shorts. Hiking boots covered her feet and ankles. She'd come dressed to convert from cold weather to the tropics. Smart girl.

It wasn't long before the pilot and copilot stripped off rain gear, stored the luggage and buttoned up the cabin. The hangar doors opened like an accordion. The twin-engine jet moved forward and stopped far enough away from the hanger that the pilots could start the engines and not affect other aircraft or buildings. With the tug unhooked and out of the way, the pilot went through the pre-flight checklist.

"Nice plane," said Marsha. "It's the right size. I love the two-two-one configuration."

"Thanks," said Heather. "It's my first and I don't know what I'd do without it."

Steve sat diagonally from Heather, facing the rear of the airplane. "How was your trip to Florida? Will the hotel deal work for you?"

"I'm letting this one go. They cut too many corners when

they built it, especially with the plumbing. The rooms smelled musty and the mold count leads me to believe there's a lot going on behind the walls."

Jack spoke up. "It's the hidden stuff that comes back to bite you."

Steve put in his opinion. "Are you talking about construction or the case we're going to investigate?"

Jack, who sat facing Heather and across the narrow aisle from Steve, reached out and touched his arm. "Both. Donnie Douglas sure had me fooled. I thought a police report would be enough to establish a baseline for the seven years. This thing keeps dragging on. I couldn't wait to hand that case off to someone else."

"Who did the family hire?" asked Marsha.

"I heard a rumor about Stevenson and Harley."

"That's not good news. They have quite the reputation."

"It's well earned."

The copilot turned toward them and announced, "We've been cleared to taxi. Flight time to Belize City will be a little over three hours. It'll be choppy until we get out of this soup, so make sure you're buckled up. Say goodbye to the cold and rain. When we land, it will be eighty-five degrees."

Heather settled into her seat for takeoff. It wasn't long before the twin jet engines whined and the plane splashed down the runway. Pointing skyward, the plane banked to the south. After bumps and rattles, sunshine broke through the cabin's windows and they winged their way to what many call a tropical paradise. Once they got there, would Steve and Marsha decide it was a fool's errand to look for a recluse that hadn't been heard from for so many years, a man who didn't want to be found in the first place? One thing she was sure of, when Steve gets to the site of the supposed abduction, his associative chromesthesia will tell him if Donnie was murdered there or if they needed to dig deeper. His 'special gift' had helped him solve more than one case during his career.

Once the plane leveled off, the copilot came out of the cockpit and offered coffee, water, or a soft drink. Steve took coffee while everyone else chose water. After the copilot delivered the beverages, Heather prompted Steve to fill her in. "What's your plan for finding out what happened to Donnie?"

"That will depend on what Marsha tells us in the next two hours."

Marsha turned in her seat to face Jack and Heather. "The international airport is northwest of Belize City. I've arranged for us to rent an SUV at the airport. From there we'll drive to the capital city, Belmopan."

"It's not Belize City?" asked Jack.

She shook her head. "It used to be, but a hurricane wiped out seventy-five percent of the homes and businesses back in the sixties. Even though they built back Belize City, and it's by far the biggest city in the country, they wanted the nation's capital away from the coast."

"How long a trip do you and Steve have to make this afternoon?"

"It's about fifty miles from the airport, but there aren't interstate highways in Belize, so it's hard to know how long it will take." Marsha took a drink from her bottle of water. "I want to start where I started last time and make sure I didn't miss something. Donnie came to Belize five years ago and worked at a golf resort in Belmopan. Of course, he used a different name there."

Steve shook his head. "Golf seems to be the common thread of this trip."

"Not really. There are only two courses in the entire country. Heather and Jack are going to the swanky one on a private island, and the other is outside the capital. Don't expect luxury accommodations."

"Are you talking about mosquitoes and cockroaches?"

"Mosquitoes for sure. After all, much of Belize is tropical forest."

"I hope you brought enough bug repellent for both of us."

Heather asked the next question. "Did Donnie's latest disappearance take place in Belmopan?"

"No, he was last seen in the town of Punta Gorda, near the southern border of Belize. That will be our second stop, unless we uncover something new in Belmopan. The town has about five thousand residents. I'll leave it up to your imagination how thorough the police investigation might have been."

"Another mosquito haven?" asked Steve.

"The hotel we'll be staying in isn't new, but it has a charm all its own and sits near the beach. There's always a pleasant breeze to shoo away the little blood-suckers."

Steve downed the last of his coffee. "How did you trace Donnie to Belize?"

"A lot of work and a little luck. I called in a favor with an analyst I worked with before I retired. She tracked him from Dallas to St. Lucia, a nation made up of a group of small islands in the Caribbean. It may be small, but it's one of many countries where you can get a second citizenship, if you invest enough in their economy."

Heather took Steve's empty cup from him, and spoke as she returned to her seat. "I did the same thing, except my second citizenship is in Ireland. I'm considering a few others for tax advantages and ease of travel."

"Is it that easy?" asked Steve.

Jack joined the conversation. "All it takes is money."

"Interesting."

It wasn't what Steve said, but how he dragged out the word that made Heather realize he'd heard something that piqued his interest.

Marsha picked up where she left off. "Donnie somehow got his name changed on his St. Lucian passport."

Steve folded his hands and nodded, but said nothing. Heather concluded he'd stored away another nugget for future use. She put her index finger to her mouth as a signal for Jack and Marsha to wait for him to speak. After twenty seconds of dead air, he said, "Let's put together what we know so far. Donnie left Texas and moved to St. Lucia to get away from the rat race. He obtained a St. Lucian passport under a different name. From St. Lucia, he moved again to Belmopan, Belize."

Marsha shook her head. "You're on the right track, but there were other countries in between, and name changes."

Heather knew what was coming and reached for a pen and a blank legal pad from a storage slot.

Steve began with a barrage of questions directed at Marsha. "Do you know all the names Donnie used?"

She rattled off five names and concluded with, "He seemed obsessed about changing his identity and keeping his real name hidden. It was only by luck that someone in Belize recognized his photo."

Marsha gave Steve a narrow-eyed look. "What are you thinking?"

"I'm thinking Donnie is a very smart man who didn't want to be found. What kind of man was, or is, he?"

"Brilliant," said Marsha as a quick response, and then gave a more thorough explanation. "Did I tell you he was socially awkward?"

"Only that he was forgettable."

"Like the invisible man," said Marsha. "No history of a significant relationship. Your prototypical basement-dwelling computer geek."

"What else?"

"A stickler for details, and fanatical about securing passwords. He'd have multiples for everything and all his work encrypted. It's what made him such a success in the gaming industry. He'd invent an impossible-to-win game and then go back and take out a firewall or two."

"Finding Donnie is beginning to sound like a challenging game."

Heather thought so, too, and this was one case she would not be left out of. She looked at her notes and determined to make phone calls after she settled in her room at Cay Chapel.

When she looked up, Jack scowled and shook his head. She cut off his words before he could speak. "There's an airstrip at Cay Chapel. We'll arrive in time to get in nine holes today."

His frown turned into a smile.

4

Steve took cautious steps down from Heather's airplane and breathed in warmth and humidity. It was nice to stand on *terra firma* and even better to leave winter's biting cold.

"I wish we could fly you to Belmopan," said Heather.

"You two go play with the rich and famous," said Steve. "I would ask you to get autographs, but that doesn't work very well for me."

"How about voice recordings?"

"Not a bad idea."

Heather took Steve's hand and patted it. "Call or send me a text when you get settled in your room. I'll expect updates twice a day. Are you sure you don't need me to go with you?"

Steve threw his voice to sound like a petulant teenager. "No mother. You'd cramp my style by helicoptering over me."

"Just for that, I'll expect updates three times a day, and keep your phone on. If you don't contact me, you're grounded for a month."

"Once a day, and that's if I remember."

"Twice."

He grumbled out something she could interpret as either a refusal or acceptance of her compromise. In reality, she knew he had no intention of calling unless they found something that required Heather's contacts or skills.

"Seriously," said Jack. "Keep us posted. We can stay on a while if you need help."

"While you were napping the last hour of the flight," said Heather, "Jack and I talked about looking around Belize for properties or business opportunities. I can't believe there are only two golf courses in the entire country, and none near Belize City. Since the hotel deal in Florida fell apart, I have time to look around."

The sound of suitcases being unloaded caught Steve's attention. After a last farewell to Jack and Heather, Marsha led him across the tarmac. They didn't get far before the faint sound of a small vehicle caught his attention. "What's this?"

"A golf cart to take us to our rental."

"Nice. I wasn't looking forward to a long walk in the sun."

After a short ride, Marsha deposited him in the passenger seat of an SUV. Compared to the quiet ride of her Tesla, the vehicle sounded like a hay bailer. Steve leaned a little to his left to make sure he caught all she said.

"You're lucky to have Heather for a business partner."

"I should have known she'd be looking for new business deals. She sees life differently than us mere mortals."

"She might be right about developing a golf course. There's a growing number of ex-pats retiring to Belize with money to spend on leisure."

"What about the golf resort we're going to?"

Marsha let out a laugh. "It's half a course, only nine holes, and to call it a resort is stretching the word until it screams."

"I pictured something like Heather and Jack are going to. This sounds ominous."

"It's safe during the day, but I wouldn't be walking around at night without a flashlight and boots."

Steve shifted in his seat. "Let's talk about something besides slithering creatures with big teeth. Why did you want to begin our search for Donnie where you started and not where you left off?"

"I told you how my boss rushed me. I'd spent so much time tracking him to Belize that I ran out of time and patience. The groundskeeper I talked to is a tight-lipped Scotsman. He told me Marcus had unexpectedly moved on to Punta Gorda, but that's all I could get out of him except he was left in a bind with a tournament scheduled the day after he quit."

"Who's Marcus?"

"That was Donnie's name while he worked at the golf course in Belmopan and in Punta Gorda." Marsha chuckled. "Don't worry about the other aliases unless we find out he used another one to leave the country."

"So the guy at the golf course knew Donnie as Marcus. You didn't speak with anyone else?"

"No time. I spent one night, found out where Marcus went, and left early the next morning."

The trip to the west side of Belmopan and the Roaring River Golf Course passed with no incidents and precious little conversation, which suited Steve. He needed to process the new information and add one more brushstroke to the canvas that would give him a multidimensional picture of the illusive Donnie Douglas.

Marsha eased the SUV to a stop and turned off the motor. "We're here."

"Is it still daylight?"

"Almost dark. Let's get checked in."

"Is it a hotel?"

"They call them chalets, but that's being overly generous. They're cabins with a river running about twenty yards behind them."

Steve cleared his throat. "I'll wait here. One less chance to step on something that doesn't like being stepped on."

"You'll have to come in. The rooms are in each of our names and you'll need to show your passport."

The hinges on the front door squeaked more than those on the SUV. Steve blamed it on the humidity.

The sound of Marsha slapping the desk bell brought footsteps their way, followed by a man's voice speaking with a thick Scottish brogue. "Ah, you made it. You're my last check in today."

"Cabins for Pennywell and Smiley."

"Cabins?"

"That's what I made reservations for," said Marsha with a hint of challenge salting her words.

"Sorry, lass, but there's only one cabin. The rest are full."

"That's not acceptable. I booked them two days ago, and they assured me I'd have two cabins."

"Aye, there were two, but that was before the idiot from Chicago had a row with his girlfriend and pulled the sink off the wall." He paused and thickened his accent. "One cabin. Take it or leave it."

Steve held up his hand. "We'll take it. No problem." He leaned into the man. "Pay no mind to the lady. She's touchy after a long day of travel."

The man mumbled something Gaelic and Marsha moaned. Steve leaned a little closer. "Would there be a place nearby where a man could get a pint?"

"Aye. It's not far. As soon as I get you two checked in, I'll be going there. Would you like to come with me?"

"Are you sure I'm not imposing?"

"Not at all. They serve decent food if you haven't eaten."

Steve turned to Marsha. "It looks like you're on your own tonight. I hope you don't mind taking care of the luggage."

It didn't surprise him that Marsha played the part of the offended woman. She didn't get to be a CIA agent without knowing how to think on the fly. "You can stay out all night as far as I care. When you come back to the cabin, don't make any noise and don't even think about climbing in bed with me."

"The thought hadn't crossed my mind, but you may have to come get me if I can't get a taxi."

"No worries," said the man. "I'll bring you home, and there's a nice couch in the living area. I'll fetch extra bedding."

Steve faced Marsha. "Don't wait up. I might be late getting back, but I'll need you to make up a bed on the couch for me."

"Don't press your luck." Without waiting for a response, she grabbed their bags and headed for the door.

"Well, I guess we're on our own." Steve put out his hand. "If we're going to have a drink together, I guess I should introduce myself. Steve Smiley."

A rough hand gripped his own. "Gavin. Nice to make your acquaintance. Let me close the office and we'll be off."

The ride to the pub lasted less than five minutes. Steve flicked his collapsible white cane and it unfurled to full size.

"Need help?" asked Gavin as he closed the car's door.

"It works best if you walk on my left side and I grab your arm." He didn't tell his new guide this also aided him by giving a sense of Gavin's height and physical condition. The voice told Steve the man leading him was no spring chicken. The sinewy bicep indicated a lean man, in good shape.

"Can you describe this place to me?"

"Aye. The name is *SCOTCHIES* and like most of the restaurants, it's open air. This one is a cluster of tiki huts. What ale do you fancy?"

"I'll take whatever you're having."

They settled at a table and for the next twenty minutes, Steve nursed a mug of something that reminded him of overcooked walnuts while Gavin downed two pints and ordered a third.

"Is the ale not to your likin'?" asked Gavin.

Steve held up a hand. "There's nothing wrong with the ale, but I need to go easy because I'm taking medicine. Getting over some sort of winter illness." Steve didn't mind telling a lie if it did no harm and the situation called for it.

Gavin's words came with less hesitancy and more opinion. "That's what comes from living in a place that goes from hot to cold. Move down here and there's two types of weather: hot and humid, or hot and raining." He tilted his head back and let out a guffaw.

By now, Steve had exhausted most of his small-talk, so he eased into a conversation he hoped would pry information out of the man. "Tell me, did you recognize Marsha when we checked in?"

His mug came down on the wooden table a little too hard. "Aye. It's been a while, but I remember her well." He paused. "She asked a lot of questions about one lad that worked for me. I din' think she was on the up-and-up."

"She meant no harm. She's an insurance investigator, looking for a man."

"Why?"

"The company she works for might owe his family a lot of money. When he left your golf course, he moved to Punta Gorda. The police say he might have come to harm. Marsha needs to find out if that's true or not."

"I'll be askin' again. Why?"

"We think the man that worked for you isn't who he claimed to be. If we're right and he's dead, someone will receive fifteen million dollars."

The Scotsman let out a low whistle. He must have leaned forward because the next question smelled of ale. "Do you work for the same company?"

"No. I used to be a cop. A homicide investigator. I still look into a few murders every year."

"A private eye?"

"Yeah."

Gavin leaned back. "Like in the movies?"

Steve chuckled. "Not exactly. I traded my gun for a white cane."

This was the moment of truth. Gavin would either agree to talk or he'd clam up like he did with Marsha.

While Steve considered how to best proceed, Gavin cleared his throat. "You're an honest man. I like that. What do you want to know?"

"We believe the man who worked for you came to Belize from St. Lucia. Is that correct?"

"Nay. He had a passport and all the proper documents from St. Kitts. Marcus Kinsey was the name."

Steve nodded. "Did he ever use another name?"

"Brandon called him Mark, if that helps any."

"Who's Brandon?"

"He worked at the clubhouse and restaurant. He and Marcus became close friends."

The sound of the server putting pint number three on the table delayed the answer for a few seconds. Gavin asked if Steve wanted to order supper.

"Not yet." He waited until the footsteps of the server faded. "Tell me more about Brandon."

"If you keep the pints comin', I'll talk all night."

"It's a deal. Drinks and dinner on me."

"I'm likin' you more all the time, Steve." The slurping sound of the first drink from the pint sounded, followed by a satisfied, "Ahh," and the sound of glass coming to rest on the table.

"Where was I? Brandon. He could charm the dew off a rose. A natural salesman when working the pro shop. He'd make the ladies and lasses feel especially welcome, if you know what I mean."

Steve nodded. "How was he with the men?"

"Smooth as silk. Not pushy, but he'd ring up a new driver before they realized they needed one. He and Marcus got to be best of chums."

"They must have had a lot in common."

The tone of Gavin's words changed to something that hinted of sympathy. "They couldn't have been more different if they were night and day. Shy was Marcus. A whiz with the computer, but no good at dealing with customers. I put him to mowing the fairways and working as a dishwasher in the kitchen. He did good work. Sometimes too good. He had to clean and stack the dishes in a way that pleased him. If they weren't perfect, he'd restack the lot of 'em."

"Why did Marcus leave?"

"That's still a sore subject with me. They left together with me havin' a tournament to run." He paused. "The odd thing is, they never called or wrote for their last paychecks."

"They left together?"

"Aye. The cook saw a taxi take 'em away early of a mornin'."

"Did either of them receive a letter or phone call that upset them?"

"No one mentioned it. Like ghosts, they were. Here one day, and poof. Gone."

———

GAVIN DEPOSITED STEVE AT THE DOOR OF THE CABIN A LITTLE after ten. Marsha met them with disdain peppering her words. "It's about time. I hope you didn't make too big of a fool of yourself."

Steve paused. "Are you talking to me or Gavin?"

That brought on a full-throated laugh from the part-owner of the golf course. "G'night, Steve. Come back any time, and we'll lift another pint."

Marsha closed the door and changed her demeanor. "Were you able to get anything useful out of the Scotsman?"

Steve threw his voice to that of a highlander. "Aye, we had a proper chin-wag."

She took his hand and tugged, but he didn't budge. "I need to discover the layout of the room on my own." He turned to the right and swept his cane across the tile floor. "Tell me what's in my way."

"A small table with a coffee service."

He walked until his cane found the legs of the table and then he turned left. "Is your bedroom or the living room this way?"

"Living room. If you had turned left at the door, you'd have run into the queen bed."

Steve backtracked and found the bed. He allowed his cane to be his guide and located the bathroom, the living room furniture, and a door leading to the back porch. He chose an over-padded chair and sat. "Where did you eat supper?"

"I drove to town. The restaurant here closed at dusk."

"It cost me dinner and drinks, but Gavin turned out to be a fount of information. I just had to prime the pump. It seems Donnie, a.k.a. Marcus, made friends with a man named Brandon Clay. They left together without giving notice."

For the next hour, Steve and Marsha discussed all the morsels of information he'd extracted from Gavin. When they both yawned, Marsha spoke what Steve was thinking. "It must be time to call it a day. Can you think of any reason for talking to anyone else here tomorrow morning?"

"I'm more interested in finding out if Brandon Clay made it to Punta Gorda with Donnie."

"I'll need to do background on this Brandon character."

"Let's give Heather something to do," said Steve. "She'll feel left out if we don't."

"Fine with me. I'm out of favors with the people I knew at the CIA."

Steve pulled out his cell phone and told it to call Heather. Music blared in the background. "Did I interrupt something?"

"Jack and I are in the hotel bar. Hang on while I get off the dance floor."

The music faded and Heather came back on. "Did you have a productive day?"

"We did, and I have a job for you. Donnie left his job at the golf course in a hurry, and he had company. I need background on a man named Brandon Clay. He came from the States and worked at the golf course for about a year before Donnie arrived. Can you call someone at the State Department and check him out?"

"No problem, but it might be Monday or Tuesday before they get back to me."

"That should give you time to land another deal."

"Speaking of, I need to get back to the bar. There's talk of building another pier for cruise ships. A golf course nearby might be in my future."

"Why does that not surprise me? Do what you can. We're off to Punta Gorda in the morning."

5

———

Steve savored an early morning cup of coffee on the screened-in back porch while Marsha showered and dressed for the day. She'd described the river and tropical forest as a winding ribbon of water that cut through dense trees and undergrowth. He used his imagination to match the sounds to her words. The land teemed with the chatter of unfamiliar birds and jungle creatures. He wondered about the sagacity of golfers searching for wayward shots.

Marsha announced his turn in the shower. As usual, he shaved while there. No need to stand in front of a mirror. It wasn't long before they hauled their bags to the rental and began the trek to Punta Gorda, some seventy-eight miles to the southeast.

"I was wondering," said Marsha, "were Donnie and Brandon good friends?"

"Hard to say. Was he mentioned in the police reports?"

"He provided a statement that said Donnie, also known as Marcus, went for a walk while he stayed at a small hotel. The hotel owners confirmed it."

Steve placed the information in a mental file. One more thing that may, or may not, lead to finding the truth.

Once out of Belmopan, Marsha played tour guide and described the landscape. It didn't take long before she ran out of adjectives and descriptors for jungle forests and small farms. Another sixty miles passed with only the drone of the engine and the sound of tires on pavement to keep him company. That suited Steve down to his shoes. He'd rather review each scrap of information than take part in a forced conversation. His mind drifted back to life with Maggie and how their conversations flowed like a lazy river.

He'd almost nodded off when Marsha announced they'd entered the coastal town of Punta Gorda, a hamlet of around five thousand souls.

"Are there any places to eat?"

"The chain restaurants haven't made it this far, but there's a place with fresh seafood, if that's what you're hungry for. Most restaurants in Belize are small and have a decent selection. Fruits and vegetables grow year 'round."

The restaurant she remembered from her previous visit offered alfresco seating and a welcoming breeze off the southern Caribbean. They each ordered bottled water and what amounted to the catch of the day.

"What's your plan for us after lunch?" asked Steve.

"It's too early to check into the hotel. Donnie's last job was seven miles from here outside a tiny village named San Felipe. He worked on an organic farm. My company summoned me home before I could visit."

"Can you find the farm?"

"It won't be hard. I have the name—Mother Nature's Garden."

Steve's thoughts harkened back to the wild sixties and seventies. "Should I wear beads and sandals?"

"I can weave a wreath of flowers for your head if you want me to."

"Serves me right for trying to be a comedian."

Having skipped breakfast, Steve fell on his food with

ravenous abandon. He didn't know what fish he consumed, but it tasted amazing. "Marsha," he said between bites, "you hit the jackpot with this place. We may have to come here again."

The SUV rattled with each bounce and swerved as it moved upward on a road that led from the coast into neighboring hills. With windows down, the scents changed from seaside to that of dense vegetation and plowed plots of fertile earth. It took but one stop and a friendly voice instructed Marsha where to turn to find Mother Nature's Garden.

When the vehicle came to a stop and the gear shift clicked into place, Steve asked, "What does this farm look like?"

"It's beautiful, but not as big as I was expecting. I'd estimate between thirty-five and forty acres, but there's an incredible variety of plants. I see a small main house and a series of six, no, eight huts with tin roofs that form a semi-circle around the house."

"Sounds like a commune."

"I wouldn't doubt it, by the looks of the woman coming toward us. Let's get out and put on our best smiles."

Marsha greeted the approaching woman with, "Hi. I hope we've come to the right place. Is this Mother Nature's Garden?"

"It is," said the woman with pride driving her words.

"I read about your work on line and we had to find out first-hand what all the buzz is about."

"Let's get out of the sun and have some fresh-squeezed mango juice."

"I'm Marsha Pennywell and this is a friend, Steve Smiley."

"We don't use last names here. I'm Lucy."

Steve nodded his greeting. He wasn't expecting the hug and kisses on both cheeks he received.

"Welcome, Steve and Marsha. I'm always glad to have guests who want to join the cause."

He wondered what cause she meant, but didn't ask.

Marsha took Steve's hand and followed their hostess to a

place where the afternoon sun wasn't beating down. Once in the shade, the heat moderated.

"Tell me how you became interested in organic farming," said Lucy.

Marsha took the lead in answering. "It's more of something I'm thinking about pursuing after I retire. For now, the best I can do is raise a small herb garden on my back patio and shop the organic aisle at the grocery store."

He wondered how much truth Marsha wove into her cover story. It sounded genuine, but didn't match up with anything she'd said or the way she'd eaten in the brief time he'd known her.

"What about you, Steve?" asked Lucy. "You're the first blind person we've had come to our garden of hope."

He cleared his throat. "I live by myself in a condo so I'm not sure what my options are."

"Your options are more than you think." Lucy's voice had zeal in it. "Do you have a back patio or a small yard?"

"Both."

"Perfect. Give me the dimensions of both and I'll make a layout of a garden that will supply a good portion of your needs for seasonal vegetables." She paused. "I take it you two have sworn off all meat and dairy?"

Marsha jumped in and answered with a resounding, "Of course. We all have to do our part to save the planet." The lie rolled off the former CIA agent's tongue.

"Cool. All the workers are in their huts, taking their afternoon naps. After that, we'll have group meditation and yoga. You're welcome to stay and join us, or you could come back tomorrow morning. We'll be in the fields harvesting and you can help. I need to make deliveries this afternoon and won't be able to show you around."

Steve answered this one. "We've already had a long day of travel. It might be best if we waited until tomorrow morning to join you. I know Marsha is dying to get her hands dirty and learn all she can about organic gardening."

"I call it Mother Nature's gift to her children."

"What time do we need to be here?" asked Marsha.

"We pay no attention to measured time. Our students are up at first light, eat breakfast, and go to the fields."

"Students?" asked Steve.

"Mother Earth is the head mistress and I'm her assistant. We never advertise, but students come to us from all over the world. They're here to learn how to save their lives from the poisons we ingest and to help others do the same. My part is showing them how to grow healthy foods without the use of chemicals or any artificial means."

"How long do they stay in your program?"

"It's not a program. It's living in harmony with the natural rhythms emitted from the earth, stars, and the entire universe. People stay until it's time to move on."

Steve nodded as if he agreed with every word said.

"This is so exciting," said Marsha. "We'll be here tomorrow morning." She took Steve by the arm. "Let's spend the rest of the day meditating on what Mother Earth wants our gardens to be."

Lucy gave a word of correction. "*Her* gardens. Mother Earth owns it all; we're invited to join her."

"Of course," said Marsha. "Her gardens."

Steve kept a straight face until road noise changed from dirt to gravel. He turned to face Marsha. "How long have we been vegetarians?"

"Since lunch. There's a good chance I'll fall off the wagon at supper."

"Glad to hear it. I've been thinking about having real Caribbean jerk chicken since I smelled it in the restaurant today."

The trip to Punta Gorda didn't seem to take as much time as the one to the farm. Before long, Marsha announced, "We're coming to our hotel. I stayed here on my last trip. It's also where Donnie and Brandon stayed. It's small, with only ten or twelve rooms. They painted the exterior white with the balcony and trim a hot pink."

"Are the rooms upstairs?"

"Ours are."

"How far from the water?"

"On the other side of the street. There's a small lobby with four tables and breakfast is included."

Steve considered his sporadic sleep patterns. "I may not be ready to leave before first light."

Marsha brought the vehicle to a stop. "I don't think Lucy has high expectations from either of us. We'll have a leisurely breakfast and get there with plenty of morning left."

"Good. An agreement exists between me and plants. If they're in the ground, I leave them alone."

MARSHA DIDN'T GET FAR WITH HER EXCUSE FOR ARRIVING late at Mother Nature's Garden before Lucy dismissed the apology. Based on what Steve learned the previous day, this farm operated with different rules, the primary one being there were no rules. Guidelines and guidance, but nothing that approached something chiseled in stone or even written.

Lucy took Steve by the arm. "I'll be with you until you catch on. Marsha, you can join any of the people in the fields you feel in harmony with. They've all been here long enough to give you an overview of our operation. Anyone here can tell you how important our work is. Feel free to join in the work. Make new friends. If you find someone to work with and your auras clash, find someone else. It's all about community and harmony."

"What about me?" asked Steve.

Lucy squeezed his arm. "I'm so excited about working with you. Mother Nature came to me last night in a dream. She said you possess a special ability that I need to help you discover. You're to help me sort tomatoes."

"I'm willing to try, but I can't promise positive results. I hope I won't waste your time."

"You can't. Time is a man-made invention. Think in terms of sunrises and sunsets, plantings and harvests, not dates."

"Ripe and picked too soon?" asked Steve.

"Exactly! That must be what Mother Nature meant. You're to sort the tomatoes we're picking this morning according to how ripe they are. I'll be with you to make sure, but I want you to trust your gift."

Marsha said farewell and left to find a kindred spirit, or at least someone who had knowledge of the missing recluse.

Lucy led Steve a short distance away, guiding him to a stool and a bar-height table. "On your left is a bushel basket of tomatoes. On your right are three smaller baskets. The first is for tomatoes that are ripe and should go to market today. The next is for those that need another day or two before they reach their peak color and texture. Basket number three is for those that need over two days to ripen."

"Any suggestions on how I'm supposed to tell the difference?"

"Let Mother Nature guide you. I have complete confidence that in no time you'll reach a state of harmonic convergence with the cosmos, soil, and the fruit of the vines."

Steve nodded, even though he thought his hyper-developed senses of smell and touch would have more to do with choosing the tomatoes than harmony between stars and tomatoes.

At first his choices were more miss than hit. Undeterred by his poor performance, Lucy proved to possess a bottomless well of patience. He heard her take about half the tomatoes out of the ripe basket and place them in one of the other two. It took time, but he noticed the slight variations in smell and firmness of the tomatoes, and his choices became more accurate.

"I knew you'd soon reach a state of harmony," said Lucy. She reminded him of an excited teen.

As the morning wore on, Steve's level of proficiency increased to where he could accomplish the task with an accuracy that surprised him. This proficiency allowed him to ask questions while he worked. He began by limiting his queries to general subjects about the differences between modern farming practices and organic, sustainable crop production. Lucy proved to be a warehouse of knowledge that flowed with quotes of statistics, studies, historical references dating back to the Neolithic era, and warnings from "experts" about what will happen to mankind without change in its practices.

Steve then brought the conversation around to the more narrow confines of the farm. "You said yesterday that people come and go as they please. Do you remember everyone who comes here?"

"I remember most of them. Using only their first name helps. I must admit that I try to forget the skeptics or those who are not in harmony with Mother Nature."

"Can you give me an example?"

"I can, but you may not like it."

"Try me."

"You're in harmony. The lady with you isn't. I didn't use her name because I don't want to remember it."

Steve considered how to ask about Donnie, or Marcus as she would have known him, and Brandon without Lucy telling him to hit the road. He needn't have worried.

"You're not here to learn about organic farming, are you?"

"No, but my trips to the grocery store will never be the same."

"Stay on the organic aisle. With your gift, you can choose the best produce available."

Steve picked up a tomato out of the basket and gave it a sniff. He pushed it away. "There's something wrong with this one."

Lucy took it. "Good catch. A worm made it past the natural barrier plants and my little soldiers. I'd have missed that if I'd only glanced at it and judged it by color."

"Do you think I can grade other vegetables?"

"As long as you stay in harmony, there's no telling what you can do."

"How do I stay in harmony with you and ask the questions I need to?"

"Is your intention good?"

"I'm trying to find out if a man is still alive. We believe he came here several years ago. When he left the States, his name was Donnie. He changed it several times, but called himself Marcus in Belize. The police say he disappeared in Punta Gorda. It's possible he came to harm there."

"That's another reason I insist on first names. Many come here to reinvent themselves." She paused. "Can you describe the man?"

"Five-feet-ten-inches tall, 165 pounds, late twenties, long, wavy brown hair, the beginnings of a receding hairline—"

Lucy cut him off. "That's Marcus, or at least it sounds like him. I assume you know he didn't come alone."

"That was going to be my next question."

"He came with Brandon."

Steve nodded. "That's the same names they used in Belmopan when they worked at a golf course. What can you tell me about their relationship?"

Lucy took in a deep breath. "Brandon was out of harmony when he came, but impressed me as a genuine seeker. Of the two, Brandon was the leader when they arrived. He talked a good game but never embraced the soil. I asked him to try his hand at making deliveries. Our customers raved about him. He badgered me to charge more than we needed to keep the farm running. It was beyond him to understand that we are here on earth to sustain her, not turn an obscene profit."

"Did he ever find harmony?"

"In his own way, but not like Marcus."

Steve knew he needed to ask more about Brandon, but that could wait. Instead, he asked, "What about Marcus?"

"Ahh," said Lucy with excitement rippling her voice. "Marcus came with deep wounds that he never discussed. He learned to work with the land. The people of our little community nurtured him the same way we do our garden, and he thrived. By the time he left, Mother Nature had grown Mark into a strong and caring soul. He became so fully orbed, he could do every task on the farm, including sales and deliveries."

Steve scratched his chin. "Did either tell you they were leaving?"

"That's not something we focus on, but Mother Nature told me they'd made plans."

"Did Mother Nature tell you anything else about Marcus?"

"What makes you ask?"

Steve cleared his throat. It was times like this that he wanted to share his deepest secret, but didn't dare. Instead, he nibbled around the subject. "You're a woman who operates with what some people call a sixth sense. It allows you to know things you can't explain."

"Do you mean when Mother Nature comes to me? I see a seed and visualize a plant and the most succulent fruit you could imagine."

"That's the general idea. I was a homicide detective for a long time, and a good one. The police in Punta Gorda believe Marcus might be dead. I sense he's not dead, only hiding."

Instead of scoffing, Lucy clapped her hands. "I knew it. There's something special in your aura. How exciting. Is there any way you can let me know when you find him? I'd like to know Marcus is alright."

"I can call, send you a text, or email you."

"It will have to be email. That's the only way we stay in contact with those who want to come to our community and our customers."

"There is one thing I'd ask of you." Steve lowered his voice. "Please don't tell anyone about my suspicion that Marcus is alive until I confirm it."

Lucy laughed out loud. "I promise, but believe me, it wouldn't matter if I did. Most people think I'm certifiable and would dismiss it as the ravings of a burned-out modern-day hippie." She caught her breath and asked. "Have you told Marsha the man you call Donnie is alive?"

"She's hoping he is for professional reasons."

"You mean she'll benefit financially?" She paused. "Beware, Steve. I'm sensing the sour fruit of greed in your quest to find Marcus."

6

———

Lucy left Steve alone to finish separating tomatoes as she checked on the workers. Before she left, he accepted her invitation to join the group for lunch. By the time voices grew in volume, he'd divided all but a few tomatoes into their baskets. He sensed someone draw near.

"Please tell me you had more luck than me," said Marsha. "Donnie left long before any of these people arrived."

"Yes, Lucy remembers him. He used the name Marcus here on the farm."

"Donnie, Marcus, or whatever else he called himself," said Marsha, as if her patience had stretched until it snapped.

"He and Brandon came and left together. I'll tell you about it on the way back after lunch."

"Are you serious? We're staying for lunch?"

Marsha's words reminded him of a snapping turtle, but he believed they'd glean more information if they stayed a while longer. "It would be rude to go. Besides, I'm curious to see what Lucy considers a proper vegetarian meal."

Marsha expressed her opinion by issuing a huff of disgust followed by, "While you've been up here in the shade and breeze, I've been in the windless valley without a hat. My face must look like a boiled lobster, and the back of my neck is on fire. The tank top seemed like a good idea this morning, but I didn't consider how close we are to the equator."

"That will give us a reason to leave right after lunch."

Lucy called everyone to come eat. Judging from the number of conversations swirling around him, Steve guessed the crowd to be fifteen or more people who made their way to a communal table under shade. Their host offered thanks to Mother Nature for the bounty. The sound of silverware clinking against the bowls and platters being passed around from person to person filled the air.

"Who's going to tell me what's on the menu?" asked Steve.

Lucy spoke before Marsha. "I'm putting a scoop of quinoa and rice on your plate."

"Where on the plate?"

"Closest to you. To the left are cucumber and onion slices. They soaked overnight in vinegar and water with salt and pepper. At the top of the plate, you'll find mashed plantains and sweet potatoes. It's served warm, and everyone loves it so much we have it three times a day. Slices of the ripe tomatoes you separated this morning are on the right side of the plate. If you find another worm, it's your own fault."

Steve dug in and had no complaints about the quality or freshness of the meal. In fact, it tasted so good that Marsha overcame her pain and disappointment long enough to issue a few moans of approval. It also didn't hurt that the worker named Jillion arrived with a bottle of aloe and presented it to Marsha as a present.

"We make it here," said the woman with a thick Scandinavian accent.

"Mangos and bananas for dessert," said Lucy. "After that you're welcome to sleep in a hammock. I'll be giving a lesson on beneficial nematodes after naps."

"Beneficial what?" asked Steve.

"Beneficial nematodes. They're naturally occurring microscopic unsegmented worms that kill hundreds of varieties of harmful insects. It's one way we cooperate with Mother Nature to produce healthy food. Those are the little soldiers I referred to earlier."

"Can I find something about it online?" asked Steve.

"It's common knowledge in the horticulture community. You might even find one of my articles."

"I can't thank you enough," said Steve. "Given Marsha's sunburn, we should call it a day. Coming here has been the highlight of my trip and the healthiest food I've eaten in years."

"Come back any time. You've convinced me I may need to recruit some vision-impaired people. You did a bang-up job separating the tomatoes."

Marsha expressed her thanks and led Steve to the SUV. Her words for the farm weren't nearly as kind on the trip home. In fact, she clarified that all she wanted was a cold shower, more aloe, and a bed. They'd meet later and he could tell her what he'd learned.

Steve went to his room, but stayed only long enough to place a call to Heather. He gave her a run-down of what he'd accomplished so far.

"It sounds like you and Marsha aren't hitting it off like I thought you would. What's your plan for the rest of the afternoon?" she asked.

"There's only one more thing left on my to-do list. I need to find the spot where the police say Donnie went missing and say his name. If I see red, that will be the end of the trail."

"And if you don't?"

"So far, Donnie has used one other alias in Belize. There's no telling how many more passports he has. I doubt Marsha's company will keep looking based on a blind guy saying he didn't see red at a murder scene."

"Did you tell Marsha about your associative chromesthesia?"

"Nope. And I'm not going to."

"That sounded definite. How many more days do you need?"

"I'll call you tonight and let you know for sure."

"Are you saying we might leave tomorrow?"

"Tell the pilot to file a flight plan." Steve paused. "How's your working vacation?"

"Awesome. There are definite possibilities for investments in Belize."

"And the golf?"

"Almost as good as the scuba diving. Jack enjoyed every minute."

"Glad to hear it. I'll call later."

Steve slipped the phone in the pocket of his shorts, grabbed his cane, and found his way downstairs to the front desk. The friendly voice of the proprietor greeted him.

"Hello, Mr. Smiley. What can I do for you?"

"Ah, Mr. Sandborne, just the man I wanted to talk to. Do you have a minute?"

"If I had as much money as I do time, I'd be rich and happy instead of just happy."

"I need to test your memory. Marsha told me you've been here a long time. Is that right?"

"June and I bought the hotel over twenty years ago. We lived in the Upper Peninsula of Michigan and came here on vacation. That's all it took to convince us to move to a place where we didn't shovel snow and wear three layers of clothes half the year."

A shiver went down Steve's back despite the tropical setting. Since losing his sight, he'd become more sensitive to the weather, especially cold. Now wasn't the time to dwell on the weather. "Some years back, a disappearance occurred here in Punta Gorda. The police said a young man named Marcus Kinsey went missing. Do you remember him?"

"Sure, I remember. Ms. Pennywell came and asked a lot of questions. She might know about the police report."

"She does, and I had her read it to me. It seemed a little sketchy. What do you remember about Marcus?"

"He and Brandon stayed here one night when they first came to town. They also stayed the night he went missing."

"What was Brandon's last name?"

"Hold on, I'll look it up in one of the old registers."

It sounded like he reached under the counter and settled a book on the counter. "Here he is. Brandon Clay."

"Yeah," said Steve. "That's the same name he used in Belmopan. Did you hear either of them call each other by any other names?"

"Sorry, that was a long time ago."

"That's what I expected. Do you remember the last place anyone saw Marcus?"

"I don't remember who last saw him, but one of our guests found a knife and a bloody towel on the beach, not far from here. The towel belonged to this hotel."

"How hard did the police search for him?"

Mr. Sandborne let out a chuckle. "I don't want to be unfair about the local constabulary, but they aren't what you might call exceptionally well trained or motivated. They had a good look at his room, but that was all. I told them about Brandon staying here, and they searched his room as well."

"Did Brandon or Mark say why they came to town to spend the night?"

"No, but they traveled light. Only a small bag each."

"And Brandon? What became of him?"

"He stayed a few days and moved on. I asked him about his plans, but he wasn't one to talk long about anything."

Steve scratched his chin. "I know this is a lot to ask, but could you take me to the spot where they found the bloody towel and the knife?"

He hesitated. "Why would you want to go there?"

"I used to be a homicide detective. It's bizarre, but I like to visit places where unusual disappearances occurred." Steve knew he had to come up with a more complete explanation. "A successful author took me under her wing and convinced me to try my hand at learning to write crime novels. It helps if I go to a location for background."

"I can't be away from the desk too long."

"If you lead me to the spot, I'll get back on my own."

The sound of a book closing caught Steve's ears as Mr. Sandborne asked, "Are you ready?"

"Have cane, will travel."

A light sea-breeze hit Steve as they crossed the street, walked down a gentle slope, and turned right on sand. He stopped counting steps when Mr. Sandborne came to an abrupt stop.

"What's shading me?"

"A palm tree. This is where they found the knife and bloody towel."

Steve nodded. "Thanks. I'll soak up the vibe of the place and dictate some notes into my phone."

He walked around the tree, running his hand against the rough bark. Was this the place the gaming genius died, or where Donnie Douglas played a game of deception? Steve listened for other voices or people rustling the sand nearby. He tilted his head to catch the noise of passing cars on the street above. Nothing. He took in a large breath and said, "Donnie Douglas." To make sure, he also spoke the other aliases Donnie used. A seagull squawked, a car passed on the nearby road, and waves lapped and gurgled, but the image of the color red did not come. Whatever happened to Donnie, his life didn't end here.

He reached for his phone and called Heather. It went to voice mail, and he waited for the prompt. "No red. The computer whiz doesn't want anyone to find him, and that's fine with me. We'll turn in our rental at the airport outside Belize City before noon tomorrow. Let's go home."

THE TIRES ON THE SUV MADE A HAPPY SINGING SOUND AS they rolled toward the airport. Marsha had skipped supper, so

Steve relayed all he'd learned from Lucy about Donnie and Brandon's stay at the farm. He also filled her in on the strange disappearance of both men from Punta Gorda.

Marsha peppered him with questions, and he answered them all, but not with complete candor. He told her he'd gone to the site of the supposed homicide and that it seemed staged. He theorized Donnie left the knife and bloody towel for the police to find. His rare gift of associative chromesthesia, the ability to see a certain color overlaying images where a homicide took place, remained his secret. He knew Donnie didn't die on the beach in Punta Gorda, Belize. It would be up to Marsha to pursue Donnie or allow the recluse to stay hidden.

"Sorry I didn't go to supper with you last night," said Marsha. "I took cold showers and slathered aloe on. I also cursed myself for not putting on sunblock."

"No problem. I went back to the restaurant we tried when we came to Punta Gorda. Their jerk-chicken is the best I ever tasted."

After a bump shifted him in the SUV's seat, he asked, "Is the sunburn any better today?"

"Not a bit."

"That's no fun."

"Neither is leaving a case unfinished."

"How long before your company settles the claim?"

"I'll delay it as long as I can, but unless something else happens, I'd say a couple of months. A lot will depend on Heather's contacts. If they can trace Donnie out of Belize, that would prove he was alive longer than we thought and wouldn't meet the seven-year threshold. It would be easier if Donnie hadn't collected passports the way some people do souvenir shot glasses."

Steve raised his voice to one that projected confidence. "I'm more convinced than ever that Donnie left Belize alive. Brandon's the one that has me scratching my head. Did he leave with Donnie or move on to a job that better suited him?"

"Who cares?"

Steve shrugged. "It's one of those loose ends that drives me nuts."

Marsha spoke with a subdued voice. "At least it's not my fifteen million dollars, but it will cost me a heathy bonus that I could use for my daughter's tuition." She raised her voice a half-octave. "What did you hear from Heather?"

"She's meeting us at the airport, and she and Jack had a wonderful vacation. It was non-stop looking at investment possibilities, playing golf, scuba diving, and dancing the night away."

"Now you've bummed me out even more. I remember when I could do all that and get by on three hours sleep."

Steve didn't say anything to cheer her. Time would take care of Marsha's disappointment and aloe would help the sunburn.

They arrived at the airport, turned in the rental, and waited on a golf cart to shuttle them to Heather's plane. By the time their ride arrived, Steve's shirt stuck to his back as sweat dribbled down his side. Their copilot's voice cut through the noise of people coming and going. "Sorry to keep you waiting. There was a mix up with reserving ground transportation."

"No problem for me, but you may have to slather Marsha with aloe on the trip home."

"Oh, my," said the copilot. "I'll get an ice pack for you as soon as we get on the plane."

"I wouldn't turn down a stiff drink, either."

"How about one while we're doing pre-flight and another on the way?"

"What about two to begin with and then we'll discuss the trip back to Texas?"

The cart's electric motor gave off a high-pitched whine as it scooted toward their destination. Heather and Jack met them on the tarmac. "Good grief," said Heather. "You poor thing. Get on board. We have the air conditioner blowing full blast."

They boarded the aircraft and buckled up for the flight. Marsha downed two drinks in quick succession and remained quiet for most of the flight home. Jack tilted his plush leather seat back as far as it would go and caught up on missed shut-eye. Heather, however, typed on her laptop and fielded calls from the office. The first three dealt with a land development on Lake LBJ. The fourth, however, caught Steve's attention.

"Are you sure?" asked Heather. "Thanks, I owe you."

Heather's on-board phone made the unique sound it did when she put it back in its cradle. Her perfume wafted stronger as he sensed her presence close to him. She whispered, "Brandon came back to the States after he left Belize. He landed in Texas."

Steve nodded, but said nothing.

———

HEATHER'S AIRCRAFT DESCENDED, PUNCHING A HOLE IN clouds that, from above, looked like a gray rug covering Conroe's airport. She'd hoped to get more done on the projects she'd taken, but wouldn't trade the memories of sun-drenched Belize for anything. The ability to relax and enjoy life had never come easy to her, but this trip showed she could mix business with pleasure. Her musings ceased when Jack brought his seat upright and gave her a broad smile.

Marsha stirred next. Her face had the hue of a bisected ruby-red grapefruit, but it didn't compare to her shoulders and neck. Fluid-filled welts raised from her skin. A couple had already popped, and she grimaced with every jolt and bump the airplane made as it touched down and taxied.

Steve looked normal with his brown hair a little tousled, clean-shaven, khaki trousers, a short-sleeve shirt, and medium-weight jacket at the ready for when he stepped into winter's cold arms. The wrap-around sunglasses stayed on until bedtime, unless he had a vexing problem to solve and he removed them to massage his temples.

"Marsha," said Steve. "Heather's sources came through with a lead for you. Brandon came back to the States after he left Belize. Nothing on Donnie."

Instead of acting surprised or even happy, she grimaced in pain. "Thanks, but I've had enough of Donnie Douglas, and that includes his buddy, Brandon."

The plane came to rest outside the hangar. As soon as the cabin's door opened, Marsha used an economy of words to express her thanks and bid Heather and Jack farewell. She then led Steve off the plane and into a cold, stiff wind.

Heather wrote off Marsha's subdued mood to the severe sunburn and not looking forward to facing Houston's traffic. She and Jack stayed on board long enough to enjoy a long parting kiss. "That needs to last you a while."

"What about this weekend? You promised."

Heather shook her head and smiled. "Aren't you tiring of me?"

"I'll let you know when that happens." They scurried down the stairs. Jack grabbed his suitcase with his left hand, and saluted with his right. "If you ever want to go to Belize again, you know my number."

The spell broke when Heather heard Steve clear his throat, his way of telling her not to leave him standing on cold concrete with the wind cutting through a thin jacket. She motioned to the pilot and copilot to take their luggage to her car and latched on to Steve.

The temperature difference between the airport in Belize and that in Conroe made her long for azure waters and gawking at fish with colors so vibrant they appeared freshly painted. Steve muttered something unintelligible through chattering teeth. After quick-marching to the parking lot, she brought the SUV to life. "The heater will kick on as soon as the engine warms. I've turned your seat's heater on high. Let me know when you get too hot."

"It may take a while for my frozen buns to get toasty. Next

time, if it's freezing or boiling hot, don't allow anyone to drag me off the plane until you and Jack finish saying goodbye."

"Sorry. We got a little carried away."

Steve flicked his wrist to dismiss the apology. "It sometimes took me and Maggie twenty minutes to break the clinch."

His reference to his deceased wife answered one of her questions. Nothing happened between him and Marsha. He'd only shown interest in one woman since he lost his wife, and that relationship seemed to have faded. At least for the immediate future.

Heather wove her way to I45 and accelerated onto the freeway. When she reached highway speed, Steve gave her additional details of his activity while in Belize. The report reminded her of sitting in a squad room when she wore the uniform of a Boston Massachusetts cop.

"It sounds like you did most of the work."

"Things worked out that way. Marsha's company pushed her too hard to get fast results the first time she was there. She could have uncovered everything I did if she'd had more time."

"Will she keep trying to find Donnie?"

"It depends on her company and how hard they want to fight the case. All she knows for sure is that Brandon came back to the States, and that's thanks to you. Donnie could be halfway across the world, using another name and passport. I doubt she'll ever find him. They might as well settle the life insurance claim with the family."

7

———

Over the next weeks, Heather tried to keep Steve from sinking into his annual Christmas funk. As in years past, her attempts at cheering him were as welcome as a root canal. Memories of his late wife visited every year with the ferocity of Dickens's ghosts of past, present, and future all rolled into one. He met most challenges head on and overcame them. Not Christmas.

Upon their return from Belize, he worked on a novella inspired by the trip. It kept his mind partially occupied, which Heather counted as a major victory. Three weeks after New Year's Day, he abandoned the work because he found the plot too confusing and couldn't think of a satisfying ending.

Heather relegated her days in Belize to the closet of fond memories until one day in February, when she turned on the news as she prepared for another day at the office. A dated photo of a young man she recognized shone on the screen. Beneath the picture ran a banner: *RECLUSE MILLIONAIRE MURDERED.* She grabbed a throw from the back of her couch, wrapped it around her, and hot-footed it next door. She found Steve in his recliner, with Max curled in a ball in his lap. "Are you watching the news?"

"The weather."

"Put it on the local news. Donnie Douglas is dead. I didn't get details."

After several long minutes the day's other stories and commercials cycled off, and the lead story looped back around. As expected, ninety percent of the broadcast involved Donnie's rise to fame and fortune, with scant details dedicated to the crime.

Steve turned off the television and picked up his phone. He instructed it to call his former partner, Houston homicide detective, Leo Vega. It rang four times before Leo moaned a greeting.

"Are you still asleep?"

"Does it matter?"

"Not really. I need you to check into something."

Leo issued a loud yawn. "Why do our conversations always include the same four words? 'I need you to...'"

Undeterred, Steve plowed on. "There's a news story this morning about a homicide on some sort of farm between Giddings and Brenham."

Leo broke in. "That's an hour's drive past the closest Houston city limit sign. Not my turf."

"I know where it is. There's not much out there, but the victim interests me. I went all the way to Belize looking for him."

Leo sounded more awake. "Are you talking about a homicide?"

"I wouldn't be calling if it wasn't. His name is Donnie Douglas, a wonder-boy of the gaming industry. News reports say he was shot and then made into a human torch."

"That sounds personal. I'll do some checking. Anything special I'm looking for?"

"Only background for now. More than what a news reporter could scrounge up, but not a deep dive."

"Anything else?"

"By noon would be nice."

"So would the steak dinner you promised me for the last favor."

The call cut off. Heather wasn't sure if Steve ended it or Leo. It was a game they played.

Max jumped down, put out with Steve for interrupting his nap with a phone call. He padded off to the kitchen, his nails clicking on the tile floor, his tail swishing back and forth. Steve rose and announced, "I'm going to the office with you today."

"Do you think Leo will call before noon?"

Steve shrugged his response. "I'm calling Marsha to check on the status of her investigation. I want you to be there to hear what she says."

"We still don't have a client."

"No, but at least there's a murder."

As usual, Heather arrived at her office at eight o'clock on the dot. It wasn't unheard of for Steve to accompany her, but it wasn't the norm. Eyebrows raised and rumors coursed through the offices whenever Steve arrived before 10:00 a.m. Heather's administrative assistants passed knowing glances to each other when Steve didn't take the time to greet them by name.

At 10:17, Steve's office phone rang. "Smiley and McBlythe Investigations," he said in an even voice as he put the phone on speaker. Heather rose from her desk on the other side of the office and joined him.

"Mr. Smiley, my name is Brandon Clay. Marsha Pennywell referred me to you. I understand you know her."

"That's correct. She and I went to Belize looking for Donnie Douglas. I understand you knew him well."

The question didn't receive an answer, but Brandon got straight to the heart of his call. "I've done nothing like this before, but I'd like to hire you to find Luke's killer."

"Who is Luke?"

"Marcus came back to the States under the name Luke Pryor. He had it changed in some other country, passport and everything. He came back on a work visa and went through the immigration process. Luke is what everyone calls him... Sorry. Luke is what everyone called him here on the farm. We don't know him as Donnie Douglas. I never did."

"Alright, to prevent confusion, we'll call him Luke. Before we get into details, I need to explain our terms and conditions for taking a case."

A ten-minute conversation followed in which Steve ironed out expectations and told Brandon that he'd have to sign a contract. The negotiations wound down to a few parting words and directions to the farm. "Heather and I will do all we can to find the person who killed Luke and bring him to justice. We also want you to know how sorry we are for your loss."

"Thank you. I'll tell Julie you're coming and relay your condolences."

"Julie?"

"Luke's wife."

Steve leaned back in his chair. "Heather and I will be there tomorrow."

As soon as the phone rested in its cradle, Heather let out a low whistle. "Now we have a murder and a client." She looked at the notes she'd taken. "Let me make sure I have everything straight. Donnie Douglas produced computer games that made him rich. He couldn't handle the pressure of being in the limelight, changed his name at least a half-dozen times, and settled for a while in Belize under the name Marcus or Mark. He then disappears and comes back to the States under the name Luke Pryor. Do I have that straight?"

"Donnie Douglas is now Luke Pryor. Since that's how they all knew him, we'll call him Luke when we go to the farm." Steve drummed his fingers on the desk. "We also have a widow and a family with expectations of being millionaires. This case could get interesting."

8

High pressure during the night pushed out winter's clouds and left the landscape scrubbed clean for the drive. It should have taken two hours to reach their destination, but an accident brought traffic down to one lane. "Good thing we left early," said Heather, trying to convince herself Houston's snarled traffic didn't bother her.

Steve grunted but said nothing. He'd grown up driving the city's streets and freeways. He didn't need to be told what happens when excessive speed and carelessness join forces. Instead of carping about irresponsible drivers, he changed the subject.

"What can you tell me about Luke's widow?"

Heather inched her SUV forward two car lengths. "Julie's the only child of an upper-middle-class family in Austin. No criminal history. She did well in high school and college but dropped out going into her senior year. A double major in theatre and accounting. She was also an artist of sorts."

"Of sorts?"

"An artist that ate ramen noodles six days a week trying to sell her work. From what I learned last night, she's using her training in accounting at the farm these days. She's put theatrical makeup and painting aside, and is into all things organic and natural."

"What else?"

"She's an alumnus of Mother Nature's Farm in Belize."

"Is that where she met Luke and Brandon?"

"They didn't grow up anywhere near each other, so I'd say that's a fair assumption."

Steve rubbed his clean-shaven chin. "Odd that the woman running the farm in Belize didn't mention they married. Perhaps that didn't happen until later."

"Finally," said Heather as the traffic gained speed, only to slow down two hundred yards later.

"Anything else?"

"Nothing of significance. Photos on Julie's social media pages show her to be an earthy, pleasant-looking woman with straight brown hair and no makeup. Based on her posts, I believe she fit in well with Lucy at Mother Nature's."

Steve nodded. "It shouldn't be much longer before we're on our way."

Sure enough, the log-jam of cars broke free, and drivers passed on both sides of the Grand Parkway, driving as if they'd pre-determined to cause the next accident. Heather took the off-ramp, merged onto Highway 290 westbound, and made good time. It wasn't long before they slid around the south side of Brenham then continued on the same US highway until the navigation system told her to turn right on a county road. After several more miles, the AI voice told her their destination lay two-hundred yards ahead.

"This place is like nothing I've ever seen," said Heather. "I bet there's a hundred greenhouses, perhaps more. They look like Quonset huts made from metal frames covered by opaque plastic."

"What are their dimensions?"

"I'm guessing about thirty yards wide and seventy-five yards long."

Heather slowed, turned onto a paved driveway, and stopped at a keypad on a pole in front of a closed gate. "I need to call Brandon and get the latest code to get in."

"The latest? How often does he change it?"

"I didn't ask him."

Heather completed her call, received the code, and noticed something else about the farm. "There's a security camera monitoring the gate." She paused. "Make that two security cameras."

"They must be proud of their cucumbers."

Heather ignored his dry sense of humor and passed through the gate that swung open and then automatically closed behind her vehicle. "Brandon said for us to follow the road to the right until we see a log cabin. He'll meet us there."

The road wound its way around a beehive of Quonset huts, all laid out in military precision. "I see a worker walking between the greenhouses," said Heather. "I bet there's a lot more I can't see. The noise you hear is a tractor pulling a flat-bed trailer. It's loaded with crates of fresh vegetables. There's another backed up to what looks like a warehouse. It's big, but not huge. I'm guessing about twenty thousand square feet. Transport trucks are backed up to loading docks."

Steve nodded. "How big are the trucks and how many?"

"Four trucks. Two loading at docks while two more are sitting off by themselves. Not semis, but medium-size bobtails. Big enough to handle about half what a semi-trailer can. Just the right size to make deliveries in a city."

"It's pushing noon. I bet other trucks left early for Houston and Austin. We need to make sure we get a tour of the facility. The way you're describing this place, it could be a high profit business, especially if they're growing everything organically. I did some study on hydroponics last night. It's one thing to raise plants in water. It's something else to have them meet the criteria required to receive the organic sticker."

"It's all I ever buy."

"You and a lot of other people. I'm not so particular, but I do like their taste."

What Heather saw next caused her eyebrows to lift. "I was expecting a rustic cabin in the woods. This place could be a hotel in Telluride or Aspen. Someone must do a lot of entertaining."

"It might be Luke's house. Or, I should say Julie's house."

"It's too big for a house, and there's a parking lot with at least forty cars. A carved sign hangs suspended over the gabled entry that reads, THE HIDDEN LODGE. A woman's coming out to meet us. If I'm not mistaken, it's Julie."

Steve had barely made it out of the passenger's seat and closed the door when the woman enfolded him in her arms.

"Thank God, you've come." It wasn't a simple declaration, but more of a gushing of words as she broke the clutch and laced Steve's right arm in her left. "I've been beside myself." She wore jeans with a legitimate work-worn hole in the right knee, sandals with socks, and a North Face jacket.

"Are you Julie?" asked Steve.

"How silly of me. Yes. Julie." Her attention shifted to Heather. "And you must be Heather. I hope you don't mind that I call you each by your first names. I can't stand formality. When I studied with Lucy in Belize, she thought it silly to use last names. The more I meditate on it, the more I agree with her."

Heather gave her a nod and a pinched smile as Steve said, "We're so sorry for your loss. Although I never met Luke, I feel as if I know him."

Julie's chin quivered. "He was the most awesome partner a woman could ever have. No one will ever take his place."

Steve nodded. "I know what you mean."

A softness filled Julie's voice. "Brandon told me when he looked you up, he saw you lost your wife a few years ago. I'm so sorry."

A nod of Steve's head acknowledged the truth of her statement as well as her condolences.

Julie's voice raised a notch. "Come, let's get out of this chilly breeze. There's a pleasant fire inside. Brandon's getting the next shipment out now, but he'll join us for lunch."

They headed up flagstone steps to the front doors. "Is this your home?" asked Steve.

"Oh no. This is where our guests stay. We have working relationships with Texas A&M and Prairie View A&M. They're not that far and some of their students take part in an internship program we patterned after Mother Nature's Farm in Belize. Other individuals with a genuine interest in hydroponics are also welcome to come as long as they agree to work in the greenhouses."

Julie led him as he tapped and scraped the ground in front of him. "It sounds like your business model is like Lucy's."

"In some ways, but not all. Luke set this up to be a for-profit business. Unlike Belize, we have to have greenhouses to grow all year round. Also, we enjoy creature comforts instead of roughing it in huts. All the rooms have en suite bathrooms. It's like a nice hotel, except we expect our interns to do their own laundry and clean their rooms at least once a week. We also allow cell phones and there's high speed Internet service."

While talking, Julie directed Steve to a chair near a crackling fireplace. He used his cane to confirm its location and felt the fabric as he settled in. "This is nice and warm," he said. "We're debating if it would be best to stay here or go back to Brenham and spend the night."

"You absolutely must stay here."

Heather wondered if fear laced Julie's declaration.

Steve leaned forward. "Are you still living in your home, Julie?"

"Oh, no. How could I after what's happened? I'm staying here in one of the VIP rooms."

"Ah."

"You'll be staying down the hall from my room. We run the lodge like a hotel, except we serve all-organic meals in the dining room. The cooks always leave snacks for the early risers and night owls. You'll each have your own room with an adjoining door so you don't have to venture out into the hallway to talk." She took a breath, following the spillage of words. "Please say you'll stay. I'd feel so much safer knowing you were right down the hall."

Heather wanted to tell Julie she'd wasted a perfectly good pout on Steve. Instead, she asked something Steve would want to know. "Do you believe someone will try to harm you?"

"People do a lot of wicked things for money. I didn't know Luke earned a fortune before I met him. All three of us, Brandon, Luke, and me said we'd never talk about our lives prior to coming to the farm in Belize. While there we reinvented ourselves."

Steve leaned back in his chair and made a steeple out of his index fingers. "Do you suspect someone in particular of killing Luke?"

"Negative energy like that drains me. I prefer to remember the good times."

"Yet you want us to discover who killed your husband and bring him, or her, to justice."

"Yes," she said with a firm voice. "I want to do all I can to save the planet and help everyone and everything live in harmony, but I draw the line at harming animals, and most certainly not humans."

"If you believe that," said Steve, "then you need to decide which is more important—being drained of positive energy or helping us find your husband's killer."

Julie covered her cheeks and eyes with her hands. Slowly, she pulled her hands down and folded them on her lap. "All right. I have no proof, but I suggest you start your investigation with Luke's closest relatives. There are two cousins, a brother and sister."

Heather jumped in. "Trey and Mary Ricks?"

"You already know about them?"

"They knew him as Donnie Douglas and tried to have him declared legally dead. They would have succeeded, but an insurance investigator started tracking him, learned about his aliases, and proved he hadn't died within the seven-year period required by law."

Julie nodded. "What you may not know is that a constable served me papers yesterday. The two cousins filed a petition this week to have our marriage declared void."

"On what grounds?"

Julie stood, walked to the fireplace, and spun around. "The paperwork said our marriage didn't meet the standards of a legal marriage because Lucy conducted the ceremony at the farm."

"Did you purchase property in both of your names?"

"Yes."

"Did you claim to be married on other legally binding documents?"

"Of course."

"And you used Luke's last name on those documents?"

"He went by Marcus in Belize and that's what's on the marriage license. Doesn't that make us married?"

Heather nodded. "I'll need to look at all his passports and the marriage document you received in Belize. That will give us a paper trail and we'll be able to prove Marcus and Luke were the same person."

Steve started to say something but stopped after the lone word, "But..."

"But what?" asked Julie.

"It's nothing."

"Yes, it is something or you wouldn't have thought it."

"I'll change my remarks," said Steve. "It may be something, but I'm not positive."

Heather and Julie looked at each other as Steve cleared his

throat. "I was thinking that filing those court papers could be a delaying tactic."

"Why?"

Heather answered. "There are two things at stake. The first is the fortune Luke accumulated under the name Donnie Douglas. We know that occurred before he dropped off the radar. The second is a multi-million-dollar life insurance policy. Until the court decides on the legality of the marriage, the rightful heir can't be named."

Steve asked, "It's important that you provide Heather with everything she asks for. The sooner she gets started, the better."

"Sure. They're in a locked file cabinet in the business office down the hall on the way to the cafeteria. I'll be back as quick as I can."

Once they were alone, Heather asked. "What's up? I know you sent her away for a reason."

"I didn't want to tell her the real reason. I need you to keep a close eye on Julie."

"Ah-ha. You believe whoever killed Luke might want to eliminate her, too."

"The thought crossed my mind and almost jumped out of my mouth. If Julie wasn't around to convince a judge that she's Luke's widow, it might be easier for those high-dollar attorneys the Ricks's hired to pull a fast one."

"Good thinking. I'll bring in the bags."

Heather made it almost to the door when a man pushed it open. He wore a baseball cap with the name "OH Farm" printed on it with a flannel shirt under a down vest, blue jeans, and hiking boots. Bourbon-colored hair went past his collar. A thick beard obscured much of his face.

"Are you Heather?"

She nodded. "You must be Brandon, one of the owners of Organic Hydroponic Farm."

"Yeah. Where's Julie?"

"Copying the papers they served her yesterday."

"Good. Have you brought your bags in yet?"

"That's what I was going to do."

"I'll have them brought up to your rooms." He looked at the fireplace. "Is that Steve?"

"Hello, Brandon."

Heather whispered. "He has exceptional hearing. Don't whisper within fifty feet of him if you don't want him to hear you."

"I heard that."

Steve remained seated as Brandon took over the chair Julie had vacated. "Thanks for coming."

Heather was surprised when Steve asked, "Why did you choose me and Heather to find Luke's killer?"

The question seemed too direct, especially from Steve. Perhaps he had found out something about Brandon she didn't know. Whether he did or not, Brandon had a ready answer for him.

"You'd already gone to Belize looking for us. You seemed like the logical choice."

"Did Lucy send you an email saying Marsha Pennywell and I tried to locate Luke?"

He tilted his head and issued what looked like a seldom-used smile. "She did some of the research for me, but I did a deeper dive. Lucy did say you're good at sorting tomatoes. That means she trusts your sixth sense."

"Good. We can skip the preliminaries. Are you as intent on finding Luke's killer as Julie is?"

"I wouldn't have called you otherwise." He looked toward the door. "There's going to be about forty-five people here in the next few minutes. Let's meet right after lunch." Brandon didn't wait for a response before he stood and walked away.

Heather moved to stand beside Steve. "That wasn't what I expected."

Steve shrugged. "I like him. He didn't tell one lie."

"He only spoke a handful of sentences."

"Some people would have filled that two-minute meeting with several lies and as many omissions."

"What about Julie?"

He scratched his chin. "She's a talented actress. I wonder if her life's an impromptu play, and she makes up lines as she goes."

9

———————

A squadron of ATVs, all identical and boasting the logo of OH Farm, thundered to a stop in front of The Hidden Lodge. Heather studied the faces of bright-eyed young adults, and several more that weren't so young, as they dismounted and made a noisy trek across the lawn. The volume decreased to whispers when the front door opened and they filed in. Each climbed the staircase leading to the upstairs living quarters.

Brandon reappeared from down a wide hallway. "You're in rooms 213 and 215. Bags are already there. There's an elevator, or you can take the stairs. Lunch will start in ten minutes in the main dining room."

"Where's that?" asked Heather.

He jerked his thumb over his shoulder like a hitchhiker. "Follow the crowd." Brandon turned on his heel and took the stairs two at a time.

Heather wondered if losing his best friend caused Brandon's economy of words. She didn't have long to ponder as Steve stood and held out his hand for her to place on his arm. "Are you ready? Lunch should prove to be a dining adventure."

"The food may not be to our liking, but there's a lot to learn here. Not all of it relates to hydroponics. And you need to keep an eye on Julie. The killer may not be through."

Julie caught up with them in the dining room, delivered papers to Heather, and took Steve's hand. She led him to a chair at one of the round tables capable of seating eight. The room had space for more tables and chairs, plenty of room to grow. Julie motioned for Heather to sit next to Steve. The kitchen staff finished sliding stainless steel rectangular pans in a steam-tray and cold dishes on beds of ice in a separate rolling cart, complete with sneeze guard.

Julie explained. "We keep things informal. Whenever you're ready, help yourself to whatever looks good and eat as much as you want. We grow most everything we serve. Don't look for meat dishes, though."

Steve tucked his napkin under his chin. "If it's half as good as what I ate at Mother Nature's Farm, I won't need meat."

A woman on the far side of the table looked up from her meal. She wore a maroon and white college sweatshirt. "You've been to Mother Nature's Farm in Belize?"

"I visited before Christmas. It was some of the freshest food I've ever tasted. Sorting tomatoes in Belize works up a powerful appetite."

The young woman giggled. "You're cute. Can I bring you a plate? I'll fill it up with all the things my dad likes."

"Perfect," said Steve.

Heather dropped in line behind the girl, and they waited for a trio of young men to fill their plates. The girl's blond braid swung as she turned to Heather. She extended her hand. "I'm Jill. Have you and your friend been interested in hydroponics long?"

"It's a recent study for both of us. My name is Heather. I'm what you might call a business opportunist. I take it you study the economics of hydroponics. Is there money to be made growing plants in water and not soil?"

"I'm convinced there is. I hope to find out after I graduate."

"Have you been here long?"

"Since the start of the semester, like all the other Aggies. It's an internship that we had to apply for. The selection process got rid of weak links in the chain."

The line cleared, and the student scooped mounds of hot vegetables onto Steve's plate. Heather followed, took half servings, and lowered her voice. "Were you and your classmates here when the murder occurred?"

The girl froze in place, then turned and nodded. "It was totally horrible. The police grilled everyone. It's lucky we sleep four to a room. Everyone had an alibi."

"I read where they determined the time of death around midnight. Couldn't someone sneak out?"

A shake of the head. "We're not locked in, but there are security cameras all over the place." After giving Heather a head-to-toe look, Jill said, "You don't look like a farmer."

"I'm an attorney and an entrepreneur."

"What about your blind friend?"

"He's my taster. If he raves about what you chose for him to eat, I'll do more research on the viability of making an investment."

Jill leaned closer. "That's awesome, but I'd be careful who I told that to. Some of these students have wild dreams but no land or money. Good water is also essential. They look at this place and see dollar signs, but don't consider the initial cash outlay."

"I've been wondering about that."

Even though Heather wasn't through filling her plate, Jill had two plates to deliver. "I should get these to Steve so he can enjoy them while they're still hot. If you want to talk some more tonight, I'm in room 202."

Heather didn't want to press it, so she half-filled a separate plate with salad and returned to the table. Steve tried talking to the man next to him, with little luck. Probably because the man sat with head down, thumbs flying over the keyboard of his phone. It occurred to Heather that this man in his mid-thirties looked as out of place as she and Steve did. The intensity of his gaze at his phone didn't mix with the upbeat sound of students talking and laughing their way through some of the best years of their lives.

Steve traded in a couple of non-responsive questions for a fork and moaned his way through the selections. "So good. Combine great vegetables with the proper seasonings, throw in an accomplished cook, and you're eating like a king."

Jill leaned forward. "Do you really like it? I thought it was just me."

"It's delicious, and I mean it."

The meal progressed, mainly in silence between Steve and Heather. They'd keep their ears open and try to catch snippets of conversations from nearby tables. When Julie sat down with her plate, she ate half of what she dished up and excused herself.

Steve leaned into Heather. "I don't know if she's still grieving or if something else is going on with her. Did you notice anything?"

Heather whispered. "Shh. Too many people. Let's compare notes after lunch."

Steve finished his lunch and spoke loud enough for those at the next table to hear him. "Best meal I've had since I left Belize. What's for dessert?"

"Grapes, strawberries, and blackberries," said Jill. "Do you want me to get you some of each?"

"I wouldn't turn it down."

The meal wound down and Jill rose to leave, but Steve stopped her. "Do you practice the afternoon siesta like they do in Belize?"

"I wish. The hour after lunch is classroom instruction and then it's back in the greenhouses until dark."

"Who teaches?"

"It rotates between one of our professors, Brandon, and Julie. Luke taught some, but not often."

"What was he like?"

"Fun. He only led the discussions twice after I arrived, but he was great. He took the time to memorize all our names before we arrived."

Heather waited for Jill to leave. "Did you hear anything useful about what she said?"

"Time will tell."

"How do you pack so much food away and not gain weight?"

"Practice. What's next for us?"

"Julie's coming back in the room. We're supposed to meet with Brandon sometime today."

***

HEATHER TOOK NOTE THAT JULIE'S OFFICE HAD NOT ONE, BUT two desks and chairs, much like the office she and Steve shared. Brandon sat behind a small, utilitarian desk with nothing but a laptop computer sitting on it. His chair made up for the money he saved on a desk. It looked as if all it needed was shoulder straps and it could go into a high-performance sports car. He glanced up when Heather led Steve into the room, but went back to typing as Julie played hostess.

"Please make yourself comfortable on the couch. Brandon will tear himself away from the computer in just a minute."

Julie then placed two chairs facing the couch. The strokes on the keyboard stopped and the computer screen came down. Brandon pushed back, stood, and joined them. Once again, he didn't mince words. "Luke was my best friend and I want his killer found. I've done more research on private detectives since we last talked, and you two have the best reputation for solving murders. What can we do to help you?"

Steve sat back. "First, we need to get some ground rules settled. If you did as much research on us as I think you did, you know we only accept the cases we want to. You already know we require you to sign a written contract. It allows us to back out of the investigation, for any reason."

"I already know all that, and we agree to the terms."

"Good. Before we talk about suspects, we'll need each of you to tell us why you went to Belize, how you met Luke, and what brought you back to the States. We already have some of Julie's story, so we'll start with you, Brandon."

"I'll speak in generalities about why I left the States. It had to do with a woman. We were engaged."

"We'll need her name."

"She's dead."

Steve nodded. "I'm sorry for your loss, but we'll still need her name, date of birth, and any other pertinent information you can give us on her."

"I don't see why."

Heather answered before Steve could. "Have you ever seen people mine for gold near a river? It takes tons of dirt to produce mere ounces of gold. The same principle applies to our investigations. The more information and data we collect and sift through, the more gold we'll find."

Brandon kept talking with his normal pattern of measured words. "Whatever it takes, we'll do it. As for Tara, the relationship ended over ten years ago and I needed to get far away to deal with it."

"Why Belize?" asked Heather.

"English is the national language. I wasn't in any shape to walk around confused by a foreign language."

Steve took his turn. "Did you start off working at the golf course in Belmopan?"

"Yeah. With only nine holes to mow, it was low stress."

"Are you sure that's all you did there?"

He hesitated. "I did some other things, working the gift shop and helping with the customers in the restaurant."

"How long were you there before Luke showed up?"

"I wasn't tracking time very well back then. At least a year and a half."

"Tell me about Luke. What was he running from?"

Julie broke in. "I don't think he was running from anything as much as he wanted to run to a new life."

"What was wrong with his old life?"

Julie shifted her gaze to a spot on the wall above their heads. "He never told me. Like I said, we agreed not to talk about what we did before Belize."

Steve shifted to a more open-ended question and directed it to Brandon. "Why did you and Luke decide to make such a hasty exit from the golf course?"

"It wasn't a quick decision. Luke studied things from all angles. He'd spend days and sometimes weeks poring over some topic and then move on. With organic farming, he studied it for months before he contacted Lucy at Mother Nature's Farm. As soon as she told us to come, we packed and left the next morning."

Steve took a deep breath and leaned forward. "Why did you and Luke stage his disappearance in Belize?"

Brandon pulled a hand down his face. "That was Luke's idea. Like I said, he liked to have a plan for everything. He never went into detail, but I could tell he wasn't hurting for money. He showed me his stash of passports after we made plans to come back to the States and start this business. We knew the cops in Punta Gorda weren't the best and the bloody towel and knife would be enough for them to look for him, but not too hard. It worked. He staged an attack that gave the appearance something bad happened to him. Without the body, they couldn't declare him dead. He used one of his many passports and came back to the States by himself."

Heather looked at Julie. "You must have been in on this plan."

She nodded. "I knew about it, but I'd already traveled back to Texas."

"What happened when you returned?" asked Steve.

"Luke had done all the research before we left. He knew how much land we needed and where he wanted to locate the farm.

We had to have a twelve-month growing season, so he decided we should grow hydroponically."

Steve turned to Heather. "I think that's enough background for now, unless you have other questions."

"I'd like to know what the local police have done so far. Have they questioned you?"

"Sure," said Julie. "They grilled me good."

"Did they arrest you or read the Miranda warning and ask if you understood your rights?"

"No, and I wondered about that."

"Do you want me to represent you if they come again?"

Brandon pinched his eyebrows together. "We know about plants, not the law. What do you recommend?"

"I'd strongly advise you talk to an attorney, but it doesn't have to be me."

"You're hired."

Steve added, "The longer the case goes unsolved, the more pressure the cops will try to put on you. Tell them you won't say anything without your attorney present."

"Is that all?" asked Brandon.

Heather added a final thought. "We try to work with the police to solve crimes. Sometimes they welcome our help; other times, not so much. Call me as soon as they try to talk to you."

Both Brandon and Julie stood and moved their chairs against a wall. Brandon asked, "Do you think the cops will come back?"

Steve nodded. "Let's get the jump on them. Who's in charge of the case?"

Brandon fielded the question. "A Fayette County detective named Adam Burris."

"We'll invite him out for a chat," said Heather.

"You're the pros. Do what's best. I have a class to teach in twenty minutes."

10

Heather and Steve retired to the privacy of their rooms. They didn't equal the quality of the Four Seasons where Heather stayed in Belize, but the rooms at The Hidden Lodge exceeded expectations. Each had a small living area, two queen-size beds, and everything you'd expect from one of the higher end chain hotels. She opened the door between her room and Steve's once she unloaded the toiletries from her suitcase, brushed her teeth, and touched up her makeup.

Steve sauntered through the door as Heather dialed the sheriff's department's non-emergency number. She gave her name and asked to be connected with Detective Burris. When asked what the call was regarding, she simply said, "The murder of Luke Pryor."

The call went through with no further questions.

"This is Detective Burris. Who am I speaking to?" His voice had a country drawl, which she expected.

"This is Heather McBlythe. I'm an attorney representing Brandon Clay and Julie Pryor. My partner and I are staying at The Hidden Lodge on the hydroponic farm. Do you have time to come by this afternoon and speak with us?"

"Funny you should call. I was planning to come out. The sheriff told me to bring Julie in for additional questioning."

"Did he tell you to arrest her?"

"Nothing like that. Just talk."

"I'll let Julie know you're coming."

"Thanks. Mighty nice of ya'. But I never said I'd—"

Heather disconnected the call, and Steve chuckled. "He has a surprise in store when he arrives."

"It will be an excellent lesson in not thinking fast enough."

"Especially when talking to attorneys."

Heather didn't respond to the intentional dig. She punched another name into her phone and waited for Julie to answer.

"Hi, Heather. What's up?"

"Detective Burris is on his way to talk to us. I want you to make yourself scarce, but stay in the building. If we need you, I'll call. How long will it take him to get here?"

"About twenty minutes to get to the front gate, but he won't be able to get in without the new code. It changes every day at noon. Do you want me to send it to him?"

"Do you have his cell number?"

"He gave me his card."

"Send me a text with the new code and Burris's cell number. Remember, you're not to speak to the police unless I'm with you or tell you to."

Trepidation filled Julie's next words. "I know you don't mean to, but you're scaring me."

Heather kept her tone all business. "It doesn't hurt to be a little afraid. It will keep you on your toes."

"I'll be in my room."

After the phone clicked off, Steve found a chair in the living room area of the suite. "What's your read on Burris?"

Heather sat on the love seat with her arm dangling over the end. "Unsure of himself, but that's only a first impression."

"What did you learn from the girl that filled my plate at lunch?"

Heather snorted out a laugh as she thought about the two plates of food stacked high. She reflected on the conversation, but more on the young woman. "She's bright and level-headed. Didn't say it outright, but it took a lot of cash to get this place up and running. I believe it's on the front end of success. If we don't have time to tour the greenhouses today, I'll ask Julie about the finances."

"What do you think she can tell you?"

Heather took the time to choose her words before she spoke. "Julie said Luke set up this farm as a for-profit enterprise. Jill convinced me it took a lot of money to get this place up and running, and there's big money to be made in selling organic vegetables. I'm not ruling out that someone killed Luke to get at this farm."

Steve scratched his chin. "You mean Julie, the grieving widow, with a lot to gain. What if it wasn't for the money he already had, but what the farm is making now, in the future, and the life insurance policy? After all, he ships high-priced organic vegetables to Houston and Austin every day."

"When did you think of that?"

"Last night, when I stayed awake doing research on hydroponics and organic food profit margins."

"Should have known." Heather snapped her fingers. "What's with the guy sitting at our table wearing out his thumbs on his phone?"

Steve shrugged. "He doesn't fit in with the rest, does he?"

"Like cross trainers with a tuxedo."

Her phone chirped with an incoming text from Julie. Heather punched in the detective's number and sent him a text with the code. "We'd better get downstairs to greet Detective Burris. Do you have your questions lined up for him?"

"Let's get a read on him first and then pump him for information."

"Sounds like fun."

Steve rose to his feet. "Admit it. You love this stuff."

"I'm not denying it. What about you?"

"It keeps me from losing the few marbles I have left."

<hr>

HEATHER PARKED STEVE BY THE FIREPLACE IN THE LOBBY. SHE sat in quiet contentment and wondered what thoughts might run through her partner's mind. Of course, sometimes instead of a profound thought, he'd issue a snore. You never knew what to expect from him.

The slamming of a vehicle's door in the parking lot brought Steve upright. "We have company."

The front door opened and in walked a man wearing inexpensive slacks, boots, a sport jacket with one frayed cuff, and no hat over his closely cropped hair. He wasn't tall or short, heavy or thin, handsome or homely. Heather thought of an empty room painted beige, including the baseboards and door jambs.

"Ms. McBlythe?" he asked, almost as an apology.

"Heather McBlythe, and this is my partner, Steve Smiley." She handed him a card, which he studied with his eyebrows knotted into a question.

"I thought you said you were an attorney, not a private investigator."

She handed him two additional cards. "Take your pick. I'm an attorney, a licensed private investigator, and I'm owner and CEO of an investment company."

Steve stuck out his hand, which Detective Burris looked at for a couple of seconds too long before he gave it a tentative shake. "Steve Smiley, former Houston homicide detective, private detective, and Ms. McBlythe's food taster."

"Huh?"

Steve let out a laugh that sounded more like a cackle. "I'm pulling your leg on the last one. Heather will lead the way to an office where we can talk without being interrupted. Take my hand and put it on your forearm. As long as you don't take off in a run, I'll keep up with you." The three walked down the hall and entered the room Steve and Heather left not more than an hour earlier.

Heather invited the detective to sit on the love seat while she brought chairs to face him. She waited for Detective Burris to speak.

"Where's Julie? I thought she'd join us."

"Perhaps later," said Heather.

"But the sheriff said I needed to bring her in for questioning."

"And I asked if you intended to arrest her."

"No, but..."

"Can you articulate probable cause for the crime you suspect her of committing in such a way that a reasonable person would believe you may detain her for questioning?"

"Huh?"

Steve held up his hands. "Now Heather, let's not be rash. I'm sure Julie has nothing to hide since she gave her last statement."

"How am I to know that without the statement?"

Burris rubbed his hand over the stubble on top of his head. "It wasn't a formal statement. Just my notes from the night of the murder."

Steve didn't hesitate. "What time did the murder take place?"

"The coroner had trouble with that because of the fire."

"I thought someone shot him."

"They did."

"Where?"

"In the back."

"Sorry, I didn't phrase the question very well. Where was Luke when the assailant shot him?"

"In his truck."

"I understand there weren't any bullet holes in the truck."

"So?"

Steve turned to Heather. "Show him."

Heather stood and gave instructions to Burris. "Come sit in my chair, and I'll pretend to be the shooter. You're Luke."

Heather walked away a few paces, turned, and quick walked toward Burris with her hand formed into a pistol at her side. She thrust it into what would be the open window of the pickup truck and hollered, "Boom!"

She kept the mock gun raised. "How are you sitting, detective?"

"Slightly turned toward you."

"What are you looking at?"

"The gun. I mean your hand."

Heather smiled and dropped her hand as Steve explained. "If someone surprises you with a pistol while you're sitting in a pickup truck, your first reaction is to identify the threat, not turn away from it."

Heather finished her part of the lesson. "If Luke didn't know the attacker had a pistol, he'd still be looking forward or out the driver's window, not facing away. Also, did you find a slug in the body or in the truck?"

"No and the crime scene guys looked everywhere, even in the field with a metal detector."

"Don't feel bad," said Steve. "I missed all kinds of things when I first started investigating homicides."

"How did you know this is my first big case?"

Steve leaned back. "A lucky guess. Let's consider what we know about the murder and put together some clues. The truck didn't have bullet holes in it. They didn't find a spent round in the body, in the truck, or anywhere nearby. The crime scene techs didn't find the spent shell. We showed how it's unlikely Luke turned his back on his killer." He paused. "What do you conclude?"

Burris shook his head while he meditated on the problem. The proverbial light bulb came on. "They didn't shoot him while he was in his truck."

"Bingo," said Steve. "That means you haven't found the original crime scene."

"Where do I look?"

Steve shrugged. "You may never find it, but it raises more questions."

"Like what?"

"Let's all think about it tonight and come back tomorrow with ideas."

"Thanks. I will. Can I see Julie now?"

Heather nodded her head. "You can see her, but unless you're ready to arrest her, she's not going with you. We want to work with you, but I have to protect my client."

"The sheriff won't like this."

Steve laughed again. "He'll be tickled pink when you explain how you figured out they didn't shoot Luke in his truck."

"You don't know the sheriff. He don't get tickled about much of anything."

Steve nodded to Heather. She gave Burris a fourth card and said, "Give him the business cards and tell him to ask around about us."

"Around where?"

"Wherever he likes," said Steve. "He can start with Houston homicide and the Texas Rangers."

Heather excused herself and went into the hallway to call Julie. "I need you in the cafeteria."

"I'm on my way."

Heather returned to Burris and Steve and said, "I'll need a few minutes to consult with my client. We won't be long."

Heather joined the widow at a table set apart from the other tables. "I need to ask some questions and give you instructions before we talk to Detective Burris."

Julie's eyes opened a little wider and she nodded. "Will he arrest me?"

"Not unless you killed your husband, or had something to do with his death."

"I didn't." Tears clouded her eyes. "I loved Luke. He was totally awesome."

"Tell me all you know about the night of his death."

"It was tax time and I had to catch up. I worked here at the office until eleven. It was so late and I had to file it the next day, so I stayed the night in my room upstairs."

"You didn't see Luke the night he died?"

"After eating supper here, he went home."

"Had it been raining?"

"There'd been a downpour that dumped half an inch of rain that afternoon. We collect rainwater, so I'm sure of the amount." She turned her head. "Why do you ask about rain?"

"Tire tracks and footprints. Their presence helps us place suspects at the scene of the crime, or their absence helps us eliminate people. Did the police take your shoes or boots?"

"No."

"What size do you wear?"

"Eight."

Heather needed to expand her questions, but she wanted Steve to be present, to pose his own and to hear Julie's responses. "I need to coach you on what to say and what not to say. The most important thing to remember is to look at me after every question. If I nod, you can answer. If I don't want you to answer, I'll say something. Detective Burris will probably read to you from a card that informs you of your rights. When he asks if you understand, say yes and nothing more. I'll take over from there."

"What if you're not with me and the cops ask questions again or arrest me?"

"That's the easiest, and the hardest, thing to do. You must tell them you won't say anything without your attorney present. But you have to be careful. A skilled interviewer will have you talking before you realize it. No matter what they say or do, keep quiet."

Heather stood and smiled. "Are you ready to talk to Detective Burris?"

She nodded. "I have nothing to hide."

The detective stood as Julie entered the office. Heather drew another chair and placed Julie between her and Steve. This also put them in the position of power, separating Julie from Burris as much as possible.

"Julie," said Burris. "You're not under arrest, but I need to read something to you, all the same."

With the rights explained, Steve spoke. "Unless I'm mistaken, Heather has some information for you."

Heather cleared her throat. "My client maintains her innocence and does not know who might have killed her husband. She told me it rained hard the day of the murder." She waited for Burris to look at her before she asked, "Did you find shoe or boot prints at or near the burned truck?"

"I don't think I'm supposed to talk about that."

"Our intention is to prove Julie wasn't there, so you can eliminate her as a suspect. She wears a size eight, and she said you didn't ask for her footwear the night of the murder."

Steve took his turn. "That means either there were no footprints or they belonged to someone with a larger or smaller shoe size. Which was it?"

Burris sighed. "Bigger. A man's size ten, but that doesn't mean she couldn't have worn her husband's."

"Do you know what size Luke wore?"

Burris dipped his head. "Nine."

"Did you get any castings of tires?"

Burris nodded his head. "We did, but there was only one set of tire tracks leading to the place the truck was burned."

"That means the murder took place somewhere else. Someone loaded Luke into his pickup, drove him away from the site of the shooting, burned most of the usable evidence, and left on foot."

Heather added, "I've heard nothing to incriminate Julie. You're welcome to get a warrant and examine her footwear, but that will only confirm what you already know."

"What about searching her house?" asked Steve. "Anything there?"

"I'm not staying at my house," said Julie.

Heather gave her a look that told her she'd violated an instruction.

Burris's eyes had the downcast look of a lost puppy. "I knew I should have stayed on patrol."

Heather gave a small shake of her head. While he was feeling sorry for himself, the man missed an opportunity to ask a follow-up question of Julie.

Heather turned to Julie. "I'm sure you have things to do. You can leave."

Steve waited until after the door clicked shut. "Don't let it get you down. It's early in the investigation, and we'll help you in every way we can. It would save you time and effort if we didn't duplicate what you've already done."

"What do you mean?"

Steve stretched his hand toward Heather. "Everyone here is after the same thing. We all want to see a killer brought to justice. It would help if we traded information. Who knows, you may already know something that you didn't recognize as important."

"Uncle Melvin will have my hide for a lampshade if he finds out I turned over sensitive information to you."

"We don't care who gets the credit when this is over. Think about it. I've found that a solved case tends to make a sheriff forget about procedures. We'll do what we can to give you information that shows you're making progress. You pass it on to the sheriff and he'll be happy."

"Like what kind of information?"

"Come back tomorrow and we'll have background research on a couple of people we've identified as possible suspects."

"You already have suspects?" He issued a sigh of capitulation. "I guess you'll be wanting something from me in return."

Steve answered with a smile and extended his hand for Burris to shake.

After Burris left, Steve settled once again in his chair. Heather leaned toward him. "Who do you want me to start with?"

"It sounded like you hit it off with the student that brought me lunch."

"Jill?"

"I should be able to remember that. You date Jack and you need to talk to Jill. Get with her tonight and pump her for information about the guy at our table that wouldn't talk. There's something about him that doesn't sit right with me. Also, tell Julie you need to look at all the interns' application forms."

"What about employees?"

"Let's leave our new friend Detective Burris something to do. Who knows, he may have already done it."

Heather uncrossed her legs. "What will you do?"

Steve stretched. "After a nap, I'll give Trey Ricks a call and see if I can't bait him into coming to talk to us."

"What about the other cousin, Mary?"

"Let's keep those two separated for now. I have a plan to get them both to come, but not at the same time."

11

S even thirty in the evening came and went before the knock sounded on Heather's door. Jill cast an approving gaze around the suite. "I wondered what the VIP rooms looked like."

"I understand you sleep four to a room."

"We call it the servants' quarters, but they're not that bad if you don't mind a bunk bed. I took the top, thinking it might be warmer. I may regret it by the end of the semester."

Heather led the way to the small living area comprised of a desk, lamp, recliner, coffee table, and a couch. "Take your pick of where you want to sit."

"If you don't mind, I'll sit in the executive chair. Someday I hope to be in one of my own."

"You're ambitious." It wasn't a question.

"More than most, but not so much that I want to climb a corporate ladder. I can't imagine being cooped up in an office every day." Jill pulled out the chair and placed it facing the coffee table and couch. She settled in, stroking the faux-leather arms as if they were satin.

Heather wanted to keep things light. "You must be near graduation."

A nod of the head. "In May."

"What then?"

"I'm hoping our conversation might lead to something."

Heather turned her head the way a confused puppy does. "Please explain."

"You're wearing designer clothes at a working farm while escorting a blind man. There are as many rumors going around about why you two are here as there are students." She paused. "I'm the only one who's figured it out so far, and I'm not telling."

"What's your guess?"

"Not a guess, more of a theory based on research. You said you came to look for an investment opportunity, but that didn't explain Mr. Smiley. You make an odd couple that has tongues wagging."

"Keep going," said Heather

"I searched the internet for both of you. Unless I miss my guess, you've already done some background checks on me and the rest of the students. Am I right?"

Heather gave a wordless single nod.

"Thought so. That's what I'd expect from a successful businesswoman who's an attorney and a private investigator. You're here to investigate Luke's murder. That explains you *and* Mr. Smiley. He may be blind, but I bet he already knows twice as much about this farm and hydroponics as Lee Paulson."

"Who's Lee Paulson?"

"I'm surprised you haven't done background on him. He's the guy that ate lunch with us and pretended to ignore Mr. Smiley."

"What can you tell me about him?"

Jill shrugged. "Not much, except he came before Christmas and doesn't know beans about beans or any other vegetable."

"What else?"

Jill leaned back in her chair. "I'll be glad to tell you what I know, and all I ask is that you remember me if you're serious about investing in hydroponic farming. I could make both of us a lot of money in an industry that checks all the boxes for profit and growth."

The door between the two rooms opened and Steve came in, sweeping his cane in front of him. "Is the recliner open?"

"It's all yours, partner. We're busted."

"I heard."

Jill's eyes narrowed. "He's been listening?"

Steve laughed as he sat in the recliner. "What did you expect from private detectives? We bugged the room so I could hear every word."

Jill burst out laughing. "Here I was, trying to get one over on you. I should have paid more attention to what I read."

"No hard feelings, I hope."

Jill wasted a pleasant smile on Steve. "None from me."

"Good. It sounds like you want to negotiate a business deal, so I'll leave that to Heather."

Heather squared her shoulders. "This offer comes with no guarantees, but I'll commit to having someone from my staff contact you. He's a land and business development expert. Between now and the time you graduate, you'll need to submit a comprehensive business plan for creating a hydroponic farm. He'll critique it and offer suggestions. I'll review the eventual plan. There's no guarantee, and I may change my mind about this idea altogether. I'll either refuse the proposal outright or, if I like what my team says, we'll hash out details. We won't talk about money until I'm satisfied the plan is viable. In return, you'll answer all our questions. Do we have a deal?"

Jill extended her hand across the coffee table. "It's a deal."

Steve rubbed his hands together. "Okay. Lee Paulson. Have you spoken to him?"

"Several times."

"What's he like?"

"Nosy."

"Paint me a word picture."

Jill straightened her posture. "He focused on the full-time employees—the cooks, cleaners, and truck drivers. Also, the professors, but only the ones that have been coming for a long time. He didn't have any use for us interns, except to ask the same questions the cops did."

Heather asked, "Why do you think that is?"

Her shoulders rose and fell. "It doesn't matter anymore. He's gone. Packed up and left after lunch."

Heather had her mouth open, ready to ask for details, but Steve interrupted. "Let's move on. What's your opinion of Detective Burris?"

"I only talked to him once. He didn't impress me as being the sharpest hoe in the tool shed. I told him the four of us were playing a game of spades in our room at the time of the murder. He lost interest fast. I asked the other girls in my room if he spoke to any of them again, and they all said no."

"How well do you know Julie?"

"She's real friendly. One of those types that wants to know all about others, but doesn't talk much about herself. She's takes care of administrative stuff, so she's out of sight most of the time."

"What about Brandon?"

"He's quiet and so smart it's scary. I don't think there's anything he doesn't know about hydroponics, but..."

"But what?"

She scrunched up her nose. "He's a little odd. He'll tell you anything you want to know, but you have to ask."

"What about Luke? Was he an introvert, too?"

"Ha. Are you kidding? Luke spent four days a week traveling to Austin and Houston, talking to customers. He took me with him twice because I wanted to know about the sales and marketing side of the business." Her gaze shifted from Steve. "What good is growing great vegetables and fruits if you don't have someone to buy them?"

"Did Luke get along with everyone here?"

Jill gave her head a firm nod. "Luke never met a stranger or anyone he didn't like."

"That's the same impression I got from people who knew

him in Belize." Steve waited long enough for a response, but none came, so he moved on. "What does everyone say about Julie?"

"Not much. She's efficient and keeps to herself. It seemed she and Luke were a bit of a mismatch. I know opposites attract, but they were like opposite sides of the globe."

"Did you ever go to their home?"

"No one I know of did, except Lee Paulson. He got curious and found where they lived. It's not on this property, but on the next tract of land behind it. It's a shipping container transformed into a tiny house."

"How do you know he went there?" asked Steve.

"Well... I... I sort of followed him." Her next words came out in a rush. "Only from a distance. It was on a weekend and I was looking out the window. He kept looking around, making sure no one was watching. When he disappeared into the trees, I got curious and followed."

Steve didn't respond, while Heather made a mental note to find the tiny house and see for herself.

"Does anyone else that works here stand out?" asked Steve.

"None of the staff do. They're locals who seem thankful to have a job. We don't hang with the truck drivers and they don't eat with us, but I hear they're locals, too."

"Were there any people who overreacted to Luke's death?"

It took Jill several seconds to respond. "It tore Julie and Brandon up, but no one else that I remember. Do you want me to ask around?"

"You'd best leave that to us. We don't want you scaring away the killer, or killers, if they're still around. Have you considered what Lee Paulson might have done to you if he'd caught you following him?"

It was Jill's turn not to respond to a direct question. Instead, she tilted her head. "Do you think a student could have killed him?"

"No one gets ruled out this early."

Heather knew Steve well enough to know he'd asked all the questions he wanted. He remained seated, but Heather thanked Jill and showed her to the door. Before Heather opened it, she handed her a card. "It might be best if you called or sent us a text instead of coming to our rooms again."

"I understand. Should I contact you or Steve?"

"It doesn't matter."

"I'm glad you trust me."

Heather smiled, nodded, and opened the door. Jill flicked the long blond braid over her shoulder and left at a quick pace.

"Describe her to me," said Steve as Heather took her spot on the couch again.

"Blond, braided hair, and curvy in all the right places. Rough hands, but I bet the men don't notice. Turned-up nose and grayish-blue eyes. The longer you look at her, the prettier she gets."

Steve nodded. "What did you think of her?"

"Ambitious and curious. Perhaps too much for her own good."

Steve uh-huhed an agreement. "It didn't take long for her to get a commitment out of you."

"Not much of one. I left myself plenty of escape clauses."

Instead of continuing the debriefing, Steve pulled out his phone. "Call Marsha Pennywell."

When Marsha answered, her words came with a hint of levity. "Are you calling to warn me of the dangers of the equatorial sun?"

"Hardly. How's the sunburn?"

"Better, but the doctor warned me I'd lose a layer of skin on my face and back."

"Heather and I are at Luke and Brandon's hydroponic farm. I wondered if your company lost track of someone."

"What are you talking about?"

"An investigator who went by the name Lee Paulson. He arrived before Christmas and left today in a hurry."

"He's not mine."

"Are you sure?"

"I'm in charge of all investigations in Texas. If he was ours, I'd have to approve it."

Steve puffed out his cheeks and exhaled. "I'd hoped he was. That means someone else sent him in to snoop."

All the levity left Marsha's voice. "Find out who hired him and you might find the killer."

"My thoughts, exactly. Thanks, Marsha."

"Keep me posted if there's anything that affects the settlement. I'm trying to stall dispersal of payment until we can get a handle on who's responsible for the murder." She paused. "Do you suspect the widow?"

"Right now, I suspect everyone, including you."

That earned a laugh. "Goodnight, Steve."

Heather waited long enough for Steve to slip the phone into his pocket. "When did you know Lee Paulson was a PI?"

"I had my suspicions when he ignored me at lunch. Jill's description of him helped, but I needed Marsha to confirm he didn't work with her."

"Do you want me to run a trace on him?"

Steve made a steeple of his index fingers. "Let's give Burris something else to keep him busy. He might get lucky and track him down, but it won't do much good, even if he finds him. He'll play the confidentiality card and hide behind a lawyer as long as he can. Let's try to peel the onion from a different direction."

Heather thought Steve had finished, but he followed with another surprise for her. "Trey Ricks agreed to come here tomorrow afternoon. I told him I'd introduce him to Luke's widow. Let's see what kind of man Mr. Ricks is. We may have to bend the rules a little, but let's put a bug in the office downstairs."

"It's a good thing I brought my lock picks."

Steve placed his hands over his ears. "I didn't hear that."

THE DOOR SEPARATING HEATHER'S ROOM FROM STEVE'S swung open at eleven thirty. "Are you ready to commit a tiny felony?" he asked.

Heather shoved a small case of lock-picking tools in the pocket of a fleece jacket. "I'm not sure a judge would agree with it being tiny, but yes. Let's get this done." They entered an empty hall. "By the way, do you have any sort of plan?"

Steve ran his cane over the carpet as they walked. "It's simple if the door's unlocked. Go in, put the bug where no one will find it, and get out as quick as you can."

"And if it's not unlocked?"

"I'll come visit you in jail."

Heather tried in vain not to chuckle. "We're in this together. I'll snitch and tell them you're the mastermind behind everything."

They reached the stairway. Steve shifted the cane to his left hand and grabbed the rail with his right. He liked to navigate stairs by himself as long as he could glide his hand down a banister or feel a wall. The stairway spilled them into the lobby with the hallway leading to the office on their right.

Steve froze. "Someone recently passed by here."

Heather scanned the long hallway, and double checked the lobby. She dropped her voice to a whisper. "I don't see anyone."

He tapped his nose twice. "A woman wearing cloying perfume. I smelled it in the hallway upstairs, too. She recently either went up or down. The smell isn't as strong down here."

"You and your hypersensitive nose." Heather checked in all directions. "I didn't see anyone upstairs and there's no one in sight."

"I heard the door close to the room next to mine as I came to get you. If you still don't see her, I think it's safe to continue on."

Still whispering, Heather stepped toward the office. "I'd feel better if we had a reason to be in this hallway."

"We do. This hall leads to the dining room and kitchen. If

anyone asks, my sweet tooth is acting up again and I want another cookie."

After another ten steps, they stopped at the office door. Heather turned the handle, and the latch released. Pushing the door open, she gasped as Brandon looked up from his laptop.

"Can I help you?" he asked.

"Sorry," said Steve. "Heather thought she left her favorite Mont Blanc pen here this afternoon. We didn't want to bother anyone, but she's a little OCD about losing things."

"I didn't notice it, but I'd be glad to help you look."

Heather held up her palm to him. "There's no need. If it's not between the cushions of the couch or under it, the pen won't be here. It will only take a minute to look."

Steve walked to a spot in front of Brandon's desk. "You're burning the midnight oil. Sorry we interrupted you."

"Julie and I are pulling extra duty since Luke's death. You're lucky you didn't find a locked door."

"And Heather would have worried about her pen all night."

Heather tented her hands on her hips. "I admit I'm too fond of that pen, but it has great sentimental value."

Steve shifted to his left, which put him between Brandon and her. She dropped to her knees and pretended to look under the couch. While hidden from view, she attached the tiny microphone to the underside of the coffee table.

"Any luck?" asked Brandon.

She shook her head, paused, and snapped her finger. "I know where it is. I put it and a yellow legal pad in the desk drawer of my room. How could I be so forgetful?"

"At least that's one mystery solved," said Brandon. "Are you making progress on Luke's death?"

Steve wiggled his hand to indicate some, but not much. "We found out something unusual about Lee Paulson. He left suddenly after lunch today. What do you know about him?"

Brandon gave a quick snort out of his nose, which told her

Lee wasn't held in high regard. "He broke into this office and planted a listening device."

Heather had to cover a gasp with a cough.

Steve kept a poker face. "How did you catch him?"

"Security cameras. There's two sets in all the common areas and rooms that might hold sensitive information."

"Two sets?" asked Heather. "I only noticed one."

"That's intentional. What you see are the big ones. The others are tiny and camouflaged. I never expected this farm to be so successful, but I'm paranoid about things going missing so I added a second set of cameras."

"That's not paranoia, it's good security," said Steve. "Especially when you have strangers staying here. Whose idea was it to take in interns?"

Luke's chair squeaked a little when he leaned back. "A group decision between Luke, Julie, and me. We wanted cheap labor, but that's hard to come by in the States. There's nothing cheaper than free, and that's interns. In fact, they pay room and board. The other people who come pay as if it's a college class."

Steve nodded. "You borrowed Lucy's business plan from Belize. What else do you know about Lee Paulson?"

"Nothing other than he used a fake name. I tried to run a check on him, but didn't get far. I watched all the footage, but he did nothing wrong besides bugging this office. I don't know if he was looking for info or was trying to find out where we keep our important papers and cash. Everything important is kept in an old safe in the shipping office. It's set in concrete and has cameras monitoring it all the time. And I know he was never in there. I can show it to Heather if you'd like to see it."

"Sure."

Brandon tapped instructions into his laptop and spun his computer around for Heather to see.

"It's big, all right."

"Did Lee Paulson talk to you or Luke very often?"

"He tried to, and it usually wasn't about hydroponics. I'm not as bad as I used to be, but I'm not one to gab if it's not work related. As for Luke, he'd carry on a conversation with a fence post and act surprised when he didn't get a response."

Steve motioned with his head to Heather. "We'll keep you posted on any developments."

Brandon shrugged. "I'd rather you wait until you know who the killer is."

Steve rose and extended a hand for Brandon to shake. "You may be the most accommodating client we've come across."

The duo left Brandon and waited until they reached Steve's room to discuss the meeting. Steve turned on the television with the volume loud enough to drown out their voices. "Did the cameras catch you planting the bug?"

"I don't think so. It's stuck on the bottom of the coffee table. I made it look like I pushed up on the table to stand when I attached it."

He nodded and raised his voice. "It's been a long day. I'm hitting the hay."

The television clicked off. "Good night," said Heather, and then stopped. The sound of the rhythmic thumping of a headboard against the wall came from behind Steve's bed. She looked at him and said, "Is that what I think it is?"

He grinned. "I smelled that perfume when we passed the room next door and I heard a man's voice."

Heather grabbed the remote, turned on the television, and shoved it in Steve's hand. "You're not old enough to listen to the movie they're playing next door."

12

———————

The interns came to breakfast wearing flannel pajamas and had that just-rolled-out-of-bed look about them. Heather didn't want to imagine how many hadn't brushed their teeth. She settled Steve in the same spot as yesterday and looked to see who might join them. A man with a bearded, professorial look settled in next to Steve and dug into a breakfast of oatmeal and fresh fruit.

"I don't smell bacon and eggs," said Steve after he introduced himself to the man and learned that he carried the title of an adjunct professor.

"Bacon and eggs," said the professor with mirth carrying his words. "Hydroponics don't lend themselves very well to growing pigs and the chickens don't like to get wet."

Steve laughed while Heather thought any joke before noon should wait.

"Are you here to study hydroponics?" asked the professor.

"We're here to learn more about it," said Steve. "Heather's an entrepreneur who's always on the lookout for the next big thing."

The professor's gaze shifted to her. "There's still time to beat the rush, and you'd be wise to get in soon."

Heather nodded, with what might have looked like agreement. "What's the most important thing for me to consider?"

Without hesitation, the professor answered. "Water. Make sure you have a plentiful supply of excellent water."

"And after water?"

"Organic certification. Profit margins and trending preferences toward organically certified fruits and vegetables are tightly correlated."

The professor took another bite of oatmeal while Heather kept the conversation going. "The management team of three wanted to set this farm up for success. Is that what you'd recommend?"

The professor put down his spoon. "As you well know, a company is only as good as its leadership. This place is a success because it's built like a three-legged stool. Brandon has the technical expertise. He's a master farmer. Julie has the administrative skills needed to keep the train on its tracks. And Luke..."

His voice trailed off, so Heather finished the sentence. "Luke knew how to sell the products."

"Exactly. Luke had a way about him. He knew exactly when to push and when to back off. I went with him on some sales calls and watched his methods. Whenever he'd call on a new customer, he'd leave a box of samples. He'd allow the products to speak for themselves before he called them back a few days later. The men respected him and the women loved him. He wasn't movie star handsome, but he didn't need to be."

"Are you saying he was a ladies' man?"

"I wouldn't know about that, but I observed he possessed a certain magnetism."

Jill arrived and sat across the table, as she'd done the previous day. She greeted Steve and asked if she could get his breakfast.

"You did such a good job yesterday I may have to hire you full time. Bring me a medium steak, two fried eggs, biscuits and gravy."

"How 'bout I bring you steel-cut oatmeal with fresh fruit and you can pretend it's steak and eggs?"

"Do like you did yesterday and bring me what your father would eat."

"I'll do what I can, but my dad's like you, a biscuit and gravy man."

Heather followed Jill to the serving line and gathered fruit and sprouted grain toast for her breakfast.

"Are you having an interesting talk with Professor Chalmers?" asked Jill.

"He seems to be a big believer in hydroponics."

"He's not like some of the other professors."

"How so?"

"He's not tenured and so set in his ways. He's fun to talk to."

"Do you know him well?"

"Only as well as the rest of the slaves."

Heather exited the line and returned to the table. Once seated, she looked for reactions from the other students as Jill sashayed to the table and presented Steve with his meal. One table of girls, in particular, dipped their heads and covered their mouths as they exchanged girl-talk that appeared to be juicy gossip.

The conversation lagged until Jill returned with her breakfast and settled in. Steve took the lead. "Jill, Professor Chalmers has been giving us a short course on what it takes to run a successful hydroponic farm. He used the metaphor of a three-legged stool comprising three types of expertise. The first is knowledge and skill in farming. Administrative skill is the second, and the ability to sell is third. What's your strongest skill of those three?"

Jill tilted her head. "That's a tough question, because I love all three."

Steve wagged his finger. "You're not getting away that easy."

Jill bit her lower lip. "If I had to choose, I'd say sales."

"And number two?"

"I guess administrative."

"That leaves knowledge and skill in farming as your weakest."

Jill's eyes sparked and her eyelids narrowed. "I didn't say I was weak in any of those areas."

Steve held up a hand. "Of course not." He turned to the professor and swept his hand across the room. "There's now a leg missing on the stool of this company. Which of these students stands out as the top candidate to fill Luke's shoes?"

The professor searched the room, but not for long. "In every group, one person stands out above the rest. This is an unusual semester because there are two who I wouldn't hesitate to put in charge of sales. Allison and Jerome have my vote."

A flush of anger rose from Jill's neck as she gave the professor a look capable of melting steel. Taking her plate and bowl, she issued a chilled excuse and left.

It didn't take long for the professor to clear his place.

Once alone with Steve, Heather asked, "What was that about?"

"I didn't want another sleepless night. Couldn't you smell her perfume? It was on both of them."

Heather's hand flew up to her mouth. She cleared her throat. "I need to find Julie and get into the personnel files and the students' applications again."

Steve nodded. "Run along. I can get back to the room by myself."

"What will you do this morning?"

"Call Detective Burris and have him try to find Lee Paulson, or whatever his name might be. After that, there's a good chance I'll take a brief nap. If I wake up in time, I'll refresh my memory on Luke's cousin, Trey Ricks. He'll be here today."

LUNCH PASSED WITHOUT INCIDENT, AND WITHOUT JILL, THE professor, or anyone else left at Heather and Steve's table. Heather told Steve the morning's study of employee records revealed little, but she acknowledged that in an investigation, that wasn't always true. Sometimes, the insignificant details helped to solve the case. Like Professor Chalmers judging the two standout students above a paramour. Jill had a good academic record, but her interest in hydroponics started last semester. It made Heather wonder if Jill's method of trying to gain favor with the professor carried over to one or more of the company owners. A love triangle?

Steve listened but said nothing except to let her know he'd heard her.

Heather admitted it might be a stretch to suspect Jill, but those committing homicides justified their actions with sometimes illogical reasons. For now, she'd put that theory on the back burner.

Steve relayed that the bug planted in the office picked up a conversation between Brandon and Julie where they discussed how to go about recruiting a new sales and marketing director. Brandon remembered an intern from last semester while Julie had her eye on Allison, one of the professor's choices. They reached no conclusion.

Steve had also called Detective Burris, who promised to get back with information on Lee Paulson, the mystery man, as soon as he had something to report.

"Something's bothering me," said Steve after he pushed his plate to one side. "We haven't located the original crime scene. Let's get Brandon or Julie to tell us where the truck burned. I want to make doubly sure the murder didn't take place where they found his body and truck."

"By seeing red?"

Steve nodded. "I already determined he didn't die in Belize. All the evidence indicates the original crime scene is somewhere else, but where? I have a feeling the location will tell us a lot about the killer."

"Anything else?"

"Talk to Julie and see how long she's planning on staying here in the lodge. You need to look at her and Luke's home."

Heather reached for Steve's plate and bowl. "The cook told me where their home is. There's a road that cuts through the back fence. It's another keypad operated gate that connects the two properties."

Steve tapped his fingertips on the table, a sign he wanted to get on with the investigation. "If we finish with the cousin in time, we'll take a walk this afternoon. You may have to climb a fence, so be sure to wear jeans."

"Are we spying on Julie?"

Steve answered the question in his own way. "You've been around Julie for a while. What's your impression of her?"

"Smart and dedicated to this farm. A bit of a loner, but not as much as Brandon. Why?"

Steve shrugged. "Was there any sign of grief today?"

"Yeah, but not like when we first met her."

"It's probably my imagination running away with me. I don't think Julie and Luke enjoyed a storybook marriage."

Heather had to admit that Steve had a vivid imagination, but he anchored it firmly in facts. "Don't discount your instincts. What are you sensing?"

"I'm having a hard time with the picture in my mind of Luke and Julie as husband and wife."

"Common law," said Heather.

Steve grabbed his cane and stood. "That's probably all it is. I'm showing my age by thinking it's not as legally binding." He pushed his chair under the table and started walking. "I'll meet you in the lobby. Trey Ricks should be here soon."

ANOTHER LOG SETTLED ONTO GLOWING COALS AS HEATHER caught up with Steve. Dust motes floated in sunshine that shone through a side window in the lobby. Like miniature snowflakes, they rode the air with no hurry to settle. The front door opened, and a man dressed in second-hand clothes walked in and cast his gaze in all directions before closing the door. Of medium height and weight, he pulled out a pocket comb and tried in vain to tame an unruly head of reddish-brown hair. After looking the wrong way once again, he turned his head and lifted his chin.

"Are you Mr. Smiley and Ms. McBlythe?"

Steve answered for both of them. "Steve and Heather. You must be Trey Ricks. I hope you don't mind if we call you Trey. It's an established custom of this place to use first names only."

Heather stood and proffered her hand for Trey to shake. "Have you been here before?"

"First time."

"Come sit by the fire."

The three settled in with Trey staring at flames as they made small leaps upward. Steve broke the ice with a general statement. "I told you on the phone that Heather and I are private detectives. One co-owner of this farm has hired us to look into who killed your cousin."

"I remember talking to you. You were nice."

Heather had her suspicions, but the longer Trey talked with clipped phrases, the more convinced she was that he had challenges in forming complex sentences.

"One thing investigators do is rule out people, especially relatives. Have the police questioned you yet?"

"Someone called Mary. She told me not to talk to anyone. Why would the police talk to me?"

"Because you and your sister are Donnie's next of kin. Your cousin made lots of money. Did you know that?"

"I make money."

Steve lowered his voice. "Did you know your cousin's marriage to Julie is common law?"

"Huh?" His eyes darted back and forth as if looking for an answer to a troublesome question. "I don't know what that is."

Heather took over. "Do you remember your cousin?"

"Not much. I was little."

"Do you know when he died?"

Trey's head bobbed like a cork with a perch nibbling the bait. "On a Tuesday. That's the day the delivery truck didn't show up, and the store ran out of milk. People got mad."

"You don't remember the exact date?"

"Mary knows."

Heather placed her hand on Trey's arm and looked into eyes that saw the world differently than most people. "Let's call Mary and see if she remembers."

Steve pulled out his phone. "Call Mary Ricks-Jones."

As they waited for the connection, Trey said, "Don't call her Ricks-Jones. She didn't like Bernie."

"Thanks," said Steve as the phone rang.

A snippy voice answered. "I don't take sales calls." The phone cut off.

Steve huffed. "Use your phone, Trey, to call your sister. Put it on speaker and tell her where you are."

After six rings, the same terse voice said, "I told you not to call unless it's an emergency."

"Don't hang up, Sis. I'm at the water farm talking to two nice people."

"You fool. I told you not to speak to anyone."

Steve broke in. "Good afternoon, Ms. Ricks. This is Steve Smiley. I'm here with my partner, Heather McBlythe. We're not the police, but we work closely with them. The investigation into your cousin's death is getting interesting. It would be in your best interest if you join your brother here at the hydroponic farm."

"I'll do no such thing."

"Would you rather we tell the police you hired a private detective to spy on Luke?"

No response came from the phone for at least five seconds. "This is blackmail."

"It's an invitation to talk to us. We should be able to get

rooms for you and your brother here tonight. Heather will call you back to confirm you'll have a place to stay. Pack for several days. That's all we need to say for now. We're taking Trey's phone from him until you arrive, so don't waste your time calling him."

Steve handed Heather the phone, and she switched it off. Trey sat wide-eyed. "Mary's mad. She does bad things when she's mad."

"You'll be fine," said Steve. "I told Mary you were at the hydroponic farm, but she didn't ask for directions. That tells me you two have been here before."

Trey's head dipped. "Mary said that was our secret."

"It isn't a secret if we already know it." Steve spoke in a calm, fatherly voice. "When were you here?"

"A couple weeks ago."

"Why did you come here?"

Trey looked around. "We didn't come here to this hotel or even to this farm. It was to a tiny house off a gravel road. I stayed in the car and Mary talked to someone. She was mad when she came got in the car."

"What happened then?"

"We went to Brenham and had supper. I got Blue Bell Ice Cream for dessert. They make it in Brenham."

"I know. It's my favorite." Steve leaned forward. "Then what did you do?"

"Mary called someone else. It was late, and I went to sleep in the back seat."

Heather excused herself. Her mental assessment of Trey had already taken place. High functioning with a low IQ. He could drive and do all the things necessary for daily living on his own. That was the positive side of the ledger. In the other column, Trey seemed easily manipulated, especially by an overbearing sister. Could she, or would she, browbeat Trey into killing their cousin?

Julie sat behind her desk, slaving over a computer keyboard. She hit the escape key as soon as Heather entered.

"Sorry to interrupt," said Heather as she wondered the cause for secrecy. "We have need of two guest rooms tonight. Are there any open?"

Julie nodded and stated, "I hope this brings you closer to finding Luke's killer."

"Steve's full of surprises today. The investigation seems to have gained speed."

"That's encouraging. Luke was such a valuable member of our team. He didn't deserve to die." Julie pushed away from her desk. "If you don't mind, I'll give you the key cards to the rooms. Please tell your guests they're welcome to join us for supper in the main dining room. I'm up to my eyes in taxes, so I'll be behind this desk for most of the night."

Instead of going to the lobby where Steve and Trey waited, Heather went to the deserted dining room. She took out Trey's phone and powered it up. "Mary, this is Heather McBlythe. Rooms are ready for you and Trey. Your brother will be in his room when you get here. Questions?"

"No questions, only a word of caution. Don't think you can push me around."

Instead of responding to the school-yard dare, Heather said, "Be sure to pick up toiletries and clean clothes for your brother. You both may be here several nights." Heather disconnected the call and turned off the phone.

On the way back to Steve and Trey, she stopped to consider something Julie had said about Luke. She'd described him as a valuable member of their team. Not the most endearing term for a murdered husband.

13

Steve pulled a stocking cap further down on his ears. "It must be near freezing out here."

"You're such a baby," said Heather as they climbed down the steps of the lodge. "You should have grown up in Boston. A nor'easter blowing in from the Atlantic will make you wish you were back in Belize."

"I'm wishing that now."

She placed his gloved hand on her arm and set off at a quick pace. "You need to spend more time in the gym and less at the pancake house."

"Don't mention a proper breakfast if there's not a decent restaurant within twenty miles of here."

"I thought you liked organic grains, vegetables, and fruits."

"They make a wonderful compliment to steak."

She shook her head and walked a little faster. "Julie referred to Luke in a peculiar way today. She said she missed him because he was a valuable member of the team."

Steve kept up the pace. "That's interesting. Do you think the marriage wasn't for real?"

"It makes me wonder. Perhaps they got carried away in that fairy tale setting of Mother Nature's Farm."

Steve pulled his hat down farther in the back. "That place casts a mean spell. Marsha Pennywell told me the people she talked to didn't have much filter when talking about each other's love lives. Hooking up with someone wasn't uncommon, but the relationships usually ended with the internship."

His words came out a few at a time because of labored breathing, but Steve didn't break stride. "I want you to talk to some of the more verbal female interns. See what they say about Luke and Julie showing affection in public. Also check out how often she stayed at the lodge before Luke's murder."

"Do you think Luke was involved with someone? Maybe Jill?"

"Not out in the open, but I bet there's more going on than meets the proverbial eye." He chuckled. "In my case, it's than what meets the ear, nose, tongue and touch."

By the time they reached the site of burned grass and scorched trees, Steve had unzipped his jacket. "It smells like an old campfire."

Heather's gaze took in the scorched ground. "Julie gave me good directions. This is definitely where Luke's truck burned with him inside it. In front of you is a large circle of burned grass. To the right are trees with charred bark and scorched leaves."

"Tell me where to stand so I'll be in the exact spot."

"Step forward ten paces."

Steve did so, and Heather spoke in a loud, clear voice. "Luke Pryor."

She waited ten seconds and said, "Donnie Douglas."

After standing motionless for several seconds, Steve turned back the way they came. "Like I suspected. Nothing. Whoever shot Luke did it somewhere else, placed his body in his truck and drove him here."

Heather placed Steve's hand on her arm again. "And then they burned him beyond recognition."

Even though Heather took a step forward, Steve stayed glued to the spot. "Why?"

"Why what?"

"Why go to all the trouble of murdering him somewhere else, lifting him into his truck, hauling him away from the scene of the murder, dousing him and his truck with gasoline and setting everything ablaze?"

He started walking, and she had to catch up to place his hand on her arm. "Another few steps and you would have run into a tree." Heather could almost hear the gears turning in Steve's mind and asked, "Of all those elements, which are the most important?"

He stopped again. "They're all related. Someone wanted the body to be very hard to identify."

"Perhaps they needed time to get away or establish an alibi."

"That's one possibility."

"What's another?"

Steve shook his head. "When I think of it, I'll let you know." He let out a sigh. "Let's start our search for the site of the murder at Luke's house. That's where Trey said he and Mary went. How far is it?"

"Less than a mile. We passed the road that leads to the locked gate on our way to the burn site."

Once again, they walked in silence. Heather pondered the list of questions Steve posed about moving and burning the body. Nothing other than buying time to get away came to her. She wondered how long it would take Steve to come up with other motives.

"We're fifty feet from the gate," announced Heather.

"Start saying 'Luke' and then 'Donnie' every ten yards."

Heather complied, and Steve gave no reaction. They stopped at a gate made of galvanized tubing.

"Does anything look out of place?"

Heather scanned the gate and the barbed wire fence that stretched in each direction from it. "Nothing. Standard fencing, trees, and keypads on each side."

"Go back and look at the keypad. See if someone tampered with it."

She left him with his hand resting on the top rail of the gate and returned with a negative report.

"Time to climb over," he said.

When Steve wanted to, he could move with speed and grace. On this bitter February day, he must not have wanted to. He climbed to the top rail with no trouble, but slipped on his way down. He landed with his feet crossed and looked like a drunk trying to walk a straight line for a cop. The dirt road had just enough grade to throw his balance off and he fell in a heap onto damp dirt in a shallow ditch.

Heather scurried over the fence to help him. By the time she arrived, he'd risen. "You should have waited for me."

He huffed. "You're twenty years younger than me. Why weren't you already on this side of the gate?"

"Don't blame me for your clumsiness. Now stand still and I'll brush you off." As she did, a chuckle escaped. She tried to tamp it down, but the giggle turned into a full-blown laugh.

"Don't you feel guilty finding humor in the misery of an old blind man?"

Instead of answering, Heather continued to laugh. "I can't help it. You looked like the guy I took in for my first arrest. His feet were all tangled up like yours and he fell into a fountain."

"I'm *so* glad I could bring back such a happy memory to entertain you. Now, go to the keypad and look for signs someone tampered with it."

Heather handed Steve his cane and continued to chuckle as she walked to the keypad. "There's a screw missing on the bottom."

When he heard her voice, Steve walked toward her. "Do you see Luke and Julie's tiny house from here?"

"Not yet. Let's follow the road."

"Keep saying his name as we walk."

Heather stopped when the road opened to a clearing and she

saw an ocean-going container transformed into a miniature home. "I believe we've arrived."

"Is there a driveway?" asked Steve.

"There's enough gravel for several cars on the far side."

"Keep going and stop when you get to the spot where you think Luke would have parked."

They walked to what appeared to be a likely spot and Heather spoke. "Luke Pryor."

Before she could speak Donnie's name Steve froze. "This is it. I'm seeing red."

Heather gasped. It never failed to amaze her when Steve identified the scene of a murder. She lowered her voice out of a sense of reverence. "It always gives me goose-flesh when you do this."

He scratched his chin. "Do you see any blood on the gravel?"

Heather scanned the rocks below them. "It could be."

Steve pulled out his phone and spoke to it. "Call Detective Burris."

On the second ring, Burris answered. "Is this Steve Smiley?"

"Yeah. I need you to bring luminol and a black light to Luke Pryor's home. I think Heather found the site where someone shot him."

"Should I call for a forensics team?"

"Not yet. We need to make sure the stain is blood."

After the call, Heather asked, "Where do you want me to park you? I'm going to have a peek in the windows."

"Take me with you and tell me what you see."

"We'll have to cross police tape."

Steve took a step toward the home. "I'll tell Burris I didn't see it."

"Duck under," said Heather as they neared the steps to the double patio. Three steps later, she said, "It's a deck made of composite material and it extends the entire length of the container. There's a fire pit and deck chairs."

"How many?"

"Three. There's also a storage shed wrapped with more police tape."

Heather turned to face the trailer. "We're only a few steps away from the sliding glass door. They pulled the curtains open, but there's a glare. Let me shield my eyes and I'll be able to see inside."

Steve dropped his hand from Heather's arm as she formed a vision tunnel with her hands. "It's small, but cute in a bachelor pad sort of way."

"Why do you say that?"

"There are clothes draped on the furniture and a sweatshirt on the floor."

"What about pictures?"

"There's a poster-size, blown-up photo of Luke, Brandon, Julie, and some other woman on the wall. Otherwise, all I see is a television and the kitchen." She took a step back. "Of course, there are smudges on the glass from fingerprint powder."

"I'd have thought Julie would have sent someone to clean up the mess the cops left by now. What can you see in the other windows?"

"They drew the curtains on all the windows in this room. I can go around the back and check, but I'll need a ladder to stand on."

"Go look. If there're curtains, don't worry."

Heather made a quick circle of the home. "No luck. Curtains all the way around."

It took another fifteen minutes before Burris arrived. He piled out of his car with a spray bottle in one hand and a special light in the other. "Where is it?"

"You parked over it," said Heather. "Back up and I'll show you."

Heather showed Burris the stained gravel. He squatted down and squirted a small amount of luminol on two or three rocks and shined the blacklight on them. His face fell.

Heather shook her head. "It needs to be darker to show up. Do you have a raincoat in the trunk?"

"I've got one of those silver thermal blankets."

"That's even better."

Burris returned and extracted the shiny sheet of material from its package to make a makeshift darkroom. He dropped on hands and knees, covered his head, and flicked on the light. A whoop of excitement preceded him throwing the silver blanket to the side. "It's blue."

Steve spoke up from the step he'd sat on. "Now you can call in a forensics team. You'll be looking for either a pistol or rifle casing and the spent round. If it's a high-caliber round, they'll be lucky to find it."

"I'll call the sheriff and let him know. By the way, he checked up on you two and told me to do whatever you said."

"There's nothing more for us to do here. Heather and I are going back and get something to drink."

By the time Steve and Heather reached the steps of the lodge, they had both removed their jackets and gloves. The sharp temperature that put color in their cheeks earlier moderated as bone-warming sunshine bore down on them. Heather blew out a breath, signaling the end of their walk. "We should have taken water."

"Two bottles each," said Steve in agreement. "Let's hydrate and rest before Mary Ricks arrives."

"I could use a quick shower." Heather swung open the front door, intending for them to go to their rooms. They only made it a few steps into the foyer before a woman blocked their way. "If you're Steve Smiley and Heather McBlythe, you've kept me waiting."

Steve turned to face the challenge. "You must be Mary. Thanks for coming. Your room is ready and waiting for you."

"I have no intention of staying here. I don't know what it is to you if I hired a private detective. I'm Donnie Douglas's cousin, or Luke or whatever you're calling him, and it's none of your business if I wanted to know something about him."

While Heather's teeth clenched, Steve maintained a calm exterior, but his words held a veiled threat. "So far, we haven't told the police that you and your brother are here. We also haven't told them you hired the private investigator long before Luke's murder, or Donnie as you knew him. That means we need to discuss this with you and we're in no mood to do that now. I strongly suggest you—"

Mary tented her hands on her hips. "Who are you to tell me what to do?"

Steve had both hands on the top of his cane. "Heather, call Detective Burris and tell him we have a suspect here who could use a long day and night of police interrogation. He's only a mile away."

"You wouldn't dare," said Mary, but her statement lacked conviction.

Steve took in a deep breath and let it out slowly. "It's a nice day. There's no need to spoil it by sending you to jail for something you can easily explain. It's your choice, Mary."

"Well..."

"Good. Consider this a mini-vacation from the hub-bub of Houston. The food is excellent and the rooms are every bit as good as a nice hotel. Heather and I have had a busy day investigating Luke's murder, and things are moving faster than we expected. I'm sure you understand an old guy like me needs to rest now and then. Did you bring a suitcase?"

The tense mood in the room eased a little, but Mary wasn't through with her complaints. "I still think you're trying to trick me. It won't work."

Steve laughed. "I spent years putting guilty people behind bars and making sure I never put an innocent one there. All we're asking for is a long chat in about an hour. That will give everyone enough time to freshen up."

Mary took a step back. "My alternatives are to stay here and talk to you, or have some hick cop put me in handcuffs. Is that right?"

Neither Heather nor Steve responded.

What sounded like a mixture of a huff and a growl came from Mary as she jerked around and took a step toward the door.

Heather held up a hand to stop her. "Did you bring toiletries and clothes for Trey?"

Mary brushed past her. "He's old enough to care for himself."

Steve took off by himself toward the stairs, causing Heather to quick-step to keep up with him. "I hope she's the one that killed Luke. There's a lot to dislike about that woman. Everything about her is like brushing against the thorns we walked past this morning. She has short, spiked red hair, and looks to be a somewhat curvy size twelve trying to squeeze into tens."

"You can't judge a horse by the size of her jeans."

Heather shook her head. "You need to work on your butchered comparisons."

They reached the top of the stairs and Steve stopped. "Please tell me there's a mini fridge in my room with bottles of water in it."

"I took care of that yesterday. When do you want to talk to Mary?"

Steve pushed back a wayward lock of hair from his forehead. "Let her stew a while longer. Tell her we'll come to her room in an hour, but I'll pretend I overslept."

"Are you sure you'll be pretending?" As usual, Steve ignored her snarky comment.

"I'll call Burris and make sure he stays nearby. Mary may need some extra coaxing to get her to talk."

14

Hot water washed away sweat from Heather's walk, but not the gut-felt dislike of Mary Ricks. What was it about the thirty-something-year-old divorcé that caused such intense feelings to rise until they spewed like a dormant volcano come to life? The water pounded and steam rose as Heather tried to put her finger on the exact cause. The way Mary spoke about her compassion-worthy brother didn't help. Perhaps it had more to do with her attitude of entitlement? Could it be her penchant for deception? Mary didn't have to come or even talk to them. Yet, here she was, and she wanted to match wits with her and Steve. Was she arrogant, foolish, or very cagey? Perhaps she had nothing to hide. Not likely since she hired a private detective before Luke's murder. Could Lee Paulson be the one who pulled the trigger and burned Luke's body?

As steam billowed, Steve's words of wisdom came to her. *Don't form conclusions without facts. Things aren't always as they seem.*

Instead of obsessing over Mary, Heather forced her thoughts to bring other suspects to mind. Faces of the two remaining owners of the hydroponic farm came to her. Did Julie or Brandon, or both of them, want to bring the number of owners down to two?

"I'll start with Julie," said Heather in a whisper. She liked to talk in the shower as much as others enjoyed singing. "Why did Julie refer to herself, Brandon, and Luke as a team? Did the fire of love she'd found with Luke in Belize burn out when they returned to Texas?"

A second thought concerning Luke and Julie came into her mind. "Luke spent a lot of time on sales calls and in hotels. Did he succumb to the temptations of the life of a traveling salesman? After all, didn't the professor say he had a way with people, especially the ladies?"

The image of Jill, the shapely and ambitious student, appeared next. "She went on sales calls with Luke. We already know she's not above earning extra credit points with her professor. I wonder if she used her charms to get her hooks in Luke? Perhaps Jill's search for a job with benefits included Julie's husband. People have killed for less, especially if Luke fit into the love-'em-and leave-'em category. Perhaps he shunned Jill and paid the ultimate price."

The hot water beat on her shoulders as she thought. "Then there's the private detective. We still know nothing about him. We'll need to get his real name out of Mary today."

Heather reached to turn off the water, but stopped. "Finally, we have Brandon. Of all the possibilities, he seems the least likely, but he's also the quietest. Steve told me to never overlook those whose waters run deep."

With the shower cut off, Heather jerked back the curtain and grabbed a fluffy towel, reveling in its quality. Someone had spent a lot of money building and equipping this lodge. Some of Luke's fortune, no doubt.

IT TOOK HEATHER LONGER THAN EXPECTED TO PUT HERSELF back together after the shower and review of suspects. Besides drying her hair, she had to reapply makeup and make a to-do list of tasks to complete after the meeting. Most related to the current investigation, but she also needed to check on the progress of a land sale and the final disposition of a beach-front apartment complex. She added a last item that brought a smile to her face. *Call Jack.*

After a last look in the mirror, she opened the door separating her room from Steve's. She found him sitting upright in a chair with hands hanging loose off the armrests. "Are you awake?"

"You took longer than usual."

"I lost track of time thinking about suspects and what I might ask Mary. How do you want to play her today?"

"Let's do the push-and-pull-back on her. She seems impulsive. We need to press her hard, but not drive her away. She's a bully, so we can't let her see weakness in us, but we need her to think she's in charge now and then."

Steve drummed his fingers on the arms of the chair. "Let's begin by focusing on the PI she hired. If we can get enough information, Detective Burris can locate him. We need to keep him busy and out of our way as much as possible."

"Where do you want to conduct the interview?"

Steve shrugged. "We have bugs in your room and the office downstairs. We can make recordings from either."

Heather considered the options as she stood. "Let's do it in my room."

"Get her."

A scowl painted Mary's face as she opened her room's door with what looked like a practiced look of disdain. She hadn't changed from the not-so-skinny jeans and knit shirt she'd arrived in. She wore the front of the blouse tucked in while the sides and back hung loose. "I hope this won't take long."

Heather wondered what brought on the sudden interest in time. Supposedly she didn't know anyone, and the farm was out in the country, miles from even a small town. As far as Heather knew, there was no place Mary needed to be. The brief trip down the hall passed in silence until Heather waved her plastic key card in front of the lock on her room's door.

"We're meeting in your room?" asked Mary. "I thought we'd go down to some office or something."

"No need to bother anyone else. Besides, we'll be more comfortable here."

Steve sat in a twin of the chair in his room and made no move to rise. He greeted Mary with a pleasant voice and invited her to sit on the couch. Heather took the executive chair from the desk for herself and positioned it facing the Mary.

"We appreciate you coming," said Steve. "If all goes well, this shouldn't take long. I've been on the phone with Detective Burris and he gave me a good idea of the information he needs us to ask you. Let's get started."

"Why isn't he here?"

"I'll explain that in a few minutes." Steve moved into his first question. "When was the last time you went to Luke's house?"

"You keep talking about someone named Luke, but I don't know anyone named Luke."

Steve nodded his head in acknowledgment. "Yes, I believe you knew your cousin as Donnie. So, when was the last time you went to his house here on the farm?"

Mary's head shook from side to side. "I've never been to his house."

"But you know where it is."

"Who says?"

Heather studied Mary and wondered why she lied about going to the tiny home.

Steve leaned forward. "We're not getting off to a good start. Let's try something else. Tell us about your relationship with Luke, or Donnie. Did you know each other as children?"

Mary scoffed. "Not much to tell. I met him once... no, twice, at stupid family reunions. The first time he must have been in, like, the fifth grade. The second time he was in high school. I thought he was a dweeb, a computer geek with old-school ear buds tethered by a white cord to a laptop. Always played some stupid game. Looking back on it, I think he was probably developing the game that made him filthy rich."

Heather took the next question. "What were his parents like?"

"Weird, like him. Real bookish and quiet. His dad worked as some sort of engineer. I never knew or cared what his mom did."

"I understand they died young."

"I guess. I don't know how old they were. I was in my senior year of high school and didn't go to the funeral even though my mom wanted me to. I didn't know them, so why should I?"

Steve took another turn. "Did you ever have contact with him while he was developing his games or gaining his wealth?"

She shook her head. "I didn't know he'd made it big until he disappeared. Back then, rich nerds were a dime a dozen. The only thing that separated Donnie from the rest of the pack of boy-wonders was when he dropped out of sight." She made tight fists out of both hands and released them in a mock explosion. "Here one day and then, POOF, GONE! The cops contacted me back then, asking some of the same questions you are."

Heather took her turn. "Years passed before you contacted an attorney about getting your inheritance. Why did you wait so long?"

Mary looked up and to the left. "I'd forgotten about Donnie until someone mentioned him. It was over a year ago when I called Jack Blackstock. I called him 'cause he helped out my mom once. Jack found out about a nosy insurance lady who got involved. Somehow she tracked Donnie to Belize, but lost the trail. The idiot cops down there said he'd disappeared, but now we know he came here." She spread her hands and looked around the room.

By this time, Mary had relaxed, as evidenced by her leaning back and using more complete sentences.

"Did you kill your cousin?" asked Steve.

Mary tilted her head. "What kind of question is that?"

Steve issued a toothy grin. "One intended to get a rise out of you. It's not one the police would ask you so directly, but I like to cut to the chase."

To Heather's surprise, Mary chuckled. "No. I didn't kill him, but I won't pretend I'm torn up about Donnie's death."

Steve added, "Or the potential of inheriting millions."

"Who wouldn't be over the moon about that?"

"Tell us how you contacted the private detective."

The sudden shift back to the detective seemed to catch Mary off guard. "Well, I didn't exactly contact him. We sort of met by chance."

Heather purposefully raised questioning eyebrows to communicate to Mary that she needed to go into detail.

"I go to Megg's on Sunday mornings, it's a little coffee shop. While I'm in line, this guy starts up a conversation. He's nice enough looking and asks if he can pay for my coffee and muffin. The next thing I know, we're talking like old friends. I give him my number and we agree to dinner. That's where we talk about what we do for a living. He tells me he's a private investigator, and that intrigued me. Somehow, we talk about how I'm related to Donnie and how he's been missing for a long time. To make a long story short, he said he'd do a few hours of work for free to find Donnie."

Mary didn't realize it, but Steve had lured her into the exact spot he wanted. She'd dropped her guard and information flowed.

Steve asked, "What did he find?"

"Not much, but it must have encouraged him enough to continue. He said he'd keep looking and for me not to worry about paying him until the court ruled Donnie legally dead and I received the inheritance."

"That's when you and Trey met him at the tiny house."

"Yeah."

"Are you still in contact with him?"

"He's out of state working on another case."

Steve nodded. "What's his name?"

"Lee Paulson."

"Can you describe him to me?"

"He's tall with rusty-red hair."

"What kind of car does he drive?"

Mary's eyebrows pinched together. "Why is that important?"

Steve chuckled and raised a single palm. "It's not, but I have theories about men and the cars they drive. I used to be a homicide detective and knew several private investigators. They all drove older cars with big, well-turned engines and a few dents. I'm wondering if Lee fits the same mold."

Mary flicked her hand in such a way as to dismiss her suspicion. "You missed it in Lee's car. He drives a new Ford Bronco."

Steve snapped his fingers. "There goes my theory. You've been very helpful, Mary. Thanks for coming by and speaking so freely with us. We may need to talk to you again tonight if we come up with anything new."

Mary stood and surveyed the room. "This is a nice lodge. How much do you think it and the farm are worth?"

Heather fielded the question with one of her own. "Are you thinking of selling your portion if you inherit it?"

"My portion?"

"There's you and your brother."

Her eyes flashed. "He'll do what I tell him."

"What about your parents?"

Mary shrugged. "There's only Mom, and she has Alzheimer's."

Heather bit down on her tongue to keep from saying what was going through her mind. Steve, however, told Mary when they served dinner and promised to save her a seat with them.

After the door clicked shut, Heather wound up to deliver a caustic review of Mary's treatment of her brother and mother. Steve held up a hand like a stop sign. "Don't say it. She's not getting my vote for sister or daughter of the year, but that doesn't mean she killed Luke."

Heather huffed. "Did you get anything useful?"

Steve nodded. "I'm more convinced than ever that we need to find Lee Paulson, or whatever his real name is. I'll call Leo and have him look for a tall, red-haired PI driving a new Bronco."

"Nothing like a friend in Houston homicide," said Heather.

"What did you pick up on?" asked Steve.

Heather knew it was a test to see if she'd found the nugget amongst the words Mary had thrown around. She took in a deep breath. "You and I are probably the only private investigators who don't have to charge for our services. Taking a job on contingency is almost unheard of."

Steve nodded. "I see two possibilities. Lee Paulson may well have killed Luke. He might be a lone wolf who traced him to the Caribbean and back to Texas."

"Or?"

"Someone else paid Paulson to come here and snoop until he had enough information on Luke's habits." Steve paused. "Mary thinks he came because of her, but what if it was someone else who actually hired him to get info and then they killed him? Of course, there's a third possibility. Mary may have made up an elaborate story about Lee Paulson being a private eye."

"But you don't think that."

Steve shook his head. "We need to find him."

The voice from Steve's phone identified the caller to be Detective Burris. When Steve answered, the wail of a siren accompanied strained words. "Steve, I'm on my way to what looks to be an accident. It's Julie. First reports are she's in terrible shape."

"Where are you?"

"On my way to Brenham."

"We'll meet you at the hospital there."

15

"Hang on," said Heather as she took the corner coming from the hydroponic farm.

"Hang on to what?" asked Steve as he fought against inertia.

"There's a handle up high on your right."

Steve groped until he found it and held on. "Has this handle always been here?"

"Uh-huh."

"Now you tell me."

"Sorry." Heather's Mercedes SUV continued to gain speed. "We'll be coming to a stop sign in a few miles. Then we'll turn onto the main road to Brenham. It's a fairly straight shot into town. I'll keep it under ninety."

It didn't take long before Steve grabbed the handle whenever Heather braked. They made it to the main road and continued on for several miles until traffic thickened.

"You're slowing. We must be close to the site of the accident. Describe the terrain."

"Rolling hills with pastures and some dense woods, especially around the creeks."

Steve nodded to say he understood, but what did he see in his mind? She didn't have long to wait, as he offered a plausible

130

explanation for the wreck. "I bet there are plenty of places where someone could get a clean shot at a passing car."

Heather jerked her gaze to the right, but only for a second. "Do you think someone shot Julie?"

His words came out guarded. "I've worried about her ever since we arrived and should have done something about it."

Traffic slowed to a crawl. They inched to the crest of a hill, which gave Heather a better view. "There's a swarm of emergency vehicles a half mile away at the bottom of the hill. Only one lane of traffic is open."

"Tell me what you see when we get there."

They moved forward, which eventually gave Heather a good view of the vehicle. "It's a van from the hydroponic farm. From the damage, I'd say it rolled two or three times." She looked to see a deputy signaling her to hurry past and clear the area.

She mashed down on the accelerator and continued talking. "It's a new van and really torn up. They cut off the driver's door. The front and side air bags all deployed. No sign of an ambulance, so they must have already transferred her."

The rest of the trip passed without incident as the onboard computer directed them to the emergency entrance of Brenham's hospital. Detective Burris awaited their arrival at the emergency entrance. "Let's find a quiet place and I'll fill you in."

"Is she still alive?" asked Steve.

"Alive and coming around as they wheeled her in."

Heather blew out a sign of guarded relief and hoped the news continued to be encouraging.

Steve asked, "Is there a place we can get a cup of coffee?"

"There's a cafeteria."

That's all it took for the trio to walk down the hall and follow the signs. Heather seated Steve and joined Burris at the coffee service. "I saw the wreckage. How many times did it roll?"

"Three."

"Let's get back to Steve with his coffee before you tell me more. No use repeating the story."

Once seated, Burris launched into his narrative. "They were cutting off the driver's side door when I arrived. Julie's lower arm was all red and puffy, but it looked like the air bags did their job. No visible cuts on her face, but that doesn't mean she doesn't have serious injuries. She must have been doing at least seventy."

"What condition were the tires?" asked Steve.

"Two flat."

"What about tread wear?"

Burris gave Heather a look that communicated he hadn't checked.

"Any sign of a blow-out?"

"I didn't check. I was busy watching EMTs extract her."

"Any idea yet if she's expected to make it?"

The detective hesitated. "She was breathing on her own."

Steve played with the sleeve that made it possible to pick up the hot paper cup. "We're probably looking at another thirty minutes before we get word on Julie's condition. We might as well bring you up to date on what we know, and you can tell us about Luke's original crime scene. You go first."

"The crime scene guys weren't encouraging about coming to a scene three weeks old, but they confirmed it's blood on the rocks in the driveway. They said they'd have the blood type today. DNA will take a while. When I left, they hadn't found brass, and weren't hopeful about finding the slug that killed Luke, either."

"I didn't expect them to find brass, but I hope we get lucky and they find the spent bullet."

The alert of an incoming call came from Detective Burris's pocket. After a quick conversation, he reported the source and nature of the call. "That was a highway patrolman. The left front tire has a hole in the sidewall. He says it looks to him like a gunshot from something powerful enough to cut through the layers of rubber and steel belts."

"Steve already guessed someone shot out the tire."

Burris looked up from his cup. "It takes an excellent shot to take out a tire on a vehicle traveling at seventy miles an hour. Any ideas who the shooter might be?"

Steve delayed his answer by taking a sip. "We have several suspects, but one stands out. I'm having my former partner from Houston homicide locate a guy that was planted at the hydroponic farm. He arrived before Luke's murder and left in a hurry when Heather and I arrived. He used Lee Paulson as his cover name, but that's likely an alias."

Heather added, "The farm requires a photo of all students and interns." She pulled out her phone and scrolled to find the photo, attached it to a text, and sent it to Burris.

Steve shifted in his chair. "There's an intern that also caught our eye. Her name is Jill. You interviewed her, so you already have her information. She took some overnight trips with Luke to Houston."

"A romantic link?" asked Burris.

Heather nodded. "She's very ambitious. We need to talk to some more of the interns and get a better read on her. What we know for sure about her is that she isn't above having a romp with her professor to get preferential treatment."

"Do you suspect her of killing Luke?"

Steve lowered his cup of coffee. "I believe she knows more than she's been willing to tell us. She may have done nothing, but I'll bet she and Luke were more than friends."

Burris shook his head. "I had Julie as the prime suspect. She had motive, means and opportunity to kill her husband. There's no will, but she seems to have a leg up on anyone else claiming Luke's millions."

"Don't be too quick to rule her out," said Heather. "There're others to consider, too. Luke's cousins are staying down the hall from us. The male seems harmless, but I believe his sister is capable of just about anything. We haven't gotten far enough with them yet to see if they have an alibi."

Steve added, "She's a real piece of work. Something tells me she has an air-tight alibi, even if she had to beg, borrow, or steal it."

"Would it do any good if I took her in for questioning?"

"Talk to the brother instead," said Steve. "He knows nothing about the killing, but it will make her worry. Read his rights in front of her. It will be interesting to see how she reacts, but be prepared for a tongue-lashing."

"I'll come by this evening."

"Concentrate your questions on what his sister knows about Lee Paulson."

A scrubs-clad woman entered the cafeteria and beat a path to their table. "Detective Burris?"

He stood.

"Doctor Kim wants to speak to you."

Burris turned to Steve and Heather. "You're coming with me."

WITH A LAST NAME LIKE KIM, HEATHER EXPECTED THE attending physician to be of Asian descent. Kim turned out to be the blond doctor's first name. Her last name proved to be an Eastern European tongue-twister that required a separate line on her name tag. After introductions, Dr. Kim began a recital of injuries, treatments, and prognosis.

"Ms. Pryor is lucky to be alive. The air bags and seatbelt did an amazing job. She suffered a severe concussion and a fracture of her left arm that has been immobilized in a splint and should heal with no problems. The MRI and CT scans show no lesions in the brain, but we'll keep a close eye on her for the next day or two. If all goes well, she'll be able to go home late tomorrow afternoon."

Steve spoke before Detective Burris had a chance to. "Can we transport her to another facility tonight?"

Doctor Kim shook her head. "That's unnecessary and not

recommended."

"We have a rather delicate situation with Julie. Someone recently murdered her husband and the preliminary reports on the wreck indicate it wasn't an accident. If transport tonight isn't possible, she'll need tight security."

"I was going to put her in a regular room, but I could put her in ICU overnight."

Steve turned to Detective Burris. "You'll need to arrange for at least one deputy to stay outside the door. Heather is armed and she'll stay at her bedside."

Heather shifted her gaze from the doctor to Steve. "I will?"

He didn't respond to Heather's tepid question. "We're going to spread the rumor that Julie's injuries are life threatening and she needs to be transferred to a hospital in Houston tomorrow."

Heather may have lagged behind Steve in his thinking, but soon matched him stride for stride. Her gaze went back to Dr. Kim. "I can arrange for a medical helicopter to transfer Julie tomorrow as soon as you say it's safe."

Dr. Kim's eyes opened a little wider. "If she's that hot of a commodity, I want her gone ASAP. You arrange air transport with appropriate staff and I'll release her tonight."

Detective Burris issued a sigh of relief. "That's good. We're short staffed as it is."

Heather nodded her thanks to Dr. Kim, who scurried off.

"Where will you take her?" asked Detective Burris.

Steve chuckled. "I have an idea, but I need to talk to Heather about it."

Heather looked at Detective Burris. "This should be interesting. Could you give us a minute alone?"

"I'm going back to the cafeteria. I missed lunch and need to update the sheriff."

After the clomp of Burris's boots faded, Steve asked, "Are we in a spot where no one else can hear?"

The waiting room stood vacant except for the two of them

and a television spouting a cooking show. Heather checked around to make doubly sure. "All clear. What's the plan?"

"Fly Julie to the airport in Conroe. Have Jack and a nurse meet the chopper and take Julie and the nurse to a hotel. The nurse will need to spend the night with her, just to be safe."

"Do you want me to hire a bodyguard?"

Steve's lip quirked. "No need. You'll be there."

"What?"

"I thought you might miss Jack. This will give you a chance to see him and guard Julie. If anyone's looking for her tonight, they'll concentrate on the major Houston hospitals. You heard Dr. Kim. Once Julie goes twenty-four hours with no trouble, she'll be fine. After the first twenty-four hours you can leave her in a hotel under a different name until we get this case sorted out."

"How long will that take?"

"Not too much longer."

Heather tented her hands on her hips, ready to give Steve grief over his vague answer, when Brandon stepped into the waiting room.

16

Heather found the remote for the television and turned the volume down. Brandon's brow furrowed with lines she interpreted as worry creases. He hung his head and mumbled, "It's all my fault."

Steve suggested they sit while he explained what they knew about Julie's injuries. Brandon sat at the very edge of his chair and dry-washed his hands. "How bad is it?"

Steve held up a single finger to keep Heather from answering. "The doctor told us she has multiple injuries. They're worried about her brain. A helicopter will take her where she'll get specialized care."

"I want her to have the best care possible."

Heather placed her hand on Brandon's shoulder and squeezed before she sat beside Steve. "This must be horrid, coming so soon after Luke's death."

He nodded and didn't respond with words, but with tears.

Steve asked, "Where were you when you heard about Julie?"

"With the strawberries. The intern named Jill came running in wailing. She grabbed me and cried until I had to push her away. It took a few minutes before she calmed down enough so she could tell me about the accident."

"Why was she so upset?"

He answered with a shrug, so Heather had to relay that Brandon didn't know to Steve. She added, "Remember, Brandon, Steve can't see you. Also, it helps after you experience something like this to talk about it. Details help people process trauma."

He took in a deep breath. "Like I said, I was working the strawberries this afternoon. I was pretty torn up when I found out the police discovered the site where Luke died."

"How did you find that out?"

"Now that you mention it, Jill told me about that, too. That occurred earlier today when Dr. Chalmers assigned her to the shipping barn. I have an office there where we monitor security cameras."

"Do you have someone monitoring all the time?"

"The interns take turns. It gives them a break. Now that I think about it, that's probably how Jill found out about the cops at Luke's."

Heather made a mental note to verify how Jill knew about the original crime site. Something else puzzled her. Why did Jill run to Brandon to tell him? Was she trying to put herself in his good graces? It's possible Jill felt it her duty to be first to tell anything, especially bad news. She'd heard Steve refer to the compulsion to spread bad news as 'the town crier syndrome.'

She didn't have long to pose silent questions to herself before Steve asked, "Did you have cameras up at Luke's house?"

"I'm sure you've guessed by now that I'm a stickler for security."

"Did the cameras record when Luke's murder occurred?"

"They should have, but we lost power and the battery back-up didn't work."

"Was power out everywhere?"

"Not to the farm. It's on a separate feed from the utility company. I still don't know why the battery backup at his house didn't work. Everything checked out fine when I tested it a few days after."

Steve folded his cane, a sign he intended to make this a longer than usual interview. "Did you ever find out the cause of the outage?"

"The utility company couldn't find anything wrong and the power came back on that night. We only lost service for a little over an hour. Detective Burris thought it was odd, and all but accused me of tampering with it."

Heather asked, "Are you saying there were no other power outages reported to the utility company?"

"That's right."

"Were you at home?"

"I was at Julie's office, going over the books." His voice softened. "Poor Julie. First Luke and now this accident."

Steve couldn't see it, but Brandon wrung his hands when he talked about Julie.

It surprised Heather when Steve came out and said, "It wasn't any more of an accident than when someone shot Luke."

Brandon blinked as if a bright light shone in his eyes. "Are you sure?"

"Someone killed Luke and now someone's tried to kill Julie. Think hard, Brandon. Who would want both of them dead?"

His chin rested on his chest. "I don't know, but I'd pay anything to have them back. They were the brother and sister I never had."

Steve didn't let up. "You're a smart guy. The police have already questioned you about where you were when Luke died. They're going to do it again, but this time it will be rougher. Do you have an attorney to represent you?"

"Why would I need one? I have witnesses and video that proves I was with the strawberries this afternoon."

"All afternoon?"

"I was in and out of the shipping barn, doing some things that Luke used to do."

"Do you have a way to get off the farm without being recorded?"

"Absolutely not."

"Are you sure?"

"One hundred percent."

Steve leaned back and let out a deep sigh. "You might be smart, Brandon, but you're not a talented liar. People who tell the truth respond with a simple yes or no. It's a dead giveaway when they exaggerate or deny something too vehemently. The worst one is, 'I swear on a stack of bibles.' You might as well have a neon sign."

Brandon's body sagged. "There's a back way, but I'm the only one who knows about it."

"What about Julie or Luke? Did they know?"

"Not even them. I've never used it, so you won't find tire tracks there."

"Where is it?"

"At the southeast corner of the farm."

"Do you have it monitored on video?"

Brandon shook his head, then must have remembered to use words to communicate with Steve, and said, "Not that one. I figured if I ever had to use it, I wouldn't come back."

The room went quiet for long seconds. Heather wondered why Steve didn't ask Brandon why he'd need to bug out. For whatever reason, Steve didn't pursue the matter. Instead, he asked Brandon a plain question that required a plain answer. "Did you kill Luke or do you know who did?"

"No to both questions."

"Why did you three come back to the States after Belize?"

"Luke thought enough time had passed that he could use one of his aliases and reestablish himself in a profession that could help people. He wanted to do his part to produce natural, environmentally friendly food."

"And you?"

"Even though Julie was his wife, she and I were along for the ride. Luke funded the entire project. He fell in love with the idea of organic hydroponics while working on Mother Nature's Farm with Lucy. She thought it would be a wonderful four-season business opportunity with greenhouses."

"Are you still in contact with Lucy?"

"Not much."

"Do you own a rifle?"

"No."

"Have you ever shot one?"

"Not even a BB gun."

"Did Luke ever talk about the games he created?"

"Some, but not much."

Heather had to listen closely as the questions and answers ping-ponged back and forth with surprising speed.

Steve kept going. "What do you know about Luke's cousins who are trying to make a claim on the hydroponics farm?"

"Not much. I know they're staying down the hall from you."

"Do you think they have a legitimate claim?"

"I don't see how they could." He looked away. "Right now, the only thing that matters is Julie getting well."

"You're not afraid of losing your job?"

"Lucy and Luke taught me to not worry about money or a job. Use your mind, and money will chase you down."

"Where were you when someone shot Luke?"

"Like I said earlier, Julie and I worked on the books in her office."

"That's right. You did already tell me that. I guess I forgot."

"No, you didn't. I studied you and Heather before I hired you. Neither of you makes mistakes like that. You tested me."

The corners of Steve's mouth turned up. "Now it's my turn to be busted."

Brandon gave Steve a pleading look, which accomplished nothing. "Can I see Julie?"

Heather answered for Steve. "They're not allowing anyone but medical personnel to see her right now."

Steve added, "Heather's driving tonight to be with her and

will keep us posted. Would you mind giving me a ride back to the farm?"

"I'd appreciate the company."

"Any chance of us sneaking off to a restaurant where I can get a hamburger before we go back?"

Brandon issued a mischievous grin.

STEVE HELD ON TO HEATHER'S ARM AS SHE LED THEIR WAY back to the cafeteria. Brandon trailed silently along while Steve wondered if he'd used his daily allotment of words, or if the hydroponic expert preferred to listen much more than he talked.

Two things attacked Steve's senses as Heather opened the door to the cafeteria: Italian seasoning for the featured meal and Mary Ricks's caustic voice. The first reminded him of awful food in middle school while the second brought back memories of Mrs. Westcott, a barracuda of an English teacher who must have owned stock in the company that made red ink for ballpoint pens. The mere thought of diagramming a run-on sentence made him cringe.

Heather whispered to him. "Mary and Trey are at a table with Detective Burris."

Mary spoke in a tone that demanded instead of asked, "Why can't you tell me how serious it is?"

"I couldn't even if I knew. It's against regulations," replied Detective Burris.

Heather spoke next, saving Steve from having to confront Mary. "All we know is they're concerned enough about Julie to fly her out as soon as possible." She patted Steve's hand. "I need to make some phone calls. I'll leave you with Brandon and keep you posted."

A nod of the head sufficed for a response, as he knew Heather needed to find a quiet place and check on arrangements to fly Julie to safety. He turned to face Mary. "Why don't we sit down and I'll tell you what I've been able to find out." He then turned to Detective Burris. "I thought you needed to go back to the site of the accident."

"Yeah. I do. If I don't see you later tonight, I'll come tomorrow." The clip-clop of Burris's boots sounded his leaving.

"Table or booth?" asked Brandon.

"Whatever is open and away from people," said Steve.

Chairs scraped against the floor as the four settled at a table. "Mary, I planned to talk to you and Trey at supper tonight, but this will have to do. There are a few things I wanted to get clarity on."

Mary shot back in her usual way. "What things?"

"How did you hear about Julie's accident?"

"Trey told me."

Steve quirked his head. "How did you hear, Trey?"

"Uh. I, uh. I overheard someone talking?"

"Who?"

"Don't know."

Mary jumped in. "Those are Trey's favorite words. I can't tell you how many times a day he says them."

"Do you two live together?"

"Heavens no. Growing up with him was more than enough for me. He lives his life and I live mine. The only reason we're here is because of the inheritance." Her next words came out lower in volume, as if she spoke to herself. "I can't wait to wave the life insurance check in the face of that awful woman who's responsible for the delay."

"Who would that be?" asked Steve, even though he already knew.

Mary all but spit out the name. "Marsha something. I can't remember her last name. She's been stonewalling the payment and I'm sick of it."

Steve wondered how far he could lead Mary on, and how Brandon would react to her. Only one way to find out. "I don't know if you've thought of this, Mary, but this accident may speed things up for you, whether Julie makes it through the night, or not."

"What do you mean?"

"Yeah, what do you mean?" asked Trey.

"Shut up, Trey. You sound like a parrot." Mary cleared her throat. "Go ahead, Mr. Smiley. Why would Julie's accident speed things up?"

"I spoke with Julie about her receiving the life insurance money and she didn't seem interested in it. She didn't deny that she'd take it, but it didn't seem important to her." He turned to Brandon. "Do you know what Julie's intentions were for receiving the inheritance?"

"I have no idea. All she cared about was Luke, me, and raising good food for people."

"Do you know if Julie has any other relatives?"

Brandon spoke with certainty. "None. We were all three alike."

Mary shot back. "Except for Donnie, uh, Luke. I'm his nearest relative."

A chair pushed back from the table. "I need to use the restroom," said Mary. "Does anyone know where it is?"

"I thought you just went," said Trey.

Venom filled Mary's rebuke. "Don't you dare say a word while I'm gone. Do you understand, Trey?"

It seemed obvious to Steve that Mary had told another lie. She likely needed to call someone and let them know about Julie's condition.

After a few minutes of silence, footsteps approached, and Mary continued where she left off. "I'm still not clear on why you think the insurance company will settle soon."

Steve held up a hand. "I'm no expert on this, but there's no doubt that Luke's dead, is there?"

"None. Dental records confirm he and Donnie are the same guy."

"And there's no doubt you and Trey are Donnie's closest living relatives?"

"No doubt."

"What's changed is that Julie may not live. The way I see it, the life insurance payout is separate from Luke's inheritance. That's assuming you and Trey are secondary beneficiaries on the policy."

"I assure you, we are," said Mary, her voice trilling with excitement. "That means I'll get control of fifteen million right away, but I'll have to wait for the rest of Luke's money until after the court rules it's mine."

"Good luck with that," said Brandon.

"What do you mean by that crack?"

Steve answered for him. "It means that Luke stashed his money all over the world behind encrypted passwords and firewalls so thick you'll never get through them."

The table creaked, which told Steve that Mary had leaned on it. "I think Brandon knows where to look. My lawyers will make him talk."

The laugh Brandon issued carried no mirth. "Luke knew what too much money did to people. He cared enough for Julie and me to not let it ruin us, so he kept us in the dark about that sort of thing. Besides, we found something better than piles of cash."

The ringing of Steve's phone put an end to the tense conversation. The mechanical voice announced a call from his former partner in homicide.

"Can you talk?" asked Leo.

"Not now."

"We found him. Call me back."

Steve told his phone to hang up and call Heather.

As soon as she answered, he said, "Change of plans. Come get me. I'm still in the cafeteria."

17

Heather spotted Steve at a table away from the few patrons that found the courage to chance the Italian fare. She approached the table and noticed Mary's flushed face, which she turned to her. "What's new on Julie's condition?"

"They're waiting on the helicopter to transport her."

Steve turned his head to face Brandon. "There might be a change of plans. Heather isn't sure she can ride in the chopper with Julie. We'll let you know as soon as we find out for sure."

This was all Heather needed to know. Steve had news for her, and he needed to share it in private. His rising from the table confirmed it.

Heather waited until they walked out of earshot before she asked for an explanation.

"Find a private place where I can call Leo."

"There's a chapel up ahead."

Steve leaned into her and whispered. "Leo said they found Lee Paulson."

"Do you still want me to go to Conroe?"

"Let's decide after we hear what Leo says."

An empty chapel awaited them, which made for the perfect over-sized phone booth for Steve to use. Leo answered on the second ring. "This reminds me of old times. You have me do all the heavy lifting while you sit back and wait for answers."

Steve paid no attention to the verbal jab and got down to business. "Heather's here with me. Tell us about Lee Paulson."

"To begin with, his real name is Paul Lee. Rusty-red hair, drives a new red Bronco."

Steve groaned. "You sure it's the same guy Mary met?"

"Positive. That little coffee shop had cameras. It's him alright."

"Paul Lee, huh? Not very creative with names, is he?"

"Don't underestimate him. He has the reputation of being a good PI."

"Good in what way?"

"Effective, but smart enough not to get his hands dirty. He's a one-man shop specializing in insurance fraud."

"Any company in particular?"

"Whoever pays the most."

Steve swept the ground in front of him with his cane as he paced. "Have you talked to him yet?"

"I didn't know you wanted me to. I have his home address if you're interested. It's on the west side, in the Cypress Fairbanks area, if you want to drop by and introduce yourselves."

"You're there now, aren't you?"

"I needed a break, so I took the afternoon off. I'm looking at his Bronco and the door to his condo."

"Send a text with his address. Heather and I are on our way."

"I'll be waiting for you. You might need someone with a real badge to get in the door."

"Thanks, Leo. We'll take you out for a steak dinner after we're finished with him."

Leo laughed out loud. "You already owe me three for other favors I've done for you."

"That's your fault for not coming to see me."

Leo mumbled something about chicken-fried steak fingers at Dairy Queen not counting as steak dinners, and hung up.

Heather didn't hesitate. "I'll call Jack and let him know I won't be coming to Conroe tonight."

"Sorry to interrupt your plans to see him, but I think it's more important to get with Leo and talk to Paul Lee."

Heather shook her head. "More name games. Do you think Leo has background on him?"

Steve lowered his voice as Heather opened the door to the chapel. "If Leo hasn't done a full background on him, he has someone working on it now. We'll walk into Mr. Lee's condo knowing more about him than his mother."

The late afternoon trip into Houston wasn't as challenging as if they tried to beat rush-hour traffic fleeing the city for the suburbs. Still, the sun had well set by the time Heather pulled her SUV into a parking spot beside an unmarked, but easily recognizable police car.

Leo piled into the back seat and handed Heather a file containing multiple sheets of handwritten notes and printouts. "For your reading enjoyment," said Leo.

Heather took it and started reading while Steve took off his seat belt and swiveled in his seat as best he could. "Is he alone?"

"No visitors since I last talked to you."

"Did anything show up in his financial records?"

"He banked some decent checks from an insurance company the last couple of months, but not enough to put a wad of cash down on a new Bronco. He's like most private eyes—feast or famine."

"What about personal history? Did anything stand out?"

"Three ex-wives and one kid with wife number two. Nothing unusual about that. He's current on child support and not too much credit card debt. Nothing stands out but the new ride to go along with his old one."

Steve quipped, "I bet the old one has a five-liter V-8 and needs a paint job."

Leo chuckled and pointed out the car to Heather. Sure enough, Steve had described the older Mustang well.

While Heather shook her head, Leo didn't mince words. "Do you think this guy killed Luke Pryor?"

Steve pulled the handle on his door and it popped open. "Let's go ask him."

It seemed odd, yet right, that Steve's hand found Leo's arm and not hers. The old partnership formed over years of working homicides welded a bond like few other jobs could. Although Leo had to lead him, Steve held the senior position and would steer the questioning. His dominance showed itself on the way to the door. "We'll stand back and let Heather get the door open. If he tries to shut it, you know what to do."

They arrived and the two men stood off to the side of the door, well away from the small peep-eye viewer. Heather knocked and turned her back so all Paul Lee could see was her long auburn hair. The door cracked open. "Can I help you?"

Heather turned to face the door. Leo shoved his badge into the opening and pushed hard enough to bump the occupant out of the way. "Houston homicide. I believe you've already met Mr. Smiley and Ms. McBlythe. They're assisting me with an investigation and I'm sure you'd like to help. Thanks for inviting us in."

By the time Paul Lee got a word in, Heather had closed the door behind her.

"All you had to do was ask. I have nothing to hide."

"Good," said Steve. "Then we can all sit down and have a nice, friendly conversation. I'll start off by asking why you skipped out on your assignment at the hydroponics farm as soon as Heather and I arrived."

"My job ended."

Leo followed with, "It's a coincidence that one PI left the same day two others showed up to investigate a murder. I don't like coincidences."

Steve added, "It makes us wonder who hired you and why?"

"That's confidential."

"I'm still standing and you haven't offered us a place to sit or something to drink," said Steve.

"Remember? You invited us in," said Leo. "Maybe I should look around to make sure everything is as it should be."

Mr. Lee raised his hands in mock surrender. "Take a seat wherever you want, but you're wasting your time. My job was on the up-and-up. I think they forgot I was still there. When you two showed up, I called the person who hired me and he told me to clear out."

"And who might that be?"

He shook his head. "No, you don't. I'm not obligated to tell you or even talk to you."

Steve nodded. "I can appreciate your desire to maintain confidentiality, so I won't ask you to reveal names. Let's talk about something else. What did you think about Luke's body being burned beyond recognition after someone shot him?"

"Not much, other than it wasn't necessary."

"Didn't it make you wonder why?"

He shrugged. "None of my business. They didn't send me there to investigate a murder."

Steve kept on. "It made me and Heather wonder why Luke Pryor was that far away from his house, the lodge, or the greenhouses. It was way off the beaten path."

"What's your point?"

"They sent you to the farm to find out if Luke Pryor was really someone else, a very rich person, a man named Donnie Douglas. Either you found out something, or someone else did. We discovered this morning that Luke wasn't killed in his truck. Someone shot him in the driveway of his house, put him in his truck, took him to the back side of the farm and destroyed as much evidence as they could. You've already admitted to being on the farm and in the employ of someone who had a lot to gain by Luke's death."

"That's speculation on your part."

"Is it? Let me tell you something that isn't speculation. You were on the farm when the murder took place. Someone hired you to provide information about Luke. Like it or not, you are neck-deep in a murder investigation, not to mention an attempted murder."

Paul Lee shot a questioning gaze at Steve. "What attempted murder?"

Steve's voice sounded like the crack of a whip. "Don't play dumb. Someone tried to kill Luke's wife today."

"What? Julie?"

Leo pulled out a notepad and pretended to read a note. "That's one murder and one attempted murder. Where were you today?"

"I never left my condo."

"Never?"

"I went to the gym and to lunch afterward."

"I thought you said you never left. You better come up with names of witnesses or you'll be looking at the inside of a cell tonight. If that happens, I might have to call the licensing board and let them know about your arrest."

Color drained from Lee's face. He drew his hand down his cheek, then snapped his finger. "Security cameras are all over this complex. They're also in the fitness center I joined. I left the complex for only an hour or two. There's no way I could have gone all the way to the farm and made it back in less than three hours."

Steve asked, "Who said the attempt on Julie's life took place at the farm?"

"Look." Beads of sweat formed on his top lip. "Someone's trying to paint me in the picture. I don't know if it's you or someone else. I also don't know who hired me. He offered me a lot more than my going rate and paid in cash. As a cover, I pretended to be interested in growing vegetables and fruit. He told me to find out what I could about Luke Pryor, Julie, and Brandon. I thought it strange that he wanted me to stay there after Luke's murder, but I don't ask too many questions with a fat payday staring me in the face."

Heather asked, "What did the man sound like that hired you?"

"Not young, not old. Sort of stilted, like he had a script in front of him. If I asked him a question, he'd hesitate before answering."

"Did he cover the receiver?"

"Now that you mention it, yeah. It made a scratching sound. How did you know?"

"Lucky guess," said Steve.

Lee made a snorting sound. "I don't think luck had much to do with it. I checked on you and Ms. McBlythe."

Steve didn't respond to the compliment, but moved on to the next item on his mental checklist. "There's a detective in Fayette County that needs to talk to you. I'll call him after we leave and tell him you'll be at the farm by ten o'clock tomorrow morning. Plan on staying a night or two. You might be useful in helping us wrap up this case."

"How? I told you I know nothing about who killed Luke, and I'm clueless about someone trying to kill Julie."

Heather asked, "How many rifles do you own?"

"Only one rifle, but several handguns."

"We'll take the rifle with us."

Paul's eyes narrowed. "You can't do that."

"I can," said Leo. "And I will. Where is it?"

Paul threw a hand in the general direction of a door off the living room. "Bedroom closet. In the rifle case."

Steve rose. "If it wasn't used to kill Luke or try to kill Julie, it will help rule you out as a suspect."

Heather didn't know if the forensic team had located a spent round yet, but this would give Detective Burris something to show the sheriff to prove he was pursuing leads.

Steve reached in Heather's direction. She took his hand and placed it on her arm. Leo exited the bedroom with a rifle case in hand a short time later. He pointed a finger at Lee and said, "Don't forget you have an appointment at the hydroponic farm in the morning. I won't be so nice if I have to look for you."

"I'll be there."

Once in the parking lot, Leo loaded the rifle case in Heather's vehicle. She extended her hand to him. "Thanks so much. It was much easier with your help. Do you know of a decent restaurant around here?"

"Yeah," said Steve, as he raised his hand and displayed his thumb and forefinger about an inch apart. "I need a slab of cow at least an inch thick. Vegetables and fruit three times a day is sending me into withdrawals."

Heather looked up to see the blinking lights of a high-flying airplane. It reminded her that Julie should have arrived in Conroe by now. "I need to call Jack and make sure Julie's safe and sound." She stepped away from Steve and Leo and waited for the call to go through.

"Hello, gorgeous."

"Hi, handsome. How's the patient?"

"Hurting, but resting comfortably. The nurse you got for her is a real hottie; at least she might have been forty years ago when she started nursing."

"I don't like competition." She paused. "Sorry about the change of plans. I think we're making good progress."

"I like the sound of that. Let me know when you're ready for Julie to come home. I'll bring her to you."

"Are you sure you can get away?"

"As long as the case doesn't stretch into next week."

"I'll tell Steve he has four days max to have it solved. Need to go. Bye."

The evening progressed at a leisurely pace as Steve and Leo relived experiences. Laughter outweighed the more somber moments as two hours flew by. When both men yawned, Heather called a halt to the night under the excuse of having a long drive to make.

By the time they reached Brenham, Steve had settled into a

mood that reminded her of a turtle, his head tucked down on his chest, virtually unmoving. He wasn't asleep, but it seemed he'd used up all his words, which suited Heather. She had so much to process from the day. What evidence had the crime scene technicians discovered? Was Paul Lee as innocent as he pretended? Why did Steve want him at the farm for two more days?

Heather pondered these things and a dozen more as the miles passed. She also thought of Jack and how much she enjoyed his company and his willingness to put his law practice on hold to join her in another of her drop-everything-and-let's-go adventures with Steve. Her thoughts were still on him as she approached The Hidden Lodge. Once parked, she retrieved the rifle case from the back of her car and led Steve up the stairway to their rooms.

They remained in silent mode until Steve stopped and pulled her back, away from a view down the hall leading to the VIP rooms. "It's Jill. I smelled her perfume and heard someone going into a room. Did you see which one?"

Heather kept her voice low. "I wasn't paying attention."

"Tomorrow I want you to make a sketch of all the rooms and label them with who's supposed to be in them."

"Knowing where Jill is supposed to be and knowing where she is at any given time are two different things. She seems to have a habit of playing musical rooms. I do know the professor's room is on this side of yours."

"Let's go. Someone's coming."

They turned the corner and Steve said, "Hello, Jill."

She stopped in her tracks. "How did you know it was me?"

"Your perfume."

"Oh. Sure." Her voice took on a cheery tone. "It's another full day tomorrow. Good night."

Heather said nothing until she delivered Steve to his room and closed the door behind her. "She's up to no good."

"Things aren't always as they seem. Good night, Heather."

Before she could leave, Steve's phone rang.

"Hello, Brandon... Yes, Julie's doing better. Heather said she's under constant supervision by a staff with years of experience in dealing with injuries like she sustained... The facility? It's the best. She's being waited on hand and foot... You're welcome... Right. I'll see you at breakfast."

18

Heather looked out her window as a crimson dawn broke over the rows of greenhouses. She whispered, "Red sky in morning, sailors take warning." Was bad weather on the way, or did the old rhyme mean imminent trouble of a different kind? No time to daydream. She'd already heard doors closing up and down the hall.

She slipped into jeans, tennis shoes, and a sweatshirt. Her hair went into a messy bun and she stepped into the hall. Brandon exited from the room toward the end of the hall wearing work clothes and carrying a heavy coat. He stopped in front of her, his eyes pleading as much as his words. "Any update on Julie this morning?"

"No change since last night." She looked toward the other end of the hall. "Why is there so much activity this morning?"

"There's a polar express bearing down on us. Rain turning to ice and snow later this morning."

"This far south?"

He nodded. "It doesn't happen often, but hard freezes in February aren't unheard of."

Heather grabbed his arm as he tried to walk past. "I realize you're in a hurry, but is there someone who can get me a list of the rooms and all the people staying here?"

"I'll leave Julie's office open for you. You may have to search for it, but I know there's a hard copy in the file cabinet. Lock up when you're finished."

"How cold is it supposed to get?"

Brandon spoke over his shoulder. "Low teens and high winds. It's all-hands-on-deck with the interns and anyone else who can help. Sorry, but I have to light the heaters in the greenhouses before it hits."

Steve opened his door and joined her as Brandon turned the corner to the stairway. "I heard. Are you dressed and ready for breakfast?"

"I have the no makeup, country-girl look about me, but I'm dressed."

"Let's see if anyone's left in the dining room."

Bleary-eyed college students didn't bother to look up from their bowls of oatmeal, grits, and fruit. Heather directed Steve to his seat as Jill beat a path to their table. She'd also foregone makeup and had a bedraggled look about her as she nodded a greeting and plopped down next to Steve.

"Good morning, Jill."

Instead of returning the greeting, Jill placed her hands on Steve's forearm. "I feel horrible about what happened to Julie. How is she?"

"Heather has the latest report."

Jill's eyebrows raised as she waited for an update.

"No change from last night." Heather looked for a response. Either Jill held Julie in high regard, or she could shed tears on command.

"I can't believe someone tried to kill her. She and Luke were so much in love. This is like living in one of Shakespeare's tragedies."

Steve eased his arm away. "How do you know they were so much in love?"

"Huh?"

"We're finding out more about Luke every day. We're hearing he had a wandering eye for other women." He took a breath. "Of course, we still need to verify the reports, but there's a rumor going around that he went on multi-day sales trips to Houston that included more than selling fruit and vegetables. Would you know anything about those?"

"Me? I'm just an intern."

"You know nothing about a blond intern and Luke hooking up?"

Jill's eyes shifted from left to right, as if she sought an exit. She answered Steve's question with one of her own. "When was this?"

"Last fall was one time."

A look of relief and a more confident voice answered, but with yet another question.

"How could I know about what happened last semester? I wasn't here."

Steve flicked his hand. "Don't pay any attention to me this morning. Yesterday was a blur. First, we found the site where Luke died which wasn't where they found his truck. Next, someone tried to kill Julie, and then we took a flying trip to Houston. We came back late, but you know that because you were visiting someone on the VIP hall."

"Uh, yeah. I had to ask my professor something." She stood. "I'm so sorry about Julie, and I hope she makes it. She really is a sweet lady. I better go."

Jill rose and took quick steps out of the room.

"How many lies did you count?" asked Steve after Jill cleared the dining room.

"The only truthful thing I heard was when she said Julie's a sweet lady."

Steve nodded. "I'll take a bowl of cereal."

"You don't want oatmeal? It's supposed to be freezing today."

"I already had my yearly allotment of oatmeal this week. Cold cereal with fruit is all I want. And coffee."

Chairs rattled and scraped as the interns and other workers slipped on winter coats and caps of all descriptions. Like a migrating herd, they cleared out on their way to save the crops from winter's icy claws.

Steve took in the sounds with his head erect. "Sounds like we'll have the dining room to ourselves."

Heather looked up. "Not all by ourselves. Trey Ricks is swimming against the stream of people and going to the serving line."

"Good. He's on my list of people to talk to. Ask him to join us."

Heather returned with Trey. By the number of bowls he carried on his green cafeteria tray, it looked like this might be his last meal before Armageddon.

When they settled, Heather asked, "Didn't you eat supper last night?"

He shook his head. "Mary never came to get me. I guess she forgot."

Considering Mary's attitude toward her brother, Heather suspected an intentional omission.

Steve's voice broke into her thoughts before she came up with a catty accusation. "Eat up, Trey. It's supposed to be a nasty day. Have you made a tour of the greenhouses yet?"

Trey had already spooned a bite of oatmeal into his mouth. Instead of swallowing, he spoke around it. "The only thing I've seen is the lobby and my room. It's real nice. The bed's big. I have a small bed."

"Why don't you and I go exploring today? We can take a tour of the greenhouses and go to the shipping warehouse."

"Do you think Mary will let me go?"

"We'll be back before she misses you."

"Can I finish my breakfast?"

"Sure. Take your time."

Steve pumped Trey for more background information. "You

arrived before Mary yesterday, so I guess you have your own car? Can you drive us to the greenhouses?"

"Yeah, I have a car. Mary lets me drive to work and back to my apartment. Coming here was kinda' like driving to work."

"Where do you work?"

"I sack groceries at a big store."

"I bet you're good at it."

This brought a smile to Trey's face. "Everyone tells me I'm the best sacker in the store. I always remember to tell the customers thank you."

It never ceased to amaze Heather how Steve could carry on a conversation with people of every age, size, shape, color, and level of education. It didn't matter if they were children or people on the downhill side of life, he could get them talking and keep them engaged until he could direct their conversation to something that would help him solve a crime. She wondered how much information he would glean from Trey. His sister Mary didn't realize it, but Steve would know a lot about her by the time he returned to meet with Detective Burris and Paul Lee.

Heather excused herself after she'd had two cups of coffee and half of a bowl of oatmeal. She went to Julie's office and found the door unlocked, just as Brandon promised. Before she rifled through files, she took stock of the personal items on Julie's desk, knick-knacks on shelves, and framed clichés of encouragement and motivation on the walls. The most prominent photo sat on her desk and showed the team of Luke, Julie, and Brandon on the farm in Belize. She'd seen the photo before, but hadn't taken the time to thoroughly study it. She picked it up and pulled it closer. "If it weren't for the beard, the color of the hair, and its length, Brandon could be Luke's brother."

Other than the one photo of the three of them, all other memorabilia seemed generic. She reached to put the framed photo back on the desk, but something in the photo caught her eye. The two men had their arms criss-crossed over Julie's shoulders. She noticed Brandon wore a simple ring on the fourth finger of his left hand. Julie had her left hand stuffed in the front pocket of cut-off blue jeans while Luke's left hand was out of the frame of the photo. Was Brandon ever married or widowed? Was there a Mrs. Brandon Clay back in Belize or somewhere else? Perhaps the death of a spouse drove him to the tropics to heal and start over. Perhaps he'd had a pretend marriage on the farm like some others.

She shrugged off the speculation and concluded it could have easily been a ring that signified nothing. "Time to get to work." It didn't take long before she located a diagram of the building, with each guest room identified by number, but didn't list the occupants. After looking underneath some papers in a drawer and thumbing through a couple of notebooks, Heather lifted the keyboard and turned it over. "Bingo. Julie should know better than to tape her password to the bottom of her keyboard."

After scanning the guests' rooms and their occupants, four possibilities existed as to who Jill visited last night: the professor, Trey, Mary, or Brandon.

STEVE WAITED FOR TREY TO MEET HIM IN THE LOBBY. THEY stepped out into the chilly, damp air with no sunshine warming the wood railing. A quick course in leading a blind person followed, and they made it to Trey's car with no mishaps.

"What kind of car do you drive?"

"It's an old Datsun station wagon."

"They quit making those a long time ago."

"Yeah, but I like it. I'll have it paid off in another year."

"How long have you had it?"

"Six years. Mary bought it for me."

"What are your payments?"

"Only two hundred a month."

Steve did a quick calculation and shook his head. Trey's

loving sister had already raked in over fourteen thousand dollars for a car that should have gone to the scrap yard years ago.

The starter ground on the first two tries, but finally caught and brought the rolling beer can to life. It chugged and bumped its way out of the parking lot.

"Where do I go?"

"Pick out any greenhouse and park as close as you can to a door." Steve needed to find out more about Mary. "I understand you and Mary don't live together."

"Not anymore. I have my room in a big house. Mary doesn't like me coming to her apartment. She has her own friends."

"You have a room and not your own apartment?"

"It's a bedroom. Other guys live there. They aren't very nice and don't stay long. We have a cook, but we have to keep our rooms clean and do chores every day."

"Do you like living there?"

He shrugged. "Sometimes the men are mean. They want money from me, but Mary takes care of all that. She had me go to the bank with her and sign something. I don't worry about people stealing anymore because Mary takes care of the money."

"Would you like to live somewhere else and have your own money to spend?"

"Mary gets real mad when I talk about that."

"What does Mary do for a living?"

"She's done lots of things, mostly what she calls a hostess. I'm not sure what that is, but she dresses nice."

"Is she married or does she have a regular boyfriend?"

"She's real popular. Her phone's been ringing a lot since she got here. I hear it through the wall."

"Can you tell who she's talking to?"

"She talks loud. But I can't make out the words."

Steve made a mental note to have Detective Burris get a record of her calls. It might be a good idea to go back and get records of calls placed and received going back several months.

Mist greeted Steve as he opened the door of the geriatric

Datsun. "We'd better get inside quick. Unless I'm mistaken, the cold front will be here any moment."

"It looks real dark in that direction."

Steve assumed Trey pointed to the north. "Come and guide me the way I taught you."

Once inside, the greenhouse covering rustled in the wind. The sound of pumps and water falling wasn't overpowering, but had a constant, soothing effect, like walking into a world of its own.

"What plants do you see?" asked Steve.

"Green beans, but they're hanging down from near the ceiling. They're growing out of holes in white pipes and wrapped around wires. It looks like a jungle."

One intern hollered. "Check the fuel level and get the heater lit. We're responsible for six more greenhouses."

Steve tugged on Trey's sleeve. "Let's stay out of their way and walk the length of the greenhouse. I want to get a better idea of how big they are."

Footsteps hurried toward them. Steve stopped and felt someone place something in his hand. A male voice said, "Sorry we can't give you a tour. Here are a few green beans to munch on. Help yourself to more." He ran in the direction Steve faced. "Let's get to the next generator."

"Something's wrong with this heater. It won't light."

"Come help me as soon as you can."

Steve and Trey made their way a few steps, and Trey stopped. "Can we go back?"

"Back to your room?"

"No. Back to the heater. I'm good at fixing things."

"Sure. Lead on."

The student trying to light the heater may have known a lot about plants, but he knew precious little about heaters. "It's the pilot light," said Trey. "It's not making a clicking sound. If you have a spare part, I can put it in. If not, I can light it with something else."

"Do whatever's fastest," said the unknown intern with anxiety painting his words.

"Do you have a piece of paper I can roll up and make a little torch?"

"I'll tear a page out of the production log."

Steve heard the raspy sound of a butane lighter igniting and smelled paper burning. He could see in his mind's eye his old water heater in the home he and Maggie owned. How many times had the pilot light gone out on their water heater and he had to relight it using the same method?

"Now we let it warm up for a few minutes and then turn the red knob," said Trey.

After the allotted time, Steve heard a whoosh as a steady stream of gas escaped and found the small flame.

"Thanks a lot, Buddy. You saved my bacon."

The young man sprinted away as Trey said, "I thought we were saving green beans."

Steve couldn't help but chuckle. "You saved both. Good job. Let's move on."

"More green beans," said Trey as he shut the door behind them on the greenhouse next door.

They walked from what Steve believed to be the front of the greenhouse all the way to the back.

Brandon's voice broke through the sounds of water circulating, motors pumping, and the wind howling. "I understand you know how to light water heaters."

"Uh-huh," responded Trey.

"I need help. Someone decided we weren't having anymore cold weather and shut off all the heaters. Could I talk you into going to all the greenhouses and making sure the heaters are working?"

Steve interjected. "He's all yours if you check on him from time to time and find someone to get me back to where we're staying."

"Jill," hollered Brandon. "Take Mr. Smiley to the lodge and get back as soon as you can. You're picking beans today."

Sleet peppered the roof of the ATV as Jill ferried Steve back to the cozy lodge. "Are you working with Brandon today?"

"I thought I was, but that all changed with the storm."

"Are you trying to get on here full time after you graduate?"

Jill's voice took on a tone to match the weather. "What makes you think that?"

"There's one, and possibly two, openings in management."

She kept quiet until the machine came to a stop. "I parked on the sidewalk. Be careful, Mr. Smiley. There may be ice on the steps and I'd hate it if you had an accident."

It took little insight to determine the words didn't match the tone of Jill's voice. Steve's questions about her angling for a job hit a nerve. He wondered how desperate she was to make her life a financial success.

19

Heather finished snooping in Julie's office and waited in the lobby for Steve to return. It was definitely a hot chocolate and fireplace day. The chugging of an ATV directed her attention to the front sidewalk shimmering with a coat of ice. She walked to the door and opened it in time to see Steve clutch the railing of the front steps. He gingerly tested each foot as he climbed the steps until his right heel hit the ice-covered wooden porch and flew out from under him. Down he came, with left hand extended to break his fall.

She moved toward him, but didn't get far before she found herself flat on her back. She inched back to safe ground and asked, "Are you alright?"

"Not sure yet. I tried to catch myself, but came down hard on my hand."

Steve tried to pull himself up, but his shoe slipped again on the ice-covered porch. "Don't come get me. I'll crawl to the door."

He let out a yelp of pain. "Must have sprained my wrist. Can't put weight on it. I'll have to roll out of the ice."

Heather took a tentative step toward him, but soon

retreated. "If you can come another four feet, you'll have good footing."

He pitched his cane in her direction, tucked his arms against his torso, and rolled until he lay at her feet. Her outstretched hands stopped his fourth roll. "Let me help you up."

"I'll get up on my own."

She backed away and felt her rump for damage. "Don't snap at me. I didn't cause the storm."

"You also didn't put salt on the steps."

She didn't appreciate the put-down, but had to admit her mind hadn't been on Steve's safety, or anyone's for that matter. The spell cast by the crackling fireplace had her thinking about Jack and a ski trip she planned for next year. Those thoughts melted like an ice cube on asphalt in August. She needed to get Steve inside and check for damage. The chair closest to the fireplace might help his sour mood.

"Do you need to lean on me until we can get you in a chair?"

"Just guide me."

Heather shut the front door behind them. "Let me help you out of your coat. Can you move your wrist?"

He grimaced when he wiggled his hand up and down. "Only a sprain. I heard you fall, too. Any damage?"

"I may have bruised my caboose, but no harm done. I'll be back as soon as I can with an ice pack and some Advil."

"Bring us both something hot to drink. This fire is too nice not to enjoy some coffee or cocoa."

One thing she appreciated about Steve was his anger would occasionally flash like lightening, but he soon put things behind him.

"Was that Jill who dropped you off?"

"Yeah. I'm not her favorite person today. I hope she didn't see me take a tumble. She might wreck from laughing so hard."

"Did you push her buttons again?"

Steve flicked his uninjured hand in her direction. "Go get the ice and something to wash the pills down. I'll tell you about my morning when you get back."

"And I'll tell you what I found in Julie's office."

Heather returned with Advil and a glass of water.

Steve whined a complaint. "This isn't coffee or hot chocolate."

"Reinforcements are coming with your ice pack, coffee, and salt for the porch, steps, and sidewalk."

A matronly woman walked in on squeaky shoes, followed by a whip-thin cafeteria worker carrying a box of rock salt. "Lord have mercy," said the woman, who went straight for Steve. "Lula, get salt on the porch and sidewalk before someone else gets hurt. Put it on thick."

The skinny woman went straight out the door while the leader of the duo took hold of Steve's arm. "Move it for me."

Steve did, but with a grimace.

"Ain't broke. That's good."

"Are you sure?" asked Heather.

"I was patching up children and students while he was riding a tricycle. If it was broke he'd be doing a lot more than flinching." She covered Steve's wrist with a dishcloth, put on the ice pack, and wrapped it with a putty-colored ace bandage. "Leave it on for twenty minutes then take it off. Come see me after that. If you don't, I'll come looking for you."

Steve thanked her, and she left as Lula came in the front door, along with a blast of cold air. "Mercy, me. We'd best double the vegetarian chili and cornbread today. Those workers are going to need winter food."

With the minor crisis over, Steve asked Heather to drape his coat over his shoulders and got down to business. "What did you see in Julie's office?"

"The diagram of rooms was easy to find, although I had to get into Julie's computer to know who's assigned to each room. We know the professor's room is next to yours, and then my room. There's two rooms vacant and then Mary's room, Trey's room, Julie's room, and Brandon has a bigger room at the end of the hall."

"What about rooms on the other side of the hall?"

"Those are vacant. I think it might be because they don't have a window. Sort of like an inside cabin on a cruise ship."

"Maggie and I stayed in one of those. She said it didn't matter, but I complained about it the whole time. Now I wouldn't know the difference."

Heather moved on before melancholy took hold. She never knew what would trigger him to slip back in time and relive the life he'd give anything to have back. "Did you hear what I said? Brandon and Julie have rooms next to each other with—?"

"I heard you. All that means is Julie *and* Luke had a room together, and Brandon had one by himself. Both were at the end of the hall. I don't blame Luke and Julie for wanting a change from the shipping container they lived in."

"You didn't let me finish. Last night Jill left someone's room on our hallway. The four possibilities are the professor, Mary, Trey, or Brandon."

Steve leaned back his head. "I see what you mean. I think we can rule out Trey. That leaves the professor, Mary or Brandon." He rubbed his chin between the thumb and forefinger of his right hand. "Interesting. What else?"

"I took a close look at a framed photo on Julie's desk. It looks like Brandon's wearing a wedding band."

"Who else is in the photo?"

"Both Julie and Luke. I'm assuming they're on the farm in Belize."

"Was it a wedding band?"

"Can't tell. Julie's left hand is in her pocket and Luke's hand didn't make it in the photo."

The front door flew open. Detective Burris came in and slammed it behind him. "Good Lord! What a mess." He walked a straight line to the fireplace. "I hope this trip will be worth me risking my life to be here. Where's this Paul Lee character?"

Heather rose from her chair. "Come sit by the fire. Mr. Lee called and said he's on his way, but the roads are like driving on an ice rink."

Burris took off a tan felt cowboy hat and put it on an end table. "I must have passed a dozen wrecks. If this keeps up, he may not make it." He paused as he studied Steve's bandaged arm. "What happened to you?"

Steve issued a one-word reply. "Ice."

Heather pulled a chair closer to the two men but didn't sit. "I'm going for a cup of something hot. Can I get you a cup of coffee, Detective Burris?"

"Might as well. I doubt if I'll be doing any interviewing this morning."

Heather returned to the sound of an ATV coming to a stop near the front steps. Jill stomped in first, followed by Paul Lee. She wore only a thin jacket, no hat, and no gloves. She didn't slow down as she made for the stairs, speaking with loud, clipped words. "This is ridiculous. I'm putting on every stitch of clothes I brought."

"Wait," said Heather. "I brought a heavy coat with a fur-lined hood. I'm not going anywhere today if you'd like to borrow it."

"Thanks. I'm still going to put on leggings and sweats under my jeans."

Steve spoke loud enough for Heather to hear as she climbed the stairs. "We'll be here by the fire when you get back."

When Heather returned, only Steve and Detective Burris sat by the fire. "Where's Mr. Lee?"

Steve raised his head. "I sent him to the dining room so we could trade notes." Steve faced the lawman. "Tell us what forensics found at Luke's property."

"They confirmed the blood on the gravel driveway is the same type as Luke's. It took them all day of searching with metal detectors, but they found the slug that went through him. They said it was in good enough shape that if they had the weapon, they could match it."

"What caliber?" asked Steve.

".357 Magnum."

"That means we're looking for a pistol and not a rifle." Steve paused. "We're also looking for a cold-blooded killer. It would have been easier to stand off at a distance and make the shot with a rifle."

Burris rose and walked to the fire, where he extended his hands. "Don't forget they shot him in the back."

Heather said, "I guess we took Paul Lee's rifle for no reason. It's a 30-06."

Steve repositioned his arm in the makeshift sling fashioned from a dish towel. "Let's not write him off yet. We made a bad assumption about the type of gun. Mr. Lee told us last night he owned several pistols. Also, he never gave us the name of the person who hired him."

"I'll get him to talk," said Burris, with confidence seasoning his words.

Steve didn't respond to the bravado, but made a poignant observation. "The way the weather's turning off, we'll have plenty of time to get to know each other."

Burris spun around. "What did you get out of him last night?"

Steve sat up straight. "Tell him, Heather."

"He claims the man that hired him communicated only by phone and paid him more than necessary to come here and try to dig up information on Luke, Julie and Brandon."

"Why all three? Luke's the only one with money or a big life insurance policy."

"That reminds me," said Steve. "I need to call Marsha and find out when the company plans to settle."

"They'll need to wait until they're sure who to make the check out to," said Heather.

Burris looked at her with a questioning glance. "I thought it was going to Julie."

"We framed the story so people believe she's at some undisclosed Houston hospital, knocking on heaven's door. Steve's idea for keeping Julie safe."

"I remember. How is she?"

"I called again while I was upstairs. She'll be fine. Jack knows a doctor that makes house calls. He checked on her this morning and said all she needs is rest and quiet for a couple of days and she'll be good to travel."

Detective Burris moved to the window. "It's turning to snow. If there's a blanket of snow over ice, it's just as well Julie can't travel." He turned to look at Heather. "I hope this place has some open rooms. It looks like no one will be arriving or leaving anytime soon."

"There are plenty of open rooms. I'll call Brandon and tell him to expect two more overnight guests."

Burris turned back to the window. "The sheriff won't like it. He wanted me to arrest Paul Lee and let him sit in a cell before he questioned him."

Steve rejoined the conversation. "Glad you mentioned that. Is there anything else you want to know about Mr. Lee before you question him?"

"Me? I thought you and Heather would do it."

"You need the practice." Steve held out his empty coffee cup to Heather. "This mug must have a hole in it. All the coffee's gone. Would you mind filling it up while you retrieve Mr. Lee?"

Heather couldn't help but shake her head. "Would you like warm cookies with that, sir?"

"That sounds good, but let's hold off on the cookies. Just coffee and a suspect, please."

Heather entered the dining room to find Paul Lee sipping on something dark in a ceramic mug and devouring a sticky cinnamon roll. "It didn't take you long to make friends with the cooks."

He swallowed. "This wasn't my idea. They brought me a cup of cocoa and this roll without me asking. I'm not sure I've tasted anything so good in my life. They're still warm."

Lula appeared with a tray topped with two pump-pots and a platter of gooey pastry. "I was on my way to bring y'all something to keep the cold away."

"You'll spoil us, especially Steve. He's not like most men who have a sweet tooth. For him it's sweet-teeth, all twenty-six of them." She gave Lula a sideways glance. "Are you sure everything in those cinnamon rolls is organic?"

"We might cheat a little, now and then. I'd best get these to Mr. Steve and that policeman before they bust down the door."

Skinny Lula led the way. She'd barely made it to the stairway when Steve announced, "Cinnamon rolls. Please tell me I'm not dreaming."

After many expressions of thanks, the unlikely quartet sat in a semi-circle in front of a picture-perfect fire, downing what Steve described as baked heaven and chasing it with their choice of coffee or hot cocoa. Heather couldn't help but notice the irony of the scene. Paul Lee, a man that should be on his way to jail, licked sticky fingers while Detective Burris issued occasional glaring glances and remained on full alert.

Heather made sure everyone had a full mug of whatever they wanted and sat back down.

The mood changed when Paul said, "I enjoy a friendly gathering as much as anyone, but I don't think you insisted I risk my life to be here to enjoy a hot drink in front of a fireplace."

"Darn right, we didn't," said Detective Burris. "I have one murder and one attempted murder to solve and you're going to help us fill in some gaps."

Steve broke in. "Don't forget, if Julie doesn't pull through there will be two homicides."

"I'm not forgetting," said Burris. "You told Steve and Heather someone paid you to come here and investigate the three people who run this place. Why all three?"

"You'll have to ask the person who hired me."

"I will as soon as you give me the name."

"Like I told them, I don't know the name."

"Yeah, and I don't believe you."

Paul leaned back in his chair and stared at the fire. "I can't help what you believe or don't. It's true. All business took place by phone."

"That won't cut it. Perhaps some time in jail will help you remember."

Steve held up his hand. "Let's take a step back. I have a couple of questions, if you don't mind."

"I'm just getting warmed up," said Burris. "But you ask your questions." He glared at Paul. "And you get used to the idea of talking."

Steve turned to face the PI. "I'm getting rusty in my old age. I forgot to ask you about the phone calls you received from the person who hired you. Did you record those calls?"

"No,"

Heather had already shifted her gaze to focus on Paul's body language. She didn't detect any sign of deceit, but she also knew the game Steve liked to play and her role in it. While she gave an unblinking stare to Paul, Steve asked her, "Is he lying?"

"All good PIs record their phone conversations with clients, suspects, and anyone else they're paid to investigate. Texas is a single-party consent state, so there's no reason he didn't record everything."

Steve asked, "We know you're a good PI. Why are you making this difficult?"

Paul heaved a sigh and lowered his shoulders to a more relaxed, yet defiant posture.

Steve kept on. "When you get home, you'll find your condo turned upside down. Houston police are very thorough when they search for evidence. I received a call from my former partner. He has your laptop and recording devices. It will save him time if you get with Detective Burris after we're finished and give him the password to your computer."

"He's nodding," said Heather. "Is there anything else?"

"Yeah," said Burris. "Who hired you?"

"I told you, I don't know. Like I said last night, it was a man's voice on the phone. He paid me in Bitcoin."

"One more question," said Steve. "Are you positive the voice belonged to a man?"

"It sounded like a man."

Burris took another swipe at Paul. "Give me a list of all the weapons you own."

Steve pointed an index finger at Paul. "Don't slip up on this one. Right now, your weapons are in a locked property room. And that reminds me, you'll need to go outside with Detective Burris and unlock your car and trunk for him to search. I'm sure you didn't leave home empty-handed. In fact, you might as well stand up and submit to a search."

Burris jerked his head to stare at Paul. "Hands behind your head and get up nice and slow."

As if watching a film in slow motion, Paul raised his hands and interlocked his fingers behind his head. "Shoulder holster under my left arm."

Heather rose to her feet and stood close enough to assist if the PI made a sudden move for his gun.

"I thought you might be packing," said Steve. "What do you carry?"

"It varies. Today I brought my Colt Python."

"That's old school. Most everyone has gone to either 9mm or .40 caliber. The .357 Magnum isn't as popular these days."

"Old and reliable. It never jams or misfires, and has better knock-down power." He looked toward the window. "There are no weapons in the car."

Heather produced gloves from the pockets of her vest. "Hand me the weapon and I'll unload it."

Burris did so and continued to search Paul. Once satisfied with the pat-down, Burris said, "I'm sure I heard you say I have your permission to search your car."

"Keys are in my coat pocket. Knock yourself out. I'm staying by the fire."

"Why don't I put you in handcuffs to make sure you're still here when I get back?"

"No need," said Steve. "Take his coat and leave it in his car and keep his keys."

Paul shrugged. "That's unnecessary. Who wants to go out in this mess when there's warm cinnamon rolls, coffee, and a nice fireplace? I didn't kill anyone or help whoever did."

Heather took in the words and pondered them. Steve had extracted more from the embarrassed PI than Paul realized. Did he intentionally help in the killing or was he used as a pawn by someone else? The puzzle pieces might be on the table, but she couldn't put them together. What else would Steve discover as the day went on?

Heads turned as Mary came down the staircase. Was that a look of recognition from Paul or simple interest in the curves under a long, bulky sweater and tight leggings?

20

Detective Burris donned his coat and hat. He took not only Paul's coat and keys, but also his driver's license before walking to the front door.

"What's this? What's going on Lee?" asked Mary.

Heather swung an open palm toward Paul and said, "Mary, I believe you know this man, but not by his real name. You know him as Lee Paulson, but his real name is Paul Lee."

Mary shrugged her shoulders. "That doesn't surprise me. He's a private detective. If he's been using a false name, I'm sure he had a good reason."

Paul stood, acting the part of a gentleman, as Mary settled into the chair next to him. "To answer your question about what's going on, Deputy Dog is making a fool of himself. He's desperate to find someone to blame for a murder."

Mary crossed her legs and leaned in Paul's direction. "He'll probably start on me as soon as he comes back from freezing his tail off."

Steve cleared his throat. "Did you miss breakfast this morning, Mary?"

Heather noted Mary's manicured nails with fake diamond chips. "I didn't see any reason to get up early."

Paul flashed Mary a smile. "The cooks made a batch of cinnamon rolls if you need a snack. We ate all they brought to us, but I could get you one and a cup of coffee."

"I shouldn't, but that sounds yummy. Do you mind?"

"Sure. I'll be right back." He rose and made for the dining room.

As soon as he was out of earshot, Mary turned to Heather, lowered her voice, and spoke with urgency. "Why is that cop so interested in him?"

Steve answered before Heather could. "Like you said, he's a private investigator. Someone hired him to do research on the owners of this place. Would you know anything about that?"

"Me? Of course not. Is he a suspect in Donnie's murder?"

"Detective Burris thinks so."

"It's obvious Burris is an idiot. What do you think?"

Heather wondered what non-committal answer Steve would give to the question. It didn't take long to find out.

"People kill for all kinds of reasons. If I was guessing, I'd say there are others with more to gain from Luke's death. Unless someone paid Paul enough to make it worth his while."

Mary challenged the response with a question. "Is there any evidence to support that theory?"

Heather took this question. "That's hard to answer. We'll know more in a day or two."

Steve changed the subject before Mary could ask for details. "I'm sure you noticed Trey isn't in his room this morning."

Mary's response followed with a huff of disgust. "What kind of trouble is he in now?"

"No trouble. He's helping Brandon and the interns in the greenhouses. It seems he's good with lighting and repairing heaters. I bet Trey's good at a lot of things."

"Don't bet on it."

Steve scratched his ear. "You said you and Trey were Luke's closest relatives. What about your mother?"

"Dear old Mom." Sarcasm dripped from the words. "She's out

of the picture. They caught her and two men robbing a jewelry store. She's a burned-out druggie with Alzheimer's who'll die in prison."

"Ah, I understand," said Steve.

"I doubt it. She left me saddled with Trey all my life. Have you ever tried to care for someone with special needs?"

Steve shook his head. "I can see where that would be an enormous responsibility. Trey told me where he lived. It sounded like a halfway house for ex-cons."

"It's a group home," said Mary with a snap in her voice.

Steve rubbed his chin. "That's a relief."

"Why?"

"It will save me a phone call. There are rules against mixing people like your brother with ex-offenders in halfway houses."

Steve couldn't see it, but Mary's lips thinned as she pressed them together. Her countenance changed as soon as Paul returned with a cinnamon roll and a cup of coffee. "Thank you. It's so refreshing to find a gentleman here."

"My pleasure."

Heather knew by his questions that Steve had already verified Mary had stuck her brother in a dangerous environment. Her opinion of Mary dropped another notch.

The front door opened again, and snow accompanied Detective Burris inside. "It's getting worse." He rejoined the group and looked down at Paul. "Go to the dining room. I need to talk to Ms. Ricks."

Mary chuckled as Paul crossed his legs at the ankles and settled in. "It's a little drafty in the dining room. I'll stay here by the fire."

Mary crossed her arms over her chest and glared at Burris. "I'm not sure I should talk to the police without my lawyer present."

Paul smiled at Mary. "That's a good idea. I'm through talking, too."

Burris pulled out a set of handcuffs. "I have plenty to arrest you, Mr. Lee. Do you want to reconsider going to the dining room?"

Mary stood and faced Burris with hands on her hips. "Where he goes, I go; and don't think you can bully me or trick me into saying anything."

"Looks like I'll have to go back to my car and get another set of handcuffs."

Steve held up his hands, palms out. "Calm down everyone. We're all stuck here and no one can leave, even if they wanted to. Let's take a break and go to our rooms." He turned his head toward Heather. "Do you know where the keys to the vacant rooms are? Detective Burris and Paul will each need a room. Let's take a break and get them settled in."

"They're in Julie's office." Heather rose from her chair, signaling everyone to do the same. "I'll call Brandon and let him know what I'm doing."

Steve added, "Let's go our separate ways, have a nice hot lunch, take a nap, and meet again about two thirty."

"Count me out for meeting again this afternoon," said Mary.

"That goes for me, too," echoed Paul.

Detective Burris shot a dagger-stare to Paul. "We'll see about that."

Heather knew Steve had something in mind, but she didn't know what. Mary whispered something to Paul and made a show of prancing out of the room. Paul's gaze followed her progress up the stairs.

Steve disrupted Paul's crooked smile when he said, "Heather, is there something in Detective Burris's room that he can handcuff Mr. Lee to?"

"I'm sure we can find something."

"Hold on. I thought you said there were plenty of rooms."

Steve leaned on his cane. "Heather might find you a room if you come to the meeting with Mary at two thirty. Otherwise, Detective Burris will have to handcuff you to something that will ensure you don't rest well."

"You wouldn't dare."

Burris rested his forearm on the pistol on his hip. "If you're a betting man, you're about to lose."

"It's your choice, Paul," said Heather.

"I'll be there, but I've got no control over Mary," he huffed.

Steve took a step toward Paul. "You'll get her to come, and then you'll make up an excuse to leave. It's her we need to talk to, not you."

Heather held her hand out like an usher directing someone to their seat. "Paul and Detective Burris, if you'll follow me, I'll get your keys and show you to your rooms."

HEATHER CHOSE THE ROOM CLOSEST TO MARY FOR Detective Burris, while Paul received an inside room across from Burris's. He took one look at the accommodations and shook his head. "There's no window. Is this supposed to be a joke?"

Heather wasn't in the mood to put up with a surly gumshoe, so she confronted Paul head on. "Instead of acting like a spoiled adolescent with overactive hormones, you should thank Steve."

"What for?"

"He's giving you freedom of movement. If it weren't for him, you'd sleep handcuffed to the arm of a chair in Detective Burris's room." She took three steps toward him and gave him the stare she'd perfected by practicing in front of a mirror. "It's not too late. If you're not satisfied with your room, I'll be glad to let Detective Burris know."

"But I did nothing illegal. I don't know why that crazy cop wants to keep me under lock and key."

"Because someone shot Luke in the back with a .357 Magnum, and you came waltzing in today with a Colt Python tucked under your arm."

Paul's eyes widened, and he swallowed hard. To his credit, he made a quick recovery. "I know how it looks, but there're plenty of .357s around. Forensics will rule me out."

Heather shook her head and told a half-truth. "You're assuming they found the shell casing, or the slug is in good shape."

He swallowed again. "I have my vices, but I didn't kill Luke. He might have had a fling with Jill, and flirted with the other interns, but that was the way he rolled."

Heather took another half-step forward. "He's not alone. You're doing a good job of putting on the stud act for Mary. I can tell Steve believes she knows something, and you're hindering a murder investigation. From one PI to another, how would you like it if our roles were reversed? What would you do if Steve or I told someone you were investigating not to cooperate?"

Heather took a step back and allowed Paul to consider her words. She lowered her voice. "You don't know who you're dealing with. Steve and I know more about Mary than you can imagine. She might look good in a sweater with those pouting lips, but she'll give you more grief than your second wife."

That caused him to take a seat on the bed. She finished with, "Keep pushing Steve and I'll make a phone call that will turn you into a pariah with half the cops in Houston. You'll be lucky if you have a driver's license two months from now, let alone a PI license."

She closed the door behind her and grinned while walking to her room. Steve sat in a chair with the window behind him. Snow danced on the wind, but the flakes looked smaller and much less fluffy. "Looks like the storm may blow itself out."

"Good. The forecast is for a hard freeze tonight, but clearing and warmer tomorrow. In a couple of days, the roads will clear."

"Is that important?"

The lights flickered and then shut off. "Uh-oh," said Heather. "The storm must have taken out the electricity."

"I'm not surprised. I wonder if there's a back-up generator."

"If there is, it hasn't kicked on."

Steve held his hand up for silence. "I hear it, but it's faint. Are the lights back on?"

"The only light in this room is coming through the window."

"Go downstairs and see if there's power to any of the building."

The hallway had a different vibe without the white noise of a fan circulating warm air, no overhead lights, and silent televisions. A door opened and Paul stepped into the hallway. "I can't see my hand in front of my face."

"I'm going to check if any of the building has power. Come with me if you don't enjoy sitting in the dark."

Mary opened her door. "What the heck is going on?" She noticed Paul and changed her accusatory tone to one more suited for a teenage romance film. "Hi there."

He acknowledged her with only a nod.

Still using her saccharine-laced voice, Mary asked, "What happened to the lights?"

"We're going to check."

Detective Burris poked his head into the hall and took a step forward. "Get back in your room, Paul."

"It's dark as a coal mine in there."

"You can come to my room," said Mary. "There's a nice soft light from the window."

"No, thanks. I have a flashlight in my car."

Mary tilted her head and narrowed her gaze before pushing her door open and allowing it to slam shut behind her.

"You can't open your car. I have your keys," said Burris.

"You also took my coat. Either you trust me long enough to get what I need, or someone else needs to get them for me. If not, I'll have to sit in front of the fire downstairs until the power comes back on."

Burris sighed and rolled his eyes. "Alright, come on. I'll get your coat."

"And my flashlight."

Heather led the way. As she turned from the bottom step, light streamed from the downstairs hallway. She went through the dining room and into the kitchen where pots boiled while bathed in bright lights. The workers looked up with helpful smiles.

"The electricity went off upstairs," said Heather.

The lead cook wiped her hands on her apron. "There's a separate generator that should have kicked on for the second floor. I'll call Brandon and let him know."

"Thanks."

Heather walked back to the lobby and gave the update. She considered telling Steve, but realized the power being off wouldn't affect him until the rooms cooled off. He'd leave his room for the warmth of the fireplace in his own time or he'd put on his coat, hat, and gloves. He might prefer to ponder alone in the cold.

Detective Burris walked with careful steps from Paul's car to the front door as Heather watched through a window etched with snow. He kicked the front door shut and stomped the snow off his boots. "It must be twenty below out there."

"It's not that cold," said Heather. "You should try spending a winter in Boston."

"No way." He raised his chin and sniffed the air. "It's getting close to noon. I smell something cooking."

Paul placed his coat and flashlight in a chair and stood in front of the fire, heating his outstretched hands. "The interns normally come in for lunch, but I don't know if they'll have time today."

A few minutes later, the rumble of ATVs answered the question. Shivering students tromped through the doorway and scurried to the dining room. Brandon and Trey brought up the end of the procession. Trey carried a tool box while Brandon spoke loud enough to be heard by Heather. "We'll check the breaker box. Hopefully, this will be a simple fix."

Heather turned to Burris and Paul. "I'll run upstairs and tell

Steve and Mary to come eat. You two might as well go to the dining room."

The two men exchanged wary glances and stepped toward the hall at the same time. It crossed Heather's mind that if the two had met under different circumstances, they'd have quite a bit in common and might become friends. As things stood, the chances of that happening looked to be as likely as a repeat ice storm in July.

Mary needed no coaxing to exit her room for a hot meal. She did, however, stop Heather with a tug on her sleeve. "What did that hateful cop say to Paul?"

"Nothing that I know of. Why?"

"He must have threatened him to stay away from me. Did you see how Paul treated me when I told him he could come to my room? I know how to read men. We had something going until that cop put the kibosh on it."

"I need to tell Steve lunch is ready. Why don't you go down to the dining room and enjoy a hot meal? Look for a guy who looks like a university professor. You and he might have something in common."

"What about that cop?"

"Cops have to eat too."

Mary turned and huffed. "That doesn't mean I have to talk to him."

Steve opened the door as soon as Heather knocked.

"You must have been at the door listening," she whispered.

"Did you threaten Paul?"

Heather lifted her chin. "I helped him see the folly of short-term pleasure to long-term negative consequences."

"You threatened him."

"Not bad." She turned and added, "Mary thinks Burris threw the cold water on their potential relationship. I didn't correct her."

"Good. Make sure Paul knows he needs to stay in his room

after lunch. We need Mary alone when we talk to her. I'll think of something to keep Burris occupied."

Heather slowed her pace. "How close are we to wrapping this thing up?"

"A couple more days should do it if two or three more things fall into place. If I'm wrong, we'll be back to square one."

21

Vegetarian chili and two different soups competed for popularity among the interns and workers. Heather chose a thick squash soup with steam rising from it like mist from a pond. Salad commanded little attention, but she bucked the trend and had a full portion. She didn't bother asking Steve what he wanted after looking into a deep tray of steaming chili. She carried their food to what looked like the teacher's table, occupied by the professor and everyone linked to the investigation, except Jill.

It came as no surprise that Mary sat next to the professor, eyes wide with interest as he waxed eloquent about varieties of tomatoes. As Heather passed Paul, he leaned back in his chair and whispered, "I owe you."

Her opinion of the private investigator went up a notch, but still had a long way to go before she'd trust him to not shade the truth. Meanwhile, Detective Burris spooned in chili while shifting his gaze to take in each face. He reminded her of a cat that pretended to be asleep, but upraised ears tuned to the direction of noises signaled its wariness.

"I was hoping you'd bring me chili," said Steve, as she placed the bowl before him. He already had a napkin tucked under his chin and spread before him in a diamond pattern. "What's it made of?"

"It's best I not tell you until you've tasted it."

Steve filled a spoon and tilted some of it out to reduce the risk of spillage. He took a tentative taste that earned a nod. "Not bad. They nailed the seasoning."

The professor gave away the secret. "It's amazing what an excellent cook can do with TVP."

Mary turned her head, making her look like a confused calf. "What's that?"

"Textured vegetable protein. It's defatted soy flour formed into various shapes. For chili they use what's called crumbles."

Steve had already taken a second bite. "I can't taste the difference between this and canned chili."

"It depends on the brand, but unless the label says it's made from one-hundred percent beef, you've eaten TVP."

"You don't say."

"TVP is high in protein and fiber and has virtually no taste or smell. All the flavors come from vegetables and spices."

Heather looked at Mary in time to see her bat her eyelashes at the professor. She placed her hand on his forearm. "You must know everything about plants."

The academic responded with a smile and made no move to pull his arm away.

The meal progressed with sparse talk until Brandon came in with an announcement directed to the interns and workers. "I hate to rush you, but there's much to do if we're going to save the crops. The heaters need constant monitoring if we're going to maintain proper temperature in the greenhouses. Some are putting out too much heat and others keep cutting off. We're working as hard as we can to get things straightened out, but the temperature will plummet tonight when the skies clear. Plan for half of you working until you're relieved at one in the morning. Group two will take your place for the graveyard shift. Professor Chalmers is making out a schedule."

Mary stuck out her bottom lip. "Does that mean you won't be here tonight?"

"Afraid so. It's the fate of a farmer to do whatever has to be done to save a crop." He rose and cleared his plate, glass, and utensils. That gave the interns their cue to shovel in what they could, stuff their pockets with cookies, and leave.

As the noise of departing students reached a crescendo, Brandon came to their table. His gaze went to Mary. "I want you to know how much I appreciate Trey helping."

A look of surprise crossed her countenance, followed by a harsh laugh. "You must be joking. What could he possibly do but get in your way?"

Brandon pulled a hand down his face. "He's been repairing and relighting heaters all morning. Right now, he's found the problem with the generator that will heat your bedroom and give you lights. You'd do well to thank him when you see him, but that probably won't be until tomorrow. He's the only decent repairman on the property." Brandon turned on a heel and made haste for the kitchen.

Mary dug into her bowl of soup as if Brandon's rebuke had never happened. She looked up as those at the table waited for her to give a more appropriate response. She finally noticed their looks. "What? He's pulling your leg. My brother couldn't change a light bulb, let alone work on heaters or generators."

Heather seethed, but Steve spoke in a calm voice. "Detective Burris, I've been meaning to ask you something. I heard they established Luke's identity by his dental records. Is that right?"

"That's correct."

"After lunch, would you give me and Heather a couple of minutes?"

"Sure, but I'll need to keep an eye on Paul."

"Put him in his room. After his white-knuckled drive from Houston and his belly full of hot food, he'll be ready for a nap."

Paul nodded. "He's right, and a nap sounds like a great idea."

Heather wondered what else Steve had up his sleeve for the

afternoon. He intended to keep Detective Burris busy while they interviewed Mary, but how?

Mary finished her meal and left her bowl, glass, and silverware on the table for someone else to pick up. Everyone else bused the table and were soon at the base of the stairway. Detective Burris looked at Paul and pointed to the top of the stairway. "I'll be up to check on you when I'm finished down here. You'd better be in your room."

"Try to be quiet when you do a bed check."

As Paul climbed the stairs, Brandon and Trey came through the front door. Both had big smiles painted across their faces. "All fixed," said Brandon. "It took longer to take off the protective covers and put them back on than it did for Trey to find the burned wire and splice in a patch."

Heather looked up at the second floor. The lights shone on their hallway. "Thanks Trey. I wasn't looking forward to sleeping in a freezing bedroom."

Brandon hooked an arm over Trey's shoulders. "Are you ready to go back to work or do you want something hot to eat?"

Trey looked at him with questioning eyes. "I thought you said the plants would freeze if we don't get the heater working in the kale greenhouse."

"They will, but I can't ask you to go without eating. All I have is two pockets full of cookies."

"I like cookies. I'd rather eat cookies than soup."

"All right, buddy. Let's go."

Steve repeated something similar to what he'd said more than once concerning this case. "Too bad Mary can't see that things aren't as they seem." He turned to face Detective Burris. "Let's sit by the fire. You're just the man to get this case unstuck."

Steve swept a path before him with his cane and found the chair he'd last vacated. Detective Burris didn't find the fire to suit his liking, so he put fresh logs on the glowing embers. Heather seated herself and waited for Steve to give Burris an assignment.

When Burris finished poking the logs, he asked, "What was it you wanted to talk to me about?"

Steve hit him with the first item. "Did you examine the report from the dentist that confirmed Luke's identity?"

"Yeah. It came from a dentist in Brenham."

"Young or old?"

"The records? I don't know. Why?"

"Not the records, the dentist. Was it a new practice or one run by a dentist who'd been there a long time?"

"A young guy, fresh out of dental school."

"Can you get me a copy of the report?"

"I don't see why not." Burris looked at Heather with his face twisted into a question. She responded with a shoulder shrug.

"Next," said Steve. "I think it's time you had a long talk with Paul."

"By myself?"

"Absolutely. Take him to your room and sit him on the couch. You sit in the roller chair because it puts you higher than him. Question everything he says to see if he can keep his story straight, but start with things you already know about him. If you take your time, it'll surprise you how much he'll tell you. People always enjoy talking about themselves. Get his entire life story. The sheriff will appreciate your thoroughness."

"Should I press him on the .357 Magnum?"

"Mention it, but don't press too hard. Ballistics will tell you if that's your murder weapon. If it is, you have your killer."

"And if it isn't the murder weapon?"

"Then you'll have to do a work-around that might require a ton of background information. If you keep him talking, you'll already have it." Steve pointed at the stairway. "You'd better go up before he goes to sleep. People get testy if you interrupt their nap."

"I'll go now."

"Don't forget to email me the report from the dentist."

Heather waited until Detective Burris made it up the stairs

and out of sight before she looked at Steve. "What are you up to? Paul won't give him the time of day."

"We needed him out of the way. Besides, Paul might slip and give Burris something that will point us to the killer."

Heather stood and warmed her outstretched hands toward the flames that danced on the logs. "I told Paul about the .357 for leverage to get him to cooperate with us."

Steve nodded. "I thought you might. You also didn't want him and Mary playing patty-cake in the room next to yours."

She shrugged, "It worked."

"Perhaps. Have you considered they might already know each other, or that they planned the murder together?"

Heather sometimes believed Steve missed his calling as a master chess player.

Steve gathered his cane from the floor beside his chair and stood. "Detective Burris should have Paul in his room by now. Let's grab some cookies from the dining room and pay a call to Mary."

As they neared the door, Steve said, "You start by telling her that Detective Burris is raking Paul over the coals. That should put her in a better mood."

Heather knocked on the door and waited for a response. Mary cracked the door open enough to ask, "What is it now?"

Steve spoke over Heather's shoulder. "We wanted to give you an update on when you might receive your payout from the insurance company. Can we come in?"

The words worked like magic to get Mary to fling open the door and bid them to enter. Heather cast an appraising gaze over the room. It looked as if someone had placed a spring-loaded device in Mary's suitcase that showered her room with clothing. It didn't seem to bother her that Heather had to move a coat from the chair so Steve could sit.

"When will I get my money?" asked Mary before Steve folded his cane and fielded her question.

"The investigation will be over in a couple of days. That will lead to one or more arrests. After that, it's up to the insurance company. I can't think of any reason they'd delay payment. Can you, Heather?"

"I'm surprised they haven't already cut the check."

Steve rubbed his chin. "Mary, do you know Marsha Pennywell?"

"She's the one who's been delaying payment. What's her game?"

"Insurance fraud investigations. Even though she works for the company that's dragging their feet in paying you, she seems like a straight shooter. I'll call her if you want me to, and see what's holding up the payment."

"There's no need for that. I'm paying some of the best attorneys in the state to get everything that's due me."

"It's really no trouble."

"Don't bother." She looked out the window. "I thought you'd be in here with Detective Burris, giving me the third degree."

"He's busy," said Heather. "He said it's time for Paul to come clean on what he knows."

Steve took over. "After all, someone hired Paul to come here and spy on Luke and Julie. It wasn't you, was it?"

Mary spun on the heels of her socks. "I know nothing about investigations except what I see on television shows, but if you find the person who hired Paul, that man is the brains behind the killing."

"What makes you think a man hired the killer?"

Mary crossed her arms over her chest. "Just a wild guess. Don't men commit most homicides?"

"She's right," said Heather in a goading tone.

Steve tapped the arm of his chair. "Statistics are on your side, but things aren't always as they seem."

"Meaning what? You don't suspect me, do you?"

Steve waved his hand. "Of course not. All I'm saying is fifteen million dollars is a lot of money—enough to tempt any man or woman. It's also plenty to split two or three ways and everyone involved would be happy. That's the problem with trying to solve murder cases that involve fortunes. Some people will do anything to get their hands on that much, even taking on accomplices."

Heather cleared her throat. "This is going to be a delicate question, but it's one that crossed our minds."

Mary's gaze narrowed. "What is it?"

Steve took over. "Like Heather said, we don't believe you're involved, but you need to be prepared to answer this if asked by the police. Do you think there's any way your brother might have been used to help kill Luke?"

She sputtered out a laugh. "You've seen my brother. He can barely put his shoes on the right foot. He's a royal pain in the neck to me, but he's harmless. I can't remember ever seeing him mad."

"What about old-fashioned greed?"

"He can't count change, let alone balance a checkbook."

"He may know more than you give him credit for." Steve made a gesture to the vent as it blew warm air. "After all, he fixed the generator that's keeping this room warm."

Heather joined in. "I watched him with Brandon. They looked like they'd known each other all their lives."

Mary stood. "I see where you're going with this. You're looking at Brandon as the person who thought up the scheme to kill Luke, and he convinced Trey to pull the trigger."

"That's one scenario," said Steve.

Mary paced the room, clicking a manicured fingernail against her teeth. She stopped and gave a pleading look. "I don't want to believe it, but I can't deny it's possible. Trey trusts everyone, especially people who treat him nice. It wouldn't be hard for someone like Brandon to pretend to like Trey, lead him to do something wrong, and tell him it was only a game. Trey likes to play computer games."

"Let's not get carried away, but what you're saying makes sense. With Trey's challenges, it's a cinch the courts would go easy on him. In fact, it's more likely he'd get to live in an alternative program than go to prison."

Heather sighed. "We need to have a serious talk with Brandon and Trey."

"Be gentle with Trey." Mary's voice had the crackle of counterfeit money. "He doesn't know right from wrong."

22

———

Neither Heather nor Steve said anything until she closed the door in Steve's room. She considered going to her room to brush the foul taste of the conversation out of her mouth. Her attempt to remain emotionally neutral and look at the case from every conceivable angle only went so far. Selling out a brother incapable of defending himself crossed the line for something Heather couldn't and wouldn't tolerate.

"Let it go," said Steve, as he pitched his cane on his bed. "It will only cloud your judgment and cause you to make poor decisions."

Heather took in a deep breath and let it out in a slow, steady stream. "I'll be all right once we put the killer away. A long run would help, if it weren't so slick outside. I guess I could do some yoga stretches—that's always a good stress reliever."

"I have some things for you to do after you get your yin and yang straightened out."

Heather took a seat on the couch and leaned back. "Are they legal?"

"Almost."

"Perfect."

196

"I need you to find out how many security cameras monitor the parking lot out front."

"I think there's only one."

"Find out for sure. We're going to need one trained on Paul's car and another on Mary's." Steve paused. "I'm assuming you brought extra cameras with you."

"I keep four in my go-bag." She rose from the couch, went to the mini fridge, and retrieved two bottles of water. "I don't mind setting up our cameras, but Brandon's cameras might have the lot covered."

Steve grinned. "That's the almost legal thing I was talking about. Before you go to so much trouble, take your lock-pick tools down to Julie's office and pretend you forgot to lock the door. Can you still log in to her computer?"

"Julie hasn't been here to change her password, and Brandon's trying to save his crops. She has the latest password taped to the underside of her keypad. I should be able to get the feed from every camera on the property."

She handed Steve his bottle. "You never drink enough water. Your body and mind won't function properly if you don't stay hydrated."

He mumbled a thanks. "The chili had just enough cayenne pepper in it to give it a burn in the back of the throat. This will help put out the last of the fires."

"What else?" asked Heather.

"Call Jack and tell him to bring Julie back late tomorrow or early the next day."

"Will we have all the answers by then?"

"I hope so, but we can't keep Julie hidden much longer without outright lying to Brandon. As soon as this weather crisis is over, he'll be looking for answers on Julie's condition."

Heather didn't say it, but Julie had slipped her mind. "Is that all?"

"Do you know someone who specializes in dental radiology?"

"What a strange question."

"Burris is sending the file that shows how they matched Luke's dental records with the body they found in the truck. A second expert opinion might reveal something they missed. I'd ask around myself, but I suspect the file will include X-rays. You'll need to be looking at those while the dentist explains what you're looking at."

Heather twisted the cap on her bottle of water. "It will take me a phone call or two to get the name of someone."

Steve eased back in his chair, a sign he'd doled out all her assignments, at least for the time being.

"What will you do this afternoon?"

Steve covered a yawn. "I'll try to act interested as Burris gives me details of everything Paul said."

Heather couldn't help but grin. Steve deserved the waste of time for sending Burris on a mission that had little chance of bearing fruit. "Is that all?"

"I almost forgot. Make sure there's a camera that gives a clear view of Jill's car. She's been too low profile lately."

"Anyone else?"

Steve raised an index finger. "Something just occurred to me. Professor Chalmers knows almost everything about this place, and he isn't very careful about student-faculty relationships. I can imagine a potential love triangle between him, Jill, and Luke."

Heather raised her hands. "This is getting too complicated. I'll be downstairs coaxing a locked door open. You unravel the romantic relationships." She opened the door to find Detective Burris with his hand raised, ready to knock.

"It's useless. Paul won't answer any questions."

Heather stepped back into the room and turned to Steve. "Did you hear?"

"Yeah. Come in, Detective."

Curiosity about what Steve would say caused her to remain.

"Tell me what happened," said Steve.

Frustration permeated Burris's words. "Nothing happened.

He had the door locked and pretended to be asleep. I banged on it until he finally opened it. He told me to come back later and went back to bed."

Steve rubbed his chin. "That may not be a bad idea. Everyone's been under a lot of stress. I've found that if I drink plenty of water and allow my body to rest, I'm much more creative in how I interview suspects." He pointed to the mini refrigerator. "Get yourself a bottle of cold water, drink it all down, and take a nap. That's what I'm doing this afternoon."

Heather covered the smile that parted her lips. She wondered if Steve had spun a yarn or if he planned all along to take a nap. It wouldn't be the first time, and he had the rest of the afternoon to complete his meager checklist of things to do.

"I'm not sure I'm supposed to sleep. If Paul were to take off, there's no telling what the sheriff would do."

Heather put her hand on Burris's arm and steered him to the door. "I'm going to make some phone calls in the lobby. I'll have a clear view of the parking lot if I move a chair by the window. Besides, Paul can't go anywhere on these roads."

Burris pointed to the window. "The sky's clearing."

Steve's mouth opened wide and he let out a loud yawn. "If he's going to make a run for it, he's much more likely to do it at night."

Burris looked toward the door. "Do you think he will?"

Steve shrugged. "If it were me, I'd get rested up this afternoon and be ready if he tries something tonight."

Heather added, "I'll monitor him while you sleep."

That proved to be the last nudge Burris needed. He took long strides toward the door and allowed the spring-loaded hinge to close it behind him.

Heather pushed open the door to her connecting room and retrieved the tools she needed to open Julie's office door. Her mind whirled with thoughts of who the killer might be and how Steve would put another case to rest. She walked as if on auto-pilot downstairs until she looked at a silver-colored door knob. After a last check in both directions, she devoted her full attention to using long, strange-looking metal tools to insert into a lock, hold back tumblers and listen for the right clicks.

Once inside Julie's office, she turned on the light and fired up the computer. A sigh of relief came when the computer received the password like a long-lost friend. A double-click on the file labeled *Security* brought up a full screen of smaller screens, each showing a different real-time image of the greenhouses, the lodge, the entrances to the property, Luke and Julie's container house, and the parking lot. Three screens gave three different views of the parking lot from as many angles. She clicked on them, one at a time, to make sure she could see every car, including Mary's. Whoever put the cameras up knew their trade. She bumped the roller on the mouse and found she could zoom in on any vehicle. Further manipulation showed she could change the camera angle.

"No need for me to put up any more," she whispered to the photo of Luke, Julie, and Brandon.

Wondering if the storm had interrupted cell phone coverage, she placed a call to Jack while checking out other security camera shots. She zoomed in on icicles hanging like stalactites from the front gate when Jack answered with a greeting that told her he didn't have a client in his office.

"Hello, gorgeous. Are you staying warm?"

"My hands are a little cold. Do you know of anyone who might warm them for me?"

"I know a guy who specializes in hand holding. Is this a social or business call?"

"Both. Is it safe for Julie to travel?"

Jack laughed. "It's not safe for anyone to be out on the roads."

"I didn't mean today. Either late tomorrow or the day after?"

"The doctor did a teleconference with Julie this morning. She's cleared for travel. The storm gave us a glancing blow, but I understand it hit you much harder. You'll have to let me know tomorrow if you think it's safe."

Heather considered what Steve had said and weighed it against safety concerns. "Plan on coming the next day."

All the while she talked to Jack, she clicked from one security camera shot to the next. In one, she saw Brandon and Trey walking from one greenhouse to the next. She shifted to a different screen and saw police tape hanging limp and covered with ice at Luke and Julie's tiny home.

"What are you doing to keep busy?" asked Jack.

"Right now, I'm living the dream of a voyeur. This place has one of the most elaborate security camera setups I've ever seen. I can watch everything that's going on in the greenhouses and most everywhere else."

"That doesn't sound exciting to me."

"The novelty is wearing off fast."

Jack's office phone rang. "Is there anything else you need? There's an embezzler on line one that will keep calling back if I don't answer."

"A suspected embezzler," said Heather, in order to get a rise out of her beau.

"Of course. All my clients are innocent until proved guilty beyond a reasonable doubt. See you in two days."

She allowed the phone to cut off without pressing the red icon. The talk with Jack did her good. He added a dimension to her life that she didn't know was missing until he helped with a prior case. With her thoughts on their relationship, her hand worked the mouse and clicked it to reveal the upstairs hallways. The screen showed no activity in the hall leading to the intern's rooms. She clicked again and up popped the second hall, which served the VIP rooms. Her finger hovered over the mouse, ready to close out the view, when a door opened. Into the hall stepped Paul. He looked both ways and eased his door closed.

"What are you up to?"

He tip-toed under an emergency exit sign, pushed open a

door, and disappeared. She tried to locate a view of the emergency stairway, but found it too late. All she caught was a glimpse of his back and a door to outside closing. Springing from the chair, she left the office door unlocked and ran down the hall to the lobby. From there, she saw him walking as fast as the snow and ice allowed across the parking lot. She thought about giving chase, but wanted to see how he planned to make his get-away without car keys.

Snow and ice covered the car. He reached under the front bumper and retrieved something.

"Extra key in a magnetic box," she whispered.

She opened the front door and stepped out onto the front porch. "Going somewhere?"

He jerked his head around. "You're not a cop and I'm not under arrest."

She walked out on the sidewalk that had a fresh dusting of rock salt. With arms wrapped across herself to stave off the cold, she approached him as he tried to insert a key in the ice-covered lock. "I'm not a cop anymore, but I have the phone number of one. Look at your car. It will take at least five minutes at a fast idle to get the defroster to warm. There's a thick layer of ice on the windshield. How long before you can see where you're going? By that time, you'll be looking down the barrel of Burris's pistol."

Heather held out her hand. Paul breathed out a full lungful of frustration, creating a small white cloud. He dropped the key in her hand and took the first step back inside.

The door closed behind them, and he asked, "What now?"

"Let's go upstairs and have a chat with Steve."

"Not Burris?"

"He's taking a well-deserved nap. Do you want me to wake him?"

He answered by shaking his head. "I'd rather talk to you and Steve."

"I thought so."

Heather couldn't tell if Steve had fallen asleep or simply

remained quiet. Instead of greeting her or Paul, he sat virtually motionless and silent. She allowed the uncomfortable mood to have its intended effect on Paul.

After a full thirty seconds, Steve asked, "Well? Does someone want to tell me why Paul is here?"

Heather nodded for Paul to give his *mea culpa*.

He cleared his throat. "I tried to leave. I keep an extra key in a magnetic box."

Steve shifted in his chair. "I didn't think you'd be so stupid to try it on a day when the roads are impassable. How far did you get?"

"I didn't get the car unlocked before Heather caught me."

"Does Detective Burris know?"

"Not yet," said Heather.

"Wake him up."

Paul shot Heather a quick, panicked glance and then shifted his gaze back to Steve. "Hold on. Heather said that wouldn't be necessary if I talked to you."

"I said no such thing."

Steve leaned forward. "We already gave you a chance to come clean. If I ask you more questions, you'll only lie or deflect again. Someone paid you enough money to withhold vital information from us and Burris. You'll either keep quiet or send us and the cops down false trails. Why should I keep talking to you?"

"I've been straight with you."

"You weren't straight when they kicked you off the force in Beaumont and you haven't changed. Gambling cost you a career, three wives, and your children. You only recently caught up on child support."

"That wasn't my fault."

Steve ignored the last statement and plowed on. "Whoever hired you is playing you. They offered twice your going rate, and they're dangling more in front of you. Someone did a deep dive into your past and found your soft spot. Tell me, did a bookie you didn't know contact you after you received your retainer?"

Paul's head dipped as he broke eye contact. "It wasn't until the second payment. I used most of the first one to keep my ex from hauling me to court."

"Can't you see what's going on? Whoever hired you is putting ten dollars in your front pocket and taking seven out of the back. All the while they used you to get information about this place and Luke's movements."

Steve let the words soak in and signaled Heather with a twitch of a finger for her to take over.

"Have a seat, Paul. I need to ask you something and it's time you told the truth."

He complied, taking up the middle section of the couch. She remained standing. "Have the threats started yet?"

His body gave an involuntary shiver, like he'd sat in an ice bath. Then he nodded and said softly, "Yeah."

"We suspected it," said Steve. "You've made yourself a target and the person or persons that killed Luke won't hesitate to get rid of you. That's why Heather will wake up Detective Burris and tell him you tried to leave. He'll arrest you for murder and hand-cuff you to something in his room until he can take you to jail. Don't worry about calling anyone. You're going to tell Heather where you've hidden your burner phone."

"But I didn't kill Luke. I was here on the property, but I didn't do it."

"We know you didn't. Somebody set you up to take the fall and we need to make them think their plan worked. It boils down to leaving you free where your chances of surviving aren't good, or you staying alive in jail."

"Do you know who's behind all this?"

"We were hoping you'd tell us."

Paul shook his head. "I wish I could. Everything I said about how they contacted me is true."

Heather motioned for Paul to stand. "Give me the phones."

He reached into the pocket of his coat and pulled out a cheap flip-phone and a regular cell phone. She put the burner phone on the coffee table and handed the other back to him. "If you don't have this on you, Burris will be suspicious. Expect him to take it. We'll keep the burner phone until we're sure we know who the killer is."

"When will that be?"

"Soon," said Steve.

Heather didn't give him time to ask for a more definite date. "Let's wake up Detective Burris. Keep treating him the same and refuse to answer questions."

Once in the hall, Paul stopped. Worry lines on his face deepened. "What did Steve mean by soon?"

"A couple of days at the earliest."

"This sounds like one of those good-news, bad-news stories. How long will I be in jail before you rescue me?"

"We'll do something before you go to trial."

Paul took a step back. "Trial? That could take six months to a year."

"It's that, or take your chances with someone who shoots people in the back with a .357 Magnum."

23

———

Steve slipped his phone in his pocket and offered an explanation without Heather having to ask who he called. "The latest weather forecast calls for a freeze tonight, but not as hard as first predicted. By late morning we can expect sunshine and temperatures in the high thirties."

"That's good news for Brandon and the workers."

"This far south it might get cold, but it doesn't stay that way for long." Steve smiled. "Not like Boston."

"You can say that again."

Steve didn't take her instruction literally and changed the subject. "Did you make Detective Burris happy by handing Paul to him?"

"He couldn't wait to put him in handcuffs. There wasn't anything to attach him to on the couch or bed, so he made him sit in the rolling chair at the desk. Paul may have a miserable night if Burris can't come up with a better way of keeping him secure."

"Attached to a rolling chair will work. Burris can move the coffee table and Paul can pull the chair next to the couch. It won't be comfortable, but it's better than sitting all night. I had to do something similar during a tropical storm. Rains flooded the streets and I couldn't get my suspect to jail until the water went down. Anyway, that's their problem. I need your help with one of my own."

"Oh?"

"Burris did what I asked and sent me the dental records. I listened to the transcription of the text, but there are pdf files and X-rays. Look at them and tell me what you see."

Heather spoke as she walked to the desk where Steve's laptop lay. "I'm no dentist so I doubt I'll be much help."

"Did you find someone to review the report and X-rays?"

"I remembered a guy in my biology class at Princeton. He became an orthodontist and will give his opinion as long as we don't use his name."

Steve had the email ready to open, so all Heather had to do was click on the images. "I'm looking at X-rays of a human jaw from various angles. It looks to me like Luke had a full set of teeth, both top and bottom. They're divided into two groups. The first is of Luke after the fire."

"What about fillings, crowns, missing teeth, gaps?"

Heather studied the images on her screen. "Nothing that I can see. Luke had nearly perfect teeth."

"Now compare them with the X-rays from Luke's dentist."

Heather manipulated his computer to do a split screen. Once again, she studied the X-rays. "All I'm seeing are two sets of teeth that look identical and perfect. Wait. There's a small chip on a lower front tooth."

Steve eased back in his chair and made a steeple of his index fingers.

Heather wondered why Steve would duplicate the identification by professionals. "I don't know what you're up to, but something tells me if I were to ask, you'd say something obtuse."

"Things aren't always as they seem."

Heather let out something between a laugh and cackle.

"You're using that phrase more and more. We must be at the point when you shut me out. You and your secrets may be the death of me."

"Sometimes my little secrets help to keep you alive. We're dealing with a person without a conscience. It's been a long time since I've come up against someone like this."

A shiver went down Heather's back and it wasn't caused by winter's chill. She cleared her throat. "What's next?"

Steve brought his hands down and rested them on his thighs. "Take a nap. That's what's on my calendar. There's nothing left to do until Professor Chalmers comes in for supper. He's a dangling thread we need to tie up."

"Literally or figuratively?"

Steve didn't reply. Instead, he walked to the bed, placed his sunglasses on the nightstand, and stretched out.

THE INTERNS CROWDED EACH OTHER IN LINE AS THEY FILLED plates with salad and steaming mounds of a Mexican vegetarian casserole. Before diving into her lunch, Heather scanned the rest of the room. Professor Chalmers sat at a table with two male interns. Jill flashed him a smile as she walked by, but otherwise pretended not to notice him and sat at a different table.

Mary made her appearance, wearing ankle-high boots, leggings and yet another sweater. She dragged a hand over the professor's shoulders as she passed him. The two students sitting at his table covered their grinning mouths and looked down at their half-eaten meals.

Heather turned to face Steve as Mary approached. She hoped the non-verbal clue to be left alone would avert a conversation the students could hear. No such luck.

"I'm sick of this weather and not having anything decent to eat. I can't wait to get back to Houston. What about you?"

Good manners and the chance to glean additional information caused Heather to turn. "Hello, Mary. My mind was back in Belize, sunning on gorgeous beaches beside a handsome man."

Mary let out a bray of a laugh that turned heads. "Girl, I need to borrow your dream. The men around here are as cold as the weather."

Heather leaned into Mary, cupped her hands around her mouth, and whispered. "If you're referring to Paul, don't count on seeing him for a long time. Detective Burris arrested him for killing Luke Pryor."

Mary's eyes widened. "Are you sure?"

"I caught Paul trying to make a run for it this morning. He won't get away this time."

Mary's front teeth clamped on her lower lip, causing her to scrape off pink, glossy lipstick. She turned to pick up silverware and took her first bite of lunch while fidgeting in her seat. After a second bite, she pushed back from the table. "I'm tired of eating with all these kids. I'll take my meal upstairs and eat in my room."

"Good idea," said Heather. "Do you want me to join you?"

"I thought you had to stay with Steve."

Heather shot a glance to where Steve sat. "I don't absolutely have to, but I guess I should. You might prefer to be alone."

"These noisy young people have me all jittery. I'll see you tomorrow."

"Yes, tomorrow it's supposed to warm and melt the ice and snow. The sunshine will brighten everyone's mood."

Mary didn't run, but didn't waste time in leaving. Heather whispered, "I told Mary."

Steve leaned into her. "Did she buy your story?"

"Like it was on sale at 90 percent off. She took her meal up to her room."

"Did you check the cameras in the hallway?"

"I'm taking my plate to Julie's office to make sure she doesn't go looking for Paul." Heather paused before she took her plate down the hall. "What about Professor Chalmers? Are you still going to talk to him tonight?"

"Let's catch him first thing tomorrow morning. Working all night will have his defenses down."

"He may not sleep after he hears what you have to say."

"Something tells me that wouldn't bother you."

"Not one bit."

THE NIGHT PROVED LONG AND WITHOUT INCIDENT AS Heather listened to financial podcasts, considered investment opportunities, and stared at a split screen of the parking lot and the hallway upstairs. At twelve forty, two of the three images of the parking lot went black on her screen. Because of a bad angle, she almost missed a hooded figure come into view and scurry toward Julie's truck. The person disappeared from sight. She remembered Mary complaining about her car and how she longed to have something new and sporty. Heather moved closer to the screen, straining to see movement. After several minutes, the crouching figure, dressed in black, sprinted from the lot into pitch-black woods.

Adrenaline coursed through Heather as she bolted from the office and ran to the front door. The sound of approaching ATV's carrying workers finishing a long shift carried on the still night air. The footsteps of interns getting ready to change shifts echoed behind her. She concluded it would be fruitless to pursue whoever went to the parking lot and stepped back into the lobby.

Her first thought turned to Mary. Had she been able to avoid the security cameras in the hallway? Surely not. Or had she? After all, Heather had focused her attention on the parking lot.

Heather bounded up the stairs, going against the flow of

bodies coming down. She hurried to her room, fumbled with the key, and told herself to calm down. This wasn't the time to make a mistake.

Steve met her at the connecting door. "What's wrong? You aren't supposed to get me until after one thirty."

"Have you heard anything in the hallway?"

"I thought I heard a door close, but it might have been a television."

"Someone dressed in black visited the parking lot a few minutes ago. They went to Julie's truck, then sprinted into the woods. Whoever it was went toward Luke and Julie's house. I was lucky to see anything. Two of the three cameras stopped working."

"What about the cameras covering this hallway?"

"I couldn't watch everything at once, but it should have recorded. I'll have to go back and check."

"Go bang on Mary's door and run back before she can open it. We need to know if she's still here."

With Mary's room close to hers, it took Heather only a handful of steps to reach the door, give five sharp knocks, and make a quick retreat. She entered her room and found Steve with his ear pinned against the wall.

He didn't need to listen so closely. The slamming of the door and muffled expletives would have brought Heather out of a deep sleep if she hadn't already been awake.

Heather covered a snicker with her hand and took Steve by the arm. "I guess that answered the question of where Mary is. Let's have a seat and talk about Julie's truck. What do you think?"

He settled in his usual spot. "If it's what I think it is, you need to be very careful. Let everyone coming in from the greenhouses get to sleep before you check her truck. Take a flashlight and don't touch anything until you're sure you know what we're dealing with."

"Do you think it's a tracking device?"

"That's one possibility."

"What's the other?"

Steve closed his fists and then opened them in a rush. "BOOM!"

Heather swallowed. "Have you ever dealt with a car bomb?"

"Nope."

"Me, either. We'd better call someone who knows what they're doing."

"I'll do it. I know the guy in charge of Houston's bomb squad." Steve patted the arm of his chair. A sure sign that the possibility of an explosion had him worried. "It's out of his jurisdiction, and he won't want to travel on icy roads for what might be nothing. You'll need to find whatever it is and take pictures of it."

"Great. That means I get to slither on my back in ice and snow."

Steve held up a hand and tilted his head. "Someone's knocking on Mary's door." He rose and walked to the wall between Heather's room and Mary's. Heather stood still as a statue. It wasn't long before she heard Mary's raised voice, but couldn't make out the words.

Steve stepped away from the wall. "The professor is going back to his room with his tail tucked between his legs. Mary accused him of allowing his students to do the knock-and-run prank. I'll not repeat what she called him, but that answers one thing for me. The professor and Mary didn't know each other before she came here."

For the next hour Heather and Steve compared notes, reviewed suspects and motives, but avoided further talk of a bomb. When the clock read 2:05 a.m., Heather put jeans over her leggings, donned a knit cap, gloves and coat.

"Be careful," said Steve.

"At least she drives something with good ground clearance." She made her way to the front steps of the lodge and stepped into the night. They'd discussed the most likely places to look for a tracking device and explosives. Ten minutes later, she sat in Steve's room. Cold, but thoroughly alive.

"What did you find?" asked Steve, his voice sounding strained but relieved.

"If it's what I think, it's a cube of C-4 taped to the firewall."

"With wires running from it?"

Heather gave a positive response as she lifted the screen to her laptop. "I'm going to look up C-4 and see if there're any pictures." It didn't take long before she let out a low whistle. "You need to call your buddy. The wires, blasting cap, and plastic explosive all look the same as what I saw."

Steve didn't rush to grab his phone. "That stuff is safe as long as nobody starts her car. Is the ice melting?"

"Not yet." Heather checked her phone. "It's twenty-seven degrees, with the wind out of the southwest."

Steve shifted in his chair. "I did some research while you were crawling on the ground. C-4 is stable on its own. It must have a blasting cap *and* a source of ignition. If you pull out the blasting cap, it won't go off, but the detonator is dangerous if it's still attached to something that sends a spark. The key to disarming it is to first pull the blasting cap out of the C-4. Then, cut the wires one at a time and keep the blasting cap and the C-4 away from each other."

Heather tented her hands on her hips. "Are you saying you want me to diffuse a bomb?"

"I'd do it if I could. The more I thought about it, an expert won't be able to come until late this afternoon. We don't know how big of a blast zone we're talking about."

Heather nodded. "Did you come across any YouTube videos on how to disarm bombs?"

"No, but that's not a bad idea. From the audio I listened to, it didn't sound that complicated. A spark sets off the blasting cap, which ignites the C-4. No spark, no boom."

Heather puffed out her cheeks and let the air escape in a

rush. "We need to renegotiate my contract to read no diffusing or disposal of bombs." A thought occurred to her. "What am I supposed to do with everything when I take it off?"

"Good question. I guess you can put it in your SUV and park somewhere a long way from here."

She put on all the cold weather gear she'd taken off. After patting her pocket to make sure she had a flashlight and a Swiss Army knife, she looked at Steve one last time. "Wish me luck."

He did and repeated his words of caution.

It wasn't long before she slithered back under Julie's vehicle. She traced the wire from the starter down to the blasting cap embedded in something that looked like a chunk of clay. Her hand shook, and it wasn't from the cold. Holding her breath, she slipped the blasting cap from the clay-like substance that could leave a crater in the parking lot. Only then did she take a breath. "So far, so good." She considered slipping the explosive into her pocket, but thought better of it. Then she remembered she carried zip-lock bags in an inside pocket of her coat in case she needed to collect evidence. These items certainly qualified. She zipped the bag shut on the plastic explosive, then focused on the wires and the blasting cap. The small pair of scissors on the multipurpose knife would have to do in cutting the thin wires. With two snips she completed the task then bagged the blasting cap with the short lengths of wires attached.

It took much longer for her vehicle to melt ice on the windshield and back glass than it did to unhook the device. She parked on the road to Luke and Julie's tiny metal home, locked the C-4 in the glove compartment, and put the blasting cap in the cargo area behind the back seat. Then, she jogged away until trees separated her from all potential danger.

As the lights of the lodge came into view, a sense of accomplishment settled on her. Relief mixed with a level of pride. She'd flirted with death and came from it unscathed. Not something she'd want to do every day, but this would be a night she'd always remember.

She yawned as her foot stepped onto the front porch. If Steve needed to keep track of Mary, he'd have to do it himself. She'd been awake for almost twenty hours and needed to recharge for what the day might bring.

24

The blackout curtains in Heather's room lived up to their name. Blinding sunlight caused her to step back when she parted them at ten thirty. Try as she might to salvage a night's sleep, she had tossed and turned after her experience of handling something so dangerous. So much for checking in with Steve at breakfast.

There was one distinct advantage to living next door to and sometimes traveling with a blind man. She never had to worry about what she wore or if her hair looked like a flock of wrens made a nest in it. She tapped on his door and heard him tell her to come in.

"You're still among the living. Glad to see it."

Heather spoke as she yawned. "Lousy sleep."

"Just as well. Only a handful of die-hard chowhounds showed up at breakfast. Burris started his vehicle and let it thaw while he and Paul grabbed a bite. Paul should be in a cell by now, while Burris will stay busy all day writing reports and receiving pats on the back for solving the murder."

"How's that going to play out tomorrow when you tell him the killer isn't Paul?"

Steve flipped his hand to express indifference. "He'll be fine as long as we deliver the real goods."

Heather reached down to touch her toes and then tried to put her palms flat on the carpet without bending her knees. She spoke as she stretched. "Any other big news while I was in dreamland?"

"Jack called. He has to be in court this afternoon and won't be free to bring Julie until tomorrow morning."

"It may take me that long to make myself look decent."

"It never bothered me what Maggie looked like. Jack and I think a lot alike on that subject."

Heather didn't know what to say until her gaze fixed on a carafe from the dining room. "Is that coffee?"

"Help yourself. I knew you'd need a full pot. It may not be hot enough now, but you can heat it in the microwave."

After filling a ceramic mug, she took a sip and found the coffee tepid. Forty-five seconds later, she clutched a steaming mug of stimulant. Her mind turned to a follow-up question from her late-night activities. "Have you done anything about the C-4?"

"I called the guy in Houston and told him what you'd done. He wasn't happy, but calmed down when I told him you'd consulted with experts, took photos of everything before you started, bagged and tagged the evidence, and parked your car a half mile away."

"Did he think watching a YouTube video qualifies as consulting with experts?"

Steve responded with a grin.

Another sip of coffee dissipated the fog in her brain a little more. "You enjoy jerking people's chains, me included. That bomb disposal guy could get me in trouble."

"You have nothing to worry about. Those guys are sticklers for doing everything by the book and they can't stand it when someone with common sense comes along and steals their glory. They also recognize the difference between taking an informed risk and recklessness. Besides, he's grateful he didn't have to do it."

His words didn't convince her and it must have showed when she didn't respond.

"You worry too much. He climbed off his high-horse when I told him I'd call ATF or Fort Hood and get some of their people to come get it."

"Nothing like threatening city cops with a federal agency to get them moving. Telling him you'd bring in the army was a nice touch."

"All part of the games people play. He'll be here this afternoon to take it off our hands. Expect him to give you grief, but it will be all bark and no bite."

"I guess I'm supposed to grovel and play the role of a dumb woman to soothe his ego." Heather sat down and continued to nurse her cup of coffee. "Is there anything else left to do before tomorrow?"

"Other than make a couple of phone calls and tell Brandon that Julie's coming home, I can't think of anything."

Heather stood and grabbed the carafe. "I'm going for a run and check on my car. I'll be back in time to shower and go to lunch."

Steve responded with a grunt, his way of acknowledging he heard her. He'd already gone someplace else in his mind.

THE LATE MORNING RUN LASTED ONLY THIRTY MINUTES, BUT the quick pace and sunshine made Heather glad to be alive. Thoughts of Jack coming tomorrow morning didn't hurt either. Everything seemed in place and the plan solid, but that didn't mean the wheels couldn't fall off at the last minute.

By the time the ATVs approached at noon, Heather had showered, blow dried her hair and put on makeup. She collected Steve, and they made their way to the dining room. When they arrived, Mary already had her meal and sat alone at what Heather called the teacher's table. She parked Steve in the seat beside Mary.

"Ah, Mary," said Steve. "How's your morning been?"

"Boring. I can't wait to get out of here. Do you think the roads will be clear enough for me to leave today?"

Heather thought about how silly it sounded that Mary had asked a blind man about road conditions. She considered the source of the question and let it pass.

Steve, however, had an answer. "Stick around until tomorrow. Now that Detective Burris has charged Paul with killing Luke, they can release the insurance settlement check. I spoke with Marsha Pennywell this morning. She's coming up tomorrow to talk to you and Julie. It wouldn't surprise me if she brings the check with her."

"I doubt that," said Mary. "My attorneys would have let me know if the company made a final decision."

"Perhaps you're right. Marsha may come up to get reports from Detective Burris. I thought you wouldn't want to miss the chance to press her on the settlement."

Heather broke into the conversation and directed her question to Steve. "It's straight vegetables today. Do you want me to pick out things I know you like?"

"Do they have cornbread?"

Mary provided the answer. "Regular cornbread, jalapeño cornbread, and corn muffins made with cream-style corn."

Steve placed his hands on the table. "I'll have whatever vegetables look good, one slice of jalapeño cornbread, and a corn-muffin."

Heather went to fill his plate and make her selections. She returned to the table and found Mary covering her mouth to keep a loud laugh from bouncing around the room. "What's so funny?"

"Steve told me how Detective Burris insisted on keeping Paul handcuffed to a chair at all times, and how he had trouble getting it through the bathroom door."

Heather shifted her gaze to Steve. "Paul had to sit in the chair and push himself backward through the doorway, then turn around and—"

She interrupted him. "I get the picture, and it's not making my lunch look any better."

Bathroom humor must have appealed to Mary. She all but doubled over laughing. While she recovered, Heather noticed Brandon enter the dining room with Trey acting as his shadow. Both men displayed hat-hair and an overall scruffy appearance. It surprised Heather when the interns broke out in applause as the two men approached the serving line.

"Why's everyone clapping?" asked Mary.

Brandon raised a hand to acknowledge and quieten the crowd. "I want to thank everyone for working so hard to save the crops, but we all know who the hero is." He turned and placed his hand on Trey's shoulder. "If it weren't for Trey repairing and keeping the heaters running, we'd have lost at least half our crop. He saved us from sure disaster. Everyone that helped save this business will receive a five-hundred-dollar bonus."

A long, standing ovation followed. Trey stood with his hands crammed deep in the pockets of stained jeans. Heather shifted her gaze to Mary, who sat with her mouth hinged open and no hint of a smile. As Brandon and Trey made for the serving line, Mary rose and left the room. Once again, she didn't bother to put her dishes where they belonged.

With his plate full, Brandon slumped in the chair next to Steve. Up close, he looked worse than at a distance. Bloodshot eyes, greasy hair, and black under his fingernails showed his need for a long, hot shower and extensive sleep. Despite the obvious fatigue, the first things out of his mouth were questions about the missing co-owner of the farm. "How's Julie? Is she any better?"

Steve put down his fork. "Much improved. In fact, she'll be here tomorrow."

Brandon hung his head and whispered, "Thank God."

Even though Steve couldn't see it, Heather caught the glisten of moisture in Brandon's eyes. Once again, the photo of the three friends in Julie's office came to mind.

Brandon looked around the room. "I thought I saw Mary."

"She left," said Heather.

Brandon stabbed a large bite of green beans. "I wanted to talk to her about something. I hope she's not planning on leaving today."

"She's not going anywhere until sometime tomorrow."

"That's good. I can barely keep my eyes open and there's something important I need to talk to her about."

Heather's gaze shifted from Brandon to Trey and back to Brandon. "I'll make sure she doesn't leave."

"Thanks. I heard Detective Burris arrested the guy that killed Luke."

"That's what the police are saying," said Steve. "Heather and I still have some loose ends to tie up then we'll be through here tomorrow."

Brandon gave Trey a smile. "All me and Trey have in mind is a hot shower and sleep until tomorrow morning."

Trey spoke a one-word response around a bite of cornbread. "Tired."

The rest of the meal passed without another word. Trey and Brandon gobbled theirs down and left.

Steve's phone buzzed, announcing an incoming call. He spoke in a hushed tone and ended the call. "Eat up. The bomb guy is here."

What she dreaded as being a severe tongue-lashing and lecture turned out to be nothing of the sort. Steve did the lion's share of the talking while Heather provided inconsequential details she hadn't told Steve. The man insisted on doing a full inspection of the truck, but found nothing except the dangling wires attached to the starter. He took photos, disconnected the wires, bagged and tagged them, and added them to Heather's evidence. In less than half an hour, he pulled away. Just another day for a guy with an unusual occupation.

Heather and Steve stood in the parking lot beside the truck that could have been in thousands of pieces if the bomb had gone off. "What do we do until tomorrow?"

"We wait and worry about what we've missed."

"Did you ever consider Brandon as a suspect in killing Luke?"

"Not over fifteen or twenty times a day."

25

———

Detective Burris arrived an hour early for the 10:00 a.m. meeting, looking both happy and tired. He explained the reason for his grin without having to be asked. "I never realized how many questions reporters asked. They come so fast you don't have time to answer them. The press conference could have been over in ten minutes if they didn't keep cutting me off."

Steve asked him to sit down. "Answering silly questions is one of the many downsides of dealing with the press."

A few seconds of awkward silence followed. Steve cleared his throat. "Detective Burris, we need to tell you about something Heather found very early yesterday morning. You were busy with Paul so we handled it on our own."

"Does it pertain to Luke's murder?"

Steve nodded. "It seems someone is serious about killing Julie, too. First, they tried shooting out a front tire of the van she drove. Then, in the early hours of yesterday morning, they planted a bomb in her truck."

Burris's head snapped up. "A bomb? What kind of bomb?"

Heather tried to look like an innocent schoolgirl and said, "Not a big one, but it would have done a lot of damage. It doesn't take that much C-4 to make a big bang."

"C-4! Are you kidding?"

Heather handed him a file folder containing multiple pages. "Here's my statement that explains everything that happened. The bomb squad in Houston came and retrieved it after I disarmed it. The name of the contact person is in my report. He's expecting a call from you later today."

Burris's eyes and mouth gaped open as he took the report. "This means I'll have to file another charge against Paul. He kills Luke and now he's trying to kill Julie." He threw up a hand in frustration.

"Paul was in custody when the person planted the bomb, so it wasn't him," said Steve. "Keep an open mind this morning. There will be several persons of interest here and you need to keep your eyes open for any sign of trouble."

"I should call for backup."

Steve held up his hand as a stop sign. "Have a couple of deputies nearby, but we don't want to spook anyone. An unexpected police presence will have a chilling effect. We need people to talk." He took a breath. "That leaves you and Heather to take care of anyone who gets out of hand."

"The sheriff needs to make that decision."

"I've already talked to him. He wants you to know he has confidence in you for whatever might happen."

That last statement might have stretched the truth a little, but it came close enough. Burris squared his shoulders and raised his chin.

Heather took over. "Let's go to the lobby and set up chairs for everyone. There's not room enough in this office."

Jack and Julie arrived as Heather and Burris arranged chairs in an oval.

"Where's Brandon?" asked Julie as soon as she entered.

"He'll be here at ten," said Heather. "How are you feeling?"

"Tylenol is taking care of the headaches, and the arm itches. What I need more than anything is to powder my nose and change. I'll be in my room."

Heather turned to Jack. "You look like you could use a cup of coffee. Come with me to the dining room."

Jack's eyebrows wiggled up and down. Dogs have tails to wag. Jack used his eyebrows.

When she and Jack returned from their quick reunion, Mary sat with legs crossed and arms folded so tight she looked as if she wore a strait jacket.

Brandon and Trey came in next. "Where's Julie?" asked Brandon without sitting down.

"In her room. She's making a speedy recovery."

Brandon took the stairs two at a time and disappeared while Trey walked with shoulders back and sat beside his sister. Mary looked at him, gave a head-to-toe appraisal, and said, "You need to comb your hair."

"Don't do no good." He pulled a knit cap from his pocket. "Keeps my ears warm, but messes up my hair."

A roll of Mary's eyes was her only acknowledgment.

Brandon wore a smile as he came down the stairs and announced, "Julie's on her way."

The front door opened again and Marsha walked in. She wore designer jeans tucked into leather boots, a cashmere sweater, and a puffy vest. She appeared completely healed of her sunburn until Heather looked closer. It's a wonder what makeup can do for a woman, but it can't work miracles. Marsha took a seat near, but not next to Steve.

"Marsha, glad you could join us. Your perfume gave you away."

"Hello, Steve. I bet you're ready to escape the frozen north and go back to Belize."

"Not really. Summers in and around Houston can last until November and start again in April. Listening to logs crackle and throw sparks isn't a bad way to spend a crisp morning." Steve spoke so everyone could hear him. "Who are we missing?"

Heather looked around. "Julie's the only one."

"I'm coming," shouted Julie as she neared the top of the stairs.

"Take your time," said Steve. "We don't want you to break the other arm."

Heather noticed Steve had abandoned the makeshift sling supporting his sprained wrist. She'd been so preoccupied with a murder and two attempted murders she couldn't say for sure when he'd ditched it.

Those standing found a seat, with Detective Burris sitting closest to the front door. Mary ended up on the opposite side of the oval from Marsha, while Brandon and Julie sat side-by-side, close to Detective Burris. Heather pushed her chair close to Steve so she could whisper about anything he needed to know, but couldn't see. Jack settled next to her. As discretely as possible, Heather motioned for him to remove a speck of lipstick she'd deposited on his lip.

Steve cleared his throat. "I wanted to give everyone an update on progress made in discovering who killed Luke. I know this is hard for Julie and Brandon to hear, so I apologize in advance. Heather and I will try to be as discreet as possible, but unless everyone hears the details, they won't understand what a clever and remorseless person we're dealing with."

Detective Burris crossed his arms. "I don't know about clever, but Paul Lee fits the bill as remorseless. He's refused to say anything and grins at me every time I ask him a question."

Jack opened his mouth, but a shake of Heather's head stilled his tongue.

"Let's begin with the crime," said Steve in a full voice. "The first thing that caught my attention was the manner in which Luke died. First came the shot in the back with what we now know is a .357 Magnum. For anyone that isn't familiar with firearms, it's a powerful weapon capable of massive injuries. The autopsy concluded that Luke died almost instantly from a single gunshot to the back."

Heads turned as Julie's silent tears accompanied a mournful

sob. Heather delivered a box of tissues and patted Julie's leg. "Hang in there. The bad part is almost over."

Julie nodded and dabbed the wet tracks that ran down her face and dripped from her chin.

Steve continued when Heather sat down. "The shooting occurred in the driveway of Luke's house. Someone loaded the body in the cab of his pickup, brought him on this property, and set the truck ablaze. I have one question for you to answer. Why?"

Detective Burris blurted out, "So they could cause a big distraction while they fabricated an alibi and made their getaway."

Steve nodded, but Heather knew it wasn't a signal that he agreed. "That's possible, but I don't think so. Fabricated alibis have a habit of falling apart. Besides, this one was too risky."

"I agree," said Marsha. "The shooting and burning of the body made me suspect the work of a psychopath and a pyromaniac. I think two people carried out the murder." She cast her gaze toward Detective Burris. "I'd make sure Paul doesn't have access to matches or anything that could start a fire."

"Can we move on?" asked Mary. "The important thing to keep in mind is I'm the closest living *real* relative Luke had, and his will clearly states I'm entitled to everything he left behind and his life insurance policy. The police have the killer in jail and this is a waste of time."

Jack spoke up. "Don't be too sure of that, Mary. I'm not involved in the inheritance case anymore, but the will states you're the next of kin *unless* he married."

Mary glared as she spoke over Jack. "You're not involved in the case. I hired real lawyers to do what you couldn't. They say the marriage wasn't legal."

Steve held up his hands. "We're getting off track, and it's obvious to me that the courts will have the final say about the inheritance. I'm here to tell you what we know about Luke's murder. As a point of interest, the outcome of this meeting will have an influence on who inherits the estate and receives the life insurance payment."

Questioning looks bore into Steve, which, of course, didn't phase him at all because he couldn't see them. He resumed where he left off. "Let's talk about motive. Who stood to gain from Luke's death?"

Once again, Steve allowed silence to prevail. It wasn't long before narrow-eyed gazes shot around the room, landing on one person then shifting to the next. Heads remained stationary but eyes shifted like the hand of a metronome set on a low speed. A few of the people squirmed in their chairs.

Mary let out a huff that broke the spell of suspicion. Steve spoke before anyone else could. "Let's take Mary, for example. She's looking forward to having more money than she can imagine. If she prevails with her claim, she and Trey will receive an insurance settlement of fifteen million dollars."

Heather added, "That doesn't count ongoing royalties held in escrow from Luke's copyrighted computer games or any other funds they can find in Luke's off-shore accounts. From what I could determine, the amount in those accounts far exceeds the insurance settlement."

"So?" said Mary, as she raised her chin in defiance. "It's my lucky day."

"Don't you mean your and your brother's lucky day?" asked Steve.

"What are you talking about?"

Steve looked relaxed, which contrasted to the steel in his voice. "Your attorneys filed a petition to declare Trey mentally incompetent and a danger to himself and others. After what he did to save the crops this week, that claim will be hard to prove."

Trey shifted his gaze to his sister. "I want to work with Brandon. He said I could."

Brandon's fists rolled into tight balls. "It's ridiculous to say Trey is incompetent or poses any sort of danger. He saved this farm and I'll do everything I can to fight that claim."

Mary answered the challenge. "Go ahead. I'll own the farm and you won't have a penny left by the time my lawyers get through with you."

Julie placed a hand on Brandon's leg. The look she issued must have communicated something to him. He settled back in his chair and said nothing else.

Steve continued. "Mary, it might interest you that we've obtained a sworn affidavit from Lucy, the woman who performed the wedding ceremony between Luke and Julie. It turns out she's an ordained minister."

"What church?" asked Marsha.

Heather answered. "That's not relevant. Lucy will come to the States or be available for a video conference and testify that the marriage is legal and properly registered in Belize."

Mary looked at Jack. "What does that mean?"

"It means the courts will have to decide who gets the inheritance and the life insurance money. Right now, things aren't looking good for you."

Worry coursed across Mary's countenance. "Who do you think will get it?"

Jack shrugged. "You'll need to consult your attorneys."

Steve held up both hands. "My purpose in going down this rabbit hole is to show that Mary had a huge motive for wanting her cousin dead. But she isn't the only one."

Movement at the top of the stairway caught Heather's attention. She leaned into Steve and whispered, "The visitor you expected is eavesdropping."

Steve tilted his head back and projected his voice even more. "Glad you could make it, Jill. Please join us. You'll be able to hear better from down here."

Necks craned to see the young woman at the top of the stairs whose face changed from flesh-tone to blotchy red.

26

———————

Detective Burris retrieved another chair and sat within arm's length of Jill. "Sit by me. I'll talk to you as soon as this is over."

"Not without an attorney present."

Burris had reached his limit of patience. "When I interviewed you the day after the murder, you told me you never associated with Luke except on this property. Since then, I've learned you and Luke had a lot more going on than raising vegetables."

"No comment."

Burris reached behind his back. "You want a lawyer? You'll get one after you're booked into jail. Stand up and put your hands behind your back." Handcuffs ratcheted shut as he read Jill her rights.

"This isn't fair."

Heather's words came in a tone of mock pity. "Such a shame, Jill. You talked yourself into a trip to jail and possibly out of a passing grade. And there's no need to send me your resume and business plan. I'm no longer interested."

Burris called for a deputy he'd stationed nearby to transport

Jill to jail. Tears tracked down her cheeks as the deputy marched her through the front door.

Burris returned to his seat with a look of self-satisfaction and his chin higher than usual.

Steve brought attention back to himself. "Sorry about the distraction. In case you're wondering, Jill had nothing to do with Luke's murder, other than being a liar and a distraction to the investigation. Keep in mind what just happened if you're tempted to shade the truth before we're finished."

He allowed the words to sink in. "Let's get back to the business at hand. Perhaps I've been too hard on Mary. She had plenty of motive, but her alibi checks out. She was miles away in Houston with a client on the night of Luke's murder."

"What kind of client?" asked Burris.

"None of your business," snapped Mary.

Steve moved on quickly. "Let's eliminate a couple more people from Luke's murder. You may not realize it, but this property has an elaborate video surveillance system. For every camera you can see, there's another you can't see monitoring almost every part of the greenhouses, perimeter gates, parking lots, and the lodge. You're being filmed by two cameras right now. Isn't that right, Detective Burris?"

"Cameras all over the place."

"You'd think this would help the police in identifying Luke's killer. However, it didn't because someone disabled the cameras that monitored Luke's driveway and house the night he was killed."

Steve crossed his legs. "Because of the double camera system, there's good news for several people in this room. Surveillance footage has ruled you out as Luke's killer."

Heather took her turn. "Brandon had no opportunity. Footage from the strawberry greenhouse shows him working there until fire trucks arrived."

"A circulation pump went out, and I had to replace it."

"Then there's Julie," said Steve. "She left her office at eleven and went to her room upstairs."

"I fell behind on a quarterly tax return. I needed to sleep as much as possible so I could finish the next morning and get it sent off before the deadline. It made little sense for me to go home that night."

"That rules two people out," said Steve. "Which brings us back to Jill. Cameras recorded her going to a Suburban in the parking lot on the night of Luke's murder. We have a statement from a certain professor who was waiting for her in the vehicle. They discussed hydroponics, among other topics, until fire trucks drove past."

Mary snorted and murmured, "Yeah, I bet they did."

Marsha spoke up. "That leaves Paul Lee."

"I'm telling you, it's him," said Burris. "He enrolled here, pretending to study water farming. He's a shady private eye who came to extort money from a millionaire. When Luke wouldn't pay, Lee killed him."

"Are you sure?" asked Steve.

"We're still tying up loose ends."

"Do you have a report back from ballistics?"

"Not yet. The weather hasn't been cooperating."

"What if it comes back that you can't match the bullet you found to Paul's pistol?"

Heather looked for signs of surprise or alarm on people's faces. Nothing.

Burris rubbed the fuzz on his close-cropped head. "He might have killed with one pistol and carried a similar one for me to discover when I searched him."

"Possible, but improbable," said Steve. He leaned back in his chair, giving everyone a break from the machine-gun exchange of questions and answers. Slowing the pace, he asked his next question. "We also haven't answered the question that should be on everyone's mind. Who tried to kill Julie?"

With no one breaking the silence, Steve plowed ahead. "And

there's one other loose end. How did the police know Luke Pryor was Donnie Douglas?"

Burris lifted his chin. "The sheriff's office got an anonymous tip that the guy in the burned-out truck was Donnie Douglas. Then the sheriff caught wind of the civil action Mary brought to have Donnie declared legally dead. I checked with the insurance company after we identified the burned body as Luke Pryor. It turns out the insurance company had tracked Donnie all over the Caribbean. Their investigation revealed Donnie Douglas and Luke Pryor were the same person."

Once again, gazes shifted from person to person. Steve allowed the people to digest the information before he offered them something else to consider. "Doesn't it make sense that the persons with the most to gain would be Mary and Trey?"

Julie shook her head as her eyes moistened again. Mary pointed at Steve and spoke through clenched teeth. "You'd better not be accusing me of something you're not ready to back up in court."

Steve came back with a question. "Did I hit a nerve? We now know that your claim to Luke's inheritance wasn't as rock-solid as you thought. I'll concede that you were otherwise occupied on the night of Luke's death, but where were you when Julie's van flipped through the air?"

"How dare you accuse me!"

"I did no such thing. All I did was ask where you were."

"None of your business."

Detective Burris spoke up. "I'm making it my business. I'm wondering if you and Paul Lee aren't in this together. He kills Luke and you get rid of Julie. You get all the inheritance and life insurance money and pay him for getting rid of Luke."

Steve added, "You'd better come up with something quick, Mary. After all, with Luke taken care of, you were only one murder away from getting everything you wanted. We checked. On the day of Julie's wreck, you left your apartment with plenty of time to get to this side of Brenham, take the shot, and get to the lodge that afternoon."

Steve's phone rang and announced an incoming call from Leo.

"I'll call you back in two minutes."

Heather stood. "Let's take a five-minute break."

27

Heather watched as people stood and stretched. Brandon, Julie, and Trey found a corner at the far end of the lobby, much too far away to hear their words. Brandon did most of the talking while Julie nodded, smiled, and gave Trey a hug with her good arm.

"Hey, gorgeous. Remember me?"

Heather snapped out of long-range surveillance and looked up at Jack's handsome face. "Aren't you the guy wearing a speck of my lipstick?"

"I'd like some more if it's part of the service at this hotel."

"First work, then play. We're on the home stretch if Leo came through for Steve."

Jack responded by holding up both hands with fingers crossed. His expression changed. "The one that left in cuffs. Her name is Jill?"

"Yeah. One of the student interns." Heather interlaced her fingers in Jack's. "She's pretty, smart, ambitious and creative."

"But?"

"She must have hidden behind a tree when they handed out morals."

"That's a shame." Jack faced her, bent down, and whispered.

"What's with Marsha? I know we didn't spend much time with her on the trip to Belize, but she ignored me completely today."

Heather shrugged. "Either she has something important on her mind, or you're not her type."

She loved it when Jack laughed. Not too loud, and not a breathy snicker.

Steve returned. "Let's take our seats and finish our business."

Chairs scraped, and conversations concluded. Steve announced, "I can now say with confidence that we know who shot Luke and why." He waited long seconds before he issued a chilling statement. "It wasn't Paul."

"You'll need to convince me," said Burris.

"Let me lay it out. From the start, this has been a case where things weren't as they seemed. You need to realize that I didn't start the investigation of Donnie Douglas's disappearance, or Luke as you all knew him. Marsha suspected he was alive and convinced her company to allow her to hunt him down. This took her to several Caribbean Islands and eventually to Belize. He changed his name multiple times and obtained numerous passports, which is easy to do if you have enough money. Luke, or Marcus as he was known in Belize, ended up working on an organic food farm with Brandon and Julie, who became his best friends. Friendship eventually turned into something more between Julie and Luke."

"Not legally," said Mary.

Steve ignored her and pressed on. "Luke staged his disappearance in Belize and returned to Texas, where he, Julie, and Brandon started this business. He had plenty of funds stashed away, so he poured part of them into this property, the greenhouses, the lodge, and everything it took to get it up and running. Then, someone found out Luke's true identity. They saw an untouched fortune and an insurance policy worth millions."

Steve shifted his head. "Mary, answer this question. Who called and told you to look into Luke's insurance policy?"

"Some man from an insurance company."

Steve nodded. "That sounds very similar to what Paul experienced. A man called and hired him to do basic background surveillance and pretend he was interested in hydroponics. In return for a fat fee, he was to live on-site, learn hydroponics, and make regular reports to the caller."

Burris spoke up. "All you're doing is convincing me that Paul killed Luke and there's a good possibility that Mary tried to kill Julie."

Steve thrust his index finger toward Burris. "You got it! That's exactly what someone wants us to think."

"That's ridiculous," said Mary.

"Not at all," countered Steve. "The bomb in Julie's truck proves someone set you up to be Julie's murderer." Gasps came from several in the room, but Steve kept talking. "Mary, did you leave your room between midnight and one in the morning the night before last?"

"Absolutely not."

"If you're going to stick to that story, Detective Burris has a set of handcuffs for you."

"You can't prove anything."

Heather jumped in. "How about security footage showing you leaving your room and using a back exit from the building thirty minutes before someone dressed in black planted the bomb? Who did you meet in the woods?"

"No one, and you don't have security footage."

Steve barely allowed her to finish the sentence. "How do you know what security footage we have or don't have?"

Mary squirmed, but clamped her lips shut while Steve allowed the question to float on the air like a foul odor.

Detective Burris rose and spoke as he walked to Mary. "Stand up. Hands behind your back. If Steve and Heather say they have video of you sneaking out of this building, that's good enough for me."

Heather continued. "We also have footage of a figure dressed in black coming out of the woods and going to the parking lot."

"Wait," begged Mary. "I'll admit I wore all black and went outside. I was to meet someone, but they didn't show."

Burris stationed himself beside Mary's chair with his hand on her shoulder.

"Keep talking," said Steve.

Mary nodded. "It was a man's voice on the phone. The same one that told me to go after the life insurance money. He never said his name."

Burris shook his head. "Nice try, but that story won't cut it."

With a softened voice, Steve cut in. "Hold on, Burris. I believe some of what you said, Mary. You went outside to meet someone. What I don't know is if you knew them, or not. What I am sure of is there's another person involved. A very smart and skilled person, who killed Luke, tried to kill Julie and planted the bomb. That person also made all three events look like you or Paul did them."

Steve turned in his chair. "Would you like to tell them who the third person is, Marsha?"

The question didn't ruffle her. "This is your story. You finish it."

Steve took in a big breath. "I didn't realize it at first, Marsha, but you used me to find Luke, or I should say, to find Donnie Douglas. When you couldn't pick up the trail to Marcus or any of the aliases he used, you decided to find Brandon Clay. You hired Paul Lee and he traced Brandon here to the hydroponics farm. To your surprise, he also found Julie and Luke Pryor, the alias Donnie Douglas was still using."

Marsha didn't react.

Steve directed his words to the entire gathering. "The insurance company ran out of patience with Marsha, and Mary's attorneys were pushing for closure. When Paul Lee told her Luke and Julie were married in Belize, Marsha hatched a plan to get rid of Luke and Julie both, and pin the murders on other people. Her plan almost worked."

For the first time, Marsha shifted in her chair.

Steve turned and spoke directly to Marsha. "You used Paul in two different ways. First, in reconnaissance and then as someone to take the blame for Luke's murder."

Marsha sat with hands in her lap, her face revealing nothing. "I didn't know about Luke's murder until I heard it on the news."

"When was that?"

"I don't remember the exact date."

"The report didn't make a splash on the news until they matched dental records with the victim."

Marsha nodded in agreement. "That cleared the way for my company to settle with Julie, or Mary and Trey."

"Which they haven't done yet."

"Not yet, but they will."

Steve wagged an index finger. "Let me amend that. The only person who will receive the settlement from the insurance company is Julie."

Heather wondered if Marsha had ice water in her veins instead of blood. Mary stared at Marsha through narrow slits. "You know about life insurance stuff. Is what Steve says true?"

Marsha gave her head a single nod. "You'll get nothing and your attorneys will drop you like a hot rock when they find out the marriage was legal and you're without funds to pay them."

Steve spoke in clear, even phrases. "Detective Burris, remind us how you knew Luke was really Donnie Douglas?"

"We received a tip."

"From who?"

"They traced the call to the insurance company Marsha works for, but the person insisted on remaining anonymous. It was him that told us Luke and Donnie Douglas were the same guy."

"And that allowed you to match Donnie's dental records in

Brenham with the man known as Luke Pryor who was shot and burned?"

Burris nodded and said, "Yes."

"Did you bring plenty of handcuffs like I asked?"

He pulled another set out of his pocket and jangled them, while everyone traded wide-eyed stares.

Steve held up his palm. "Hold off on cuffing her until I get the whole story." He lowered his voice. "Mary, you told us that a man called you about making a claim on Donnie's life insurance policy. Is that right?"

She snapped back. "Yes. How many times do I have to tell you?"

"Are you sure it was a man?"

"Yes!"

"What if I told you police searched Marsha's condo this morning and found a device that changes voices? She can make her voice sound just like a man."

Confusion etched wrinkles in Mary's forehead.

Steve kept talking. "Voice expert technicians will take samples of Marsha's voice, run it through her device, and get a match."

He took a breath. "They also recovered a .357 Magnum. It belonged to Marsha's ex-husband who confirmed she took it as a souvenir of their marriage. I'm willing to bet ballistics will prove that's the pistol used to kill Luke."

Steve kept going. "Marsha set you up, Mary. How much of the inheritance were you supposed to give the man on the phone for planting the bomb in Julie's truck? And don't deny it."

Mary slumped in her seat and squeaked out, "Five million, but I didn't plant the bomb. The voice said all I had to do was wear all black and hang around outside and he'd come to me. When he didn't show I figured the deal was off." She glared at Marsha. "I guess it wasn't a *man* after all."

Mary sprang from her chair, lunging at Marsha.

Burris caught her and pulled her arms behind her. Handcuffs ratcheted over her wrists.

Mary struggled against Burris's hold. "Conniving witch! You used me. The bomb was your idea, and I'll swear in court that's the truth."

Burris called the deputy on duty in the hall. "Saunders, you have a customer."

Mary's stream of venomous words faded and quiet fell over the room when the front door closed.

Steve turned toward Marsha. "And then there was one. Five million dollars would have sent your daughter to law school in style, with enough left over for you."

Heather stood with her small, but deadly, pistol drawn when she saw Marsha's calculating gaze assessing the room.

With her gun pointed at center mass, she said, "Burris, a little help, please."

With the handcuffs tightened and Burris's firm grip on Marsha's arm, Heather slipped her right hand under Marsha's vest and withdrew a black semi-automatic. "Nothing like coming to a party prepared."

A tall, broad-shouldered man wearing a western suit and a felt cowboy hat came from the hallway. When his jacket parted, Heather saw the small, circular badge of a Texas Ranger. The Ranger nodded at Heather and held open a plastic evidence bag to receive Marsha's weapon. He turned to Detective Burris. "Good job. I'll take this one."

The Ranger took hold of his prisoner and started toward the front door.

Silence covered the room until the door latch clicked.

Burris looked at Steve and said, "Looks like you were right all along. It wasn't the PI like I thought."

Steve stood and held out his hand to Burris. "No need to be down on yourself. You've got the makings of a fine detective. It just takes time."

Burris shook Steve's hand. "Thanks for all you did. It's been good working with you, Steve. You, too, Ms. McBlythe."

"Same here, Detective," said Heather.

As Burris walked away, Steve held up a hand. "Make sure you get the murder charges against Paul Lee dropped."

Once Burris cleared the front door, Trey looked around the room that boasted four empty chairs. "Can I go to work this afternoon?"

Steve and Heather both chuckled.

Julie hooked her good arm in Trey's. "You'll be working with us every day, from now on."

"But first," said Steve, "we need Trey to help Jack take our bags to Heather's car. She and I need to talk to Brandon and Julie in her office before we leave."

28

Heather looked at Brandon. "We'll join you in the office in just a few minutes."

Heather and Steve stayed by the fireplace as the room emptied. She heaved a sigh of relief. "That went just like you planned. Having the Ranger standing in the hall was a nice touch. Marsha didn't look so confident when he walked in."

"Let's get this next part over and go home. Max gets cranky if we're gone too long."

The office door stood open when they arrived. Brandon and Julie had already seated themselves in chairs, leaving the couch for Steve and Heather.

Julie spoke as soon as Heather shut the door. "I can't thank you enough for all you've done for us."

Heather nodded as Steve folded his cane. "Solving murders is what we do. Everyone has their strengths and weaknesses."

Brandon grinned as he said, "I told Julie to expect a big bill from you and it will be worth every penny. We don't know how you figured out Marsha planned everything to make it look like Paul killed Luke and Mary tried to kill Julie."

Steve brushed away the compliment with a wave of his hand. "The case had its challenges with all the names Luke used. I still can't believe some of the things he did to make sure nobody found him."

After a few awkward moments of silence, Steve said, "There's one more thing we haven't mentioned, even to the police."

Julie's eyebrows raised. "I'm not sure I can stand much more intrigue, but I have to know. What is it?"

Steve waited a few more seconds. "Luke Pryor is still alive."

Julie gasped as the muscles in Brandon's jaw flexed.

Heather bit down on the inside of her lip to keep from grinning. Steve had kept this last surprise from everyone but her.

He kept talking. "Isn't that right, Luke? Or should I call you Donnie, or Marcus, or Brandon? That's not to mention the other names you used in the Caribbean. To avoid any further confusion, I'm going to use your birth name until we get this sorted."

"My name is Brandon Clay." His words and tone held no conviction. Steve had scored a direct hit and Brandon's ship of deception was sinking.

Steve leaned forward and lowered his voice. "Like I said, your birth name is Donnie Douglas, and for the purpose of this conversation, that's who you're going to be."

Julie grabbed Donnie's hand. "Please don't tell anyone. It will ruin everything."

"How did you find out?" asked Donnie as he stood and paced the floor.

"I first suspected it at the organic food farm in Belize. I should have become suspicious at the golf course when I learned about the differences in personalities between you and the real Brandon. You're the true introvert, a brilliant young man who spent so much time and energy developing computer games that you didn't know how to interact with people. After you became friends, you noticed the real Brandon bore a striking resemblance to you. That's when you hit on the idea of changing roles. You made a plan to trade identities on the way from the golf course in Belmopan to Mother Nature's Farm. You became like the hero in your most popular game, the one who changes into someone, or something else."

Donnie returned to his seat. "You can't imagine what being around too many people did to me. I could never get away from them as long as I was Donnie Douglas."

"He's getting better," said Julie with a look of admiration on her face.

Steve forged ahead. "You wanted to come back to the States and Julie wanted to come with you, but you couldn't come back as yourself. That's when you presented your plan to the real Brandon. The two of you would trade identities. You'd take on the name Brandon Clay and he would take the name Luke Pryor. You looked enough alike that you could get by with it."

Donnie hung his head.

"You and Julie wanted to get married, but feared someone would find out and destroy the one thing you had to have—anonymity. The question was how to have a marriage, and stay hidden."

Julie straightened her back, but didn't say anything.

Steve took a deep breath and continued. "Then I remembered your obsession with redundancy. It's built it into your games, your security, and all the different names you used. You decided to create a redundant fake husband to round out the deception."

Julie took in a deep breath. "You know about that, too?"

Steve issued a professorial nod. "Once you had the how figured out, you and Julie got married in Belize. When you all returned to the States, Julie and the fake Luke pretended they were husband and wife. You pulled out all the stops to keep your identity hidden."

Julie turned to Steve. "What made you suspect the marriage wasn't real?"

"I had my suspicions when Heather looked in the tiny house and said it looked like a bachelor pad. When she saw the architectural drawings of the rooms here at the lodge, yours are side-by-side with a connecting door."

Julie nodded her head with emphasis. "To keep up appearances, I'd sleep in the tiny house whenever Brandon went on sales trips."

Heather couldn't help herself from asking the next question. "How did you fake the dental records?"

Steve spoke before Donnie could. "They didn't. The fake Luke went for regular appointments at a local dentist's office. I'm guessing Donnie Douglas's dental records no longer exist. Money can make things like old X-rays disappear. Can't they, Donnie?"

"You're right about everything. It was like I was playing a game, except it was real. As for my old dental records, I took care of those before I left the States. Nothing illegal, like a fire or a burglary. My dentist was still old school, X-ray films and paper records. He died before I left and his widow asked if I wanted my records sent to another dentist. I told her I already had an appointment and I'd be glad to deliver them. In truth, there was no new dentist."

Heather broke in with a question. "Is that when you started collecting passports and new identities?"

"Yeah. That became a game, too. Like all games, you tire of playing them after a while. I married Julie in Belize, just like you said. Brandon and I faked my disappearance. I took his passport, and I gave him one of mine. We went our separate ways and didn't meet again until we were back in Texas. We got the farm going and we each played our part. Privately, he lived his life and we did too."

"As evidenced by him living in the tiny house and Julie staying in her room here," said Steve.

Steve interlocked his fingers. "What did you have to give Brandon to keep him from giving away your secrets?"

Julie straightened her posture. "Half the profit from the farm, and he earned every penny."

Donnie took over. "Brandon and I thought alike about so many things. We both found something to believe in when we discovered organic farming. Julie knew she wanted to spend her life growing healthy food. We were all friends. Real friends."

Donnie cast his gaze to his boots and said, "I guess you have to tell all this to the police."

Steve tilted his head toward Heather. "Do you know of any laws they've broken?"

"Nothing that can be proved. At least not yet."

Julie didn't hesitate. "Not yet?"

"Since the real Donnie Douglas is alive and well, it would be fraud if you collected on the life insurance policy."

Steve added, "Right now, we're the only four people in the world who know that the man who used to be called Donnie Douglas is alive. If you refuse to accept the insurance settlement, that's the way things will stay with me and Heather."

Julie and Brandon launched into each other's arms.

"But..." said Steve. "You'd be wise to keep up the charade of living separate lives until the trials are over and the press moves on. Then, if you want to get remarried under Brandon's name, go for it."

Julie nodded like a bobble-head doll. "Expect a wedding invitation."

Steve rose, unfurled his cane, and went to the door without another word. Heather said goodbyes for both of them and promised they'd be at the wedding. She caught up with Steve in the hall. "You big softy. On the verge of choking up, weren't you?"

He cleared his throat. "Nothing of the kind. My brain is like oatmeal from too much thinking, and my body is screaming for meat. Romantic sentiment has nothing to do with it."

Heather chuckled, "A wise man once told me things aren't always as they seem."

Thanks for reading *The Name Game Murder.* I hope it satisfied your appetite for a good mystery and kept you turning the pages to find out 'whodunit.' I would be very grateful if you would take a minute to leave a review at your favorite retail site, Bookbub or Goodreads. Reviews are the lifeblood of books and you, the reader, can keep that lifeblood flowing!

To stay abreast of Smiley and McBlythe's latest adventure, and all my book news, join my Mystery Insiders community. As a thank you, I'll send you a *reader exclusive* Smiley and McBlythe mystery novella.

You can also follow me on Amazon, Bookbub and Goodreads to receive notification of my latest release.

Thanks again for reading!
Bruce

Scan above image to sign up or go to brucehammack.com/the-smiley-and-mcblythe-mysteries-reader-gift/

**Three families. Two murders. One blind PI.
Has he finally met his match?**

Blind PI Steve Smiley's former homicide partner is in trouble. If Leo can't solve an eighty-year-old cold case murder, he'll be put out to pasture before his time.

When Smiley offers to help out his old partner, what he finds is a generations-long feud between three families. With no love lost between any of them, Smiley's field of suspects grows and Leo's future looks bleak.

Before Smiley can help his friend solve the cold case, the feuding families are rocked by another murder. Is history repeating itself? Are the two killings connected? With a real live killer on the loose, can Smiley connect the dots and solve the cases, or will another murder be relegated to the cold case files?

Scan below or go to
brucehammack.com/books/murder-down-the-line/

About the Author

Drawing from his extensive background in criminal justice, Bruce Hammack writes contemporary, clean read detective and crime mysteries. He is the author of the Smiley and McBlythe Mystery series, the Fen Maguire Mystery series and the Star of Justice series. Having lived in eighteen cities around the world, he now lives in the Texas hill country with his wife of thirty-plus years.

Follow Bruce on Bookbub and Goodreads for the latest new release info and recommendations. Join his newsletter list at brucehammack.com and receive a free short story.